A CHARM OF MAGPIES

A REGENCY ROMANCE

EVITA O'MALLEY

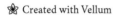 Created with Vellum

For my darling husband
Thee and me
Always

ACKNOWLEDGMENTS

To my sister, without whom I might never have typed a single word of a single story. You challenged me to write you a book, and because I do enjoy a challenge, I did. I cannot thank you enough for setting me on this path to a creative passion I never realised I possessed.

To my friends and family who have listened to my book chatter with endless patience, I couldn't have done this without you. Special shoutout to my papa whose Sunday afternoon analysis has often given me the boost of inspiration and enthusiasm I needed to get the right words on the page.

To the wonderfully talented writers in the Edinburgh Creative Writers Club who have been a phenomenal source of support, encouragement and constructive critique, thank you.

To all the writers who have filled my life with their stories, I will forever be grateful for the love, laughter, heartache, tears, adventure, magic and mystery your words have brought me.

CHAPTER 1

Westbury, Warwickshire. March 1813

"Find a husband or die, Catherine—" announced Lady Westbury, sweeping into the library where her husband and two daughters sat in quiet pursuit of an afternoon's distraction.

"Is that an ultimatum, Mother?" Lady Catherine cut in, fleetingly drawing her dark brown eyes up from her book.

The countess scowled, though not a soul in the room was paying mind enough to notice. "Do not be so absurd," she said, her pitch rising. "You know perfectly well I had not finished speaking. Why do you insist on interrupting me? Why do you insist on provoking me?"

"Why do you insist on making dramatic declarations when you know it provokes me to provoke you?" Catherine replied, pulling at an errant gold thread in her seat's upholstery, not in the least swayed by her mother's bluster. "Really, you are the instrument of your own doom."

"Westbury, do you hear this? Do you hear how she speaks

1

to me?" the countess cried, her agitation with her eldest daughter rising to the fore with splendid promptness.

The earl, sitting at the far end of the room, hidden behind his newspaper and the large wings of his high-back chair, mumbled from behind the safety of his broadsheet, determined, as was his habit, to remain oblivious to the scene unfolding just pages away. He knew all too well that any mindfulness on his part would invite his being drawn into whatever drama his wife and daughter were concocting to sustain their mutual irritation. But what real sport was there to be had in such a game, he often wondered, when all the advantage lay with one player? For his wife could never hope to match their daughter's sharpness of mind ... or tongue.

And so it fell to Lady Rose, as it always did, to pacify her mother. Laying aside her book, she crossed the room to join the countess who still stood at the door, rigid with frustration.

"Now, Mama, do not take on so. You know Catherine merely teases," she said, taking up her mother's hand and patting it gently. "What was it you were saying? You see, we are all listening," Rose continued, though neither her sister nor her father so much as glanced in their direction.

The countess smiled at her second daughter, who's politeness and hushed tone was always enough to undo the damage wrought by her sister's harshness. Rose's golden curls and light blue eyes were a mirror to her own, though the countess' gold turned more to silver every day – a fault she laid at the feet of her first-born, for Catherine's wilful and stubborn nature was enough to try the best of souls.

Once settled in a large armchair, with Rose ready to pour her tea and generally fuss and ensure her comfort, Lady Westbury continued, "I am back from tea with Lady Jenners," she said, ignoring Catherine whose eyes rolled high into her head on hearing the name, "and she told me of a story she had read about a spinster who died and was eaten by her cat."

"Lord! Where could she have read that?" Rose asked, with a seriousness that caused her sister to close her book and stare across at the pair.

"Well, I doubt it was in *The Times*," Catherine said, before her mother could answer. "Rose, do not give a moment's thought to this nonsense. Lady Jenners will have picked her way through one of those tiresome rags she somehow manages to acquire, the ones where, I am certain, they create news to turn the heads of silly women and children."

In response to her daughter's disdain and in a fit of commendable drama, the countess clutched at her breast. "How can you be so harsh? I am simply trying to protect you. You have not yet secured a husband; you do not even seem to be trying, and what if your bloom fades? Will you end up like that poor woman?" she said, before reaching for a small sugared biscuit. She added with a surprising degree of calm, "Though you know, I cannot help but wonder about the size of her cat."

At this, Catherine could remain no longer. Rising to leave the room, she glanced toward her father's seat, but the earl remained resolutely hidden behind his paper. "Of all the ridiculous notions I can lay at the feet of Lady Jenners and her fanciful tales of terror," she said, turning her attention once more to her mother, "I do believe this is the worst. Pray, do not concern yourself with my fading bloom – I am but twenty-one. I think I might see a season or two yet before I must resign myself to spinsterhood. And if it will please you, Mother, in this instance, I assure you there will be no danger."

The countess beamed, hopeful she had at last convinced her daughter of the necessity of finding a husband.

"Yes," Catherine quipped, reaching for the door, "I shall simply never own a cat."

∾

"Catherine, must you be so cruel to Mama?" Rose scolded on following her sister from the library.

"If the woman insists on being ridiculous, I insist on pointing it out to her."

"But it really is terribly cruel," Rose said, taking hold of Catherine's arm to draw her full attention.

Catherine shook herself free of her sister's hand and moved to one of the small tables that flanked the staircase. "It has long been my habit to tease our mother. Why do you take such a keen interest in it now?" she asked, turning a vase on the table and pulling at the flowers within it, upsetting their previously neat arrangement.

"You were never so sharp before, your humour never quite so biting. And I ..." Rose worried at the corner of her lower lip. "I do not even believe you find amusement in it anymore. I cannot recall when I last heard you laugh."

Catherine's hand dropped from the flowers, and she stood, momentarily dumbstruck by her sister's observations. She started to turn toward her, but afraid her sister might read the truth in her face, she stared instead at the solid front door not ten paces away.

"I laugh," she replied weakly, uncomfortable with the growing tension between them – the realisation that her sister was right adding to her discomfort.

"You know Mama means well," Rose said.

"She means to marry me off, and as the topic is now raised daily, I think she means to do so quite soon," Catherine replied, turning fully to face Rose, no longer reluctant to meet her sister's steady gaze.

"You do not think she has a husband in mind? Surely, she is not serious. She cannot believe the tale about the spinster and the cat."

A wry smile cut through Catherine's rather serious expression as she regarded her sister, once more amazed at Rose's unwavering faith in others. "You really are too good, you know. You cannot help but see the best in people. Can you even imagine a person acting to preserve themselves at the expense of others?"

"But Mama wishing to see you married must be to ensure your happiness and security."

"Oh, I do not doubt such concern has a part to play, but I believe fears for her own security hold a far greater sway. If she must, she will sell all hope of my being happy to ensure her own well-being."

Turning away from Rose, Catherine started up the stairs toward her bedroom. Rose followed closely behind and took a seat at Catherine's vanity table, her face screwed in confusion at her sister's earlier speech. She lifted a brush and began, distractedly, to loosen the curls set about her face. "Are things as bad as all that? Is Papa in difficulty?"

Catherine sat on the edge of her bed, her shoulders rounded and her head hung low, wearied by all she knew of how completely the family's wealth had been devastated by their father's fruitless speculations.

"We have a title," she replied, after a moment or two, "but that is all. He has lost all that was to be lost and mortgaged everything else."

Rose shook her head. "That is not possible, not ruin, not without us knowing. He would have warned us. Mama would have warned us."

"Would they?" Catherine asked, pulling at the bed cover on either side of her and trapping it tightly between her fingers as they curled against her palms to form fists. "Would either of them hint at trouble if it meant facing their own failures? No. Better they keep their secrets and save face than prepare us for what is to come."

"If they were so determined this was to be kept from us, then how is it you know?"

Catherine's head shot up. "I will not be lied to. I will not be kept ignorant," she said, her voice hard. On seeing Rose flinch, she softened her tone, though she knew her words would still be painful to hear. "My future, our future, is at the mercy of the decisions and mistakes they make. I found ways to become informed. Papa is ruined, and I fear marriage is the only hope for salvation – for us, and for Westbury."

Rose, who had noticed her father's agent attended the house far more frequently of late but had not allowed herself to dwell on the possible reasons why, stared, wide-eyed and silent. To hear now that their family was ruined, and from so trusted a source as Catherine, was too much. After a moment, the hairbrush fell to the floor as she raised her hands to cover her face, sobs causing her shoulders to shake, tears forcing their way through her fingers.

Catherine, drawn out of her own self-pity by her sister's distress, was quickly beside her. She knew Rose could not have been spared the truth but was determined she would be spared further hurt. She picked up the brush and ran it through her sister's hair while gently humming, soothing curls and soul with bristle and song. Rose's breath slowed, and she looked up at Catherine's reflection in the mirror.

"We shall be safe. Mama and Papa will not see us wed if we cannot be happy, will they?"

Catherine gently kissed the top of her sister's head. "Of course not. Do not upset yourself; I am tired, that is all. And you know that I am wont to see the worst in every situation." On seeing her sister brighten a little, she added, "And perhaps, if I at least try to be agreeable, I might dupe a man into marriage who is wealthy enough to secure the fortunes of us all."

~

Catherine was saddened by the changes in Rose during the week after her revelations about their family circumstance. It was not simply that her sister cried often, but that, when she smiled, it was with less heart. That Rose should be brought so low, when Catherine had it in her power to protect and restore her, was a pain greater than she could have imagined.

So, I will be married, she argued with herself, pacing her bedroom floor. *It was always going to be so. I was always going to be some man's wife. It will simply be sooner than I had hoped, and my choices will be limited,* she told her reflection on taking a seat at her vanity table. *There were always limitations on the man I would choose – I was never fully free – but if I do this, Rose will be saved. If I marry well enough, she may be free to follow her heart, and,* she continued, hoping to convince herself, *I may be happy. Happiness is not yet lost.*

~

The countess reacted to the news of her daughter finally agreeing to marry in the way Catherine had expected – with drama and animation. That her delight could hardly be contained but could scarcely be voiced, at least not in any manner befitting the moment, gave rise to a curious sort of convulsion, words and emotions struggling for expression.

"My daughter married. Oh, Catherine, such happy news," the countess finally gushed. "And so much to do, so much to plan. We must start making arrangements at once."

"Surely, I should secure a man before I spend what

remains of my inheritance on silks, Mother," nipped Catherine testily, already regretting her announcement.

"Hush now, we shall have no such talk," replied her mother. "Things are not as bad as all that." She smiled, looking about her to see if any of the servants were nearby. "Really, there is nothing at all to be concerned about on that account. Now, first things first. We must have Lady Jenners to tea. She is the best person to help us plan. And I am certain she will agree that we must all be in London within the fortnight … and then there is the dress, and so much to …"

Catherine groaned as she sat beside her mother. She nodded but no longer listened. *London, of course.* How had it not occurred to her that, to find a husband, she would be subjected to a season in London?

For Rose, all of this is for Rose, she told herself, continuing to nod at her mother. *Smile, for pity's sake, smile,* she reminded herself as Rose was called to share in the happy news.

CHAPTER 2

Arlington Street, London. April 1813

*L*ondon was as drab as Catherine remembered. Rain beat against the drawing room window at her back, and the fire that had been blazing for half an hour was scarcely warm and bright enough to chase away the unrelenting cold, grey aspect of the day. The prospect of spending a season in town, forced to attend every party and being exhibited as a prize, only added to her displeasure. Indeed, the only comfort she had managed to find in the whole affair was the change she could see in her sister. In Westbury, Rose had suffered such low spirits that Catherine had feared her sister might not recover. Her face had taken on a frightful pallor and her usually bright eyes seemed dulled and ever rimmed with red. Now in London, with the family engaged in securing Catherine a husband, Rose appeared happy, carefree, and delighted by everything – all signs of her earlier depression dispatched with no trace remaining. She was Rose once more.

"Have you ever seen such a wonderful display of colour?"

Rose asked, halfway through a conversation Catherine had been paying little mind to. "I had almost forgotten London could provide so many delights, and the people such affability and charm, and you have been quite the favourite."

Catherine, who was less delighted by their situation, unpicked the misshaped stitches in her needlepoint and barely raised a smile in reply. She could offer no utterances of excitement to match Rose's, at least, none that would sound sincere, and so she remained silent. In truth, she had hated their engagements, and no remembrances of coloured silks or favour garnered could alter that.

"Oh yes, quite the favourite," agreed Lady Westbury. "At last night's dance, I could not have been prouder of you. You were delightful. I had not thought you capable of such charm – not one unpleasant remark the entire evening."

"I could make amends for that now if you wish, Mother," Catherine said, casting aside her needlework, unhappy at the recollection of her crawling politeness, the reminder of the previous evening adding to her already sour mood.

The countess chose to ignore Catherine's bite, as she often did now, for having at last secured her daughter's agreement to marry, she no longer seemed affected by Catherine's commentary and criticism.

"And the favouritism of one man could not have gone unnoticed," the countess continued. "Lord Royston was decidedly attentive. I hope another meeting – and the swift intervention of your father – might secure a formal agreement there."

Before Rose could express her opinion, Catherine, who was now pacing back and forth in front of the tall bookcase beside the fireplace, barked a loud, short laugh. "Heavens, we are in danger if you have set your hopes on Lord Royston. He is an outrageous fop. The man had eyes for no one but himself. For half our conversation, he looked past me to the mirror behind, checking and rechecking the coif of his hair. I would sooner be eaten by cats than claim that man as a husband!"

The countess shifted uncomfortably in her seat. This was not the reaction she had hoped for. Still, it was only the first flush of the season, and a speedy conclusion to the business of marrying her daughter off could not have been counted upon.

"Well then," she mused, "perhaps a little prudence is the thing. We must not allow our heads to be turned too readily by a handsome face and pleasing manner. Though I think we need not hint at any disinclination, for given time, you may find the man more agreeable. Can we be patient, dear Catherine? Patient and pleasant until decisions must be made."

"I assume you mean to ask: Can I temper my tongue? Can I fawn and feign favour, disguising contempt and checking ridicule?" Catherine sniped, snatching a book from the nearest shelf, opening it and snapping it shut almost immediately. "Based on the display I managed last night, it seems I can."

The bitterness in her daughter's reply and the paltriness of her victory were lost on the countess. "Wonderful, dear, simply wonderful," she said, clapping her hands in delight and calling for fresh tea.

"Rose, you have been smiling in the most ridiculous manner all afternoon," chided Catherine as soon as the countess was called from the drawing room and the sisters were left alone and free to talk among themselves. "What on earth so delights you?"

"Everything," Rose said, laughing lightly as Catherine

rolled her eyes heavenward at her reply. "Come now, you must feel happy being out of Westbury too? There was such a gloom about the place, but here, there is hope and possibility. You must feel it."

Catherine set aside her task of sorting through the little pile of calling cards that had been left for them in the last few weeks. "I am pleased you think so, and to see you happy is happiness enough for me," was all she could manage in reply.

"But you must be thrilled at how well we have been received. Mama is beyond happy, though she was born for such engagements and is entertained by the whirl of it all, but even Papa seems brighter here."

Unnoticed by her sister, Catherine winced at the mention of their father who had spent much of their time in London between the card table and his club – where, she had no doubt, he was already spending as though a husband had been found and a deal had been struck.

"His spirits are lifted," Rose continued, "and it comforts me to see him less burdened. The distraction and the giddy commotion are just what we needed to lift us out of the gloominess of the previous month."

Catherine bit her tongue to prevent herself pointing out that the change in attitude likely had more to do with the prospect of avoiding financial ruin than the change in location. But seeing Rose so animated was peace enough, and so she remained quiet, allowing her sister to talk on excitedly, her enthusiasm sufficient enough to raise even Catherine's hopes.

The reprieve offered by Rose's enthusiasm lasted the rest of the afternoon, and Catherine's happy mood continued throughout the day as she endured, with greater grace than before, the preparations for that evening. She did not notice when extra attention was given to ensuring her hair was just so, with not one curl out of place. She did not pass comment when her green and turquoise silk dress was laid out, and it was not until her mother suggested she wear diamonds that any sort of objection was made.

The countess smiled. "I could not help myself, Catherine, such brilliance in cut and colour pales only in the light of your beauty this evening. I do not think I have ever seen you so radiant."

Catherine blushed. She had grown so accustomed to her mother's criticism she barely noticed it, but praise was new, and she could not recall the last time her mother had called her "beautiful". This, and her continued high hopes for the future, led to a rather swift and unexpected agreement to the countess' request. With the diamonds secured about her throat, Catherine set off to the Jenners' with the rest of her family. For the first time since they had come to London, she felt at ease and looked forward to a quiet and pleasant evening solely in the company of her mother's oldest friends, with as little talk of marriage as she could possibly manage.

Alas, such hope and high spirits barely lasted beyond stepping across their hosts' threshold. Catherine had just stepped foot out of the waiting room when Lady Jenners was upon her, eager to make an introduction to the Honourable Robert DeChancey, second son of the Earl of Macklesford.

CHAPTER 3

Manchester. April 1813

"But I love her," protested Captain James Garbrae as he strode into the library, refusing to let lie the argument that had begun in the breakfast room and echoed along the main hallway of their home as the son stalked the father through the house.

"Love, boy? Do not speak to me of such things. You are twenty-five; what can you know of love? Lord, I have twice your years and know little enough of the matter," his father replied. "You will not marry Miss Harrington, and that will be an end to it."

"It most certainly will not be an end to it," said the captain as he swung the door shut with a resounding bang. "I cannot imagine what objection you have to the match. Mr Harrington has been a friend to you for more than twenty years. What is it about the man or his daughter that is unsuitable?"

Mr Garbrae ignored his son's theatrics, picked up the morning paper from the sideboard, and headed across the room for a seat by the window. "I have not said anything to slight the Harringtons. You know perfectly well the regard I have for Mr Harrington as a businessman and a friend, and his daughter is a pleasant enough young woman," he said, noting his son continued to glare at him.

"Then, damn it, what is your objection to our being engaged?"

"Watch your tone!" Mr Garbrae snapped, tossing his newspaper on an empty seat, unhappy at the continuing challenge. "I will not be addressed in such a way, by you or any man. I did not get where I am by allowing such disrespect to stand."

The captain raised his hands in surrender. "Forgive me, Father," he relented, not wanting to antagonise him further, "but you must understand my frustration. You acknowledge the virtues of the family, you allude to nothing that makes Miss Harrington unsuitable, yet you refuse to provide support for an engagement that would secure our happiness."

Mr Garbrae sat in his usual chair and reached across to the seat opposite to collect up the scattered sheets of the morning paper. He motioned to his son to sit. "You know I have always acted in your best interest, that I have always provided you with any advantage I could to make your life better, to give you a chance at more than was ever provided me by my father."

The captain acknowledged this with an abrupt nod of his head as he took up a seat.

"When you were younger, I put you to work; you had to earn every privilege. I did this so you would understand those we employ and those who must earn, in preparation for when you assume control of the business. I had you enlist in the navy so you would appreciate what it is to fight for a cause and learn the importance of leadership, order, discipline, and honour. These values, I believe, are important, and

I needed to impress their importance upon you. You know I was right in both of these matters, so please, trust that I still act in your best interest."

The captain flicked at the edge of the small oriental rug that ran beneath his chair with his boot. "I trust you," he said, "but I do not understand you. Explain to me how giving up this prospect for happiness could possibly be in my best interest."

"Son, Miss Harrington is a good girl – pleasant, accomplished, and pretty, but what would she bring to your marriage? She carries with her no social advantage, nothing to help in your advancement. All the benefits of the match fall in her favour. What is there for you to gain?"

"Is love not enough?" the captain asked, looking his father squarely in the face. "Could I not be complete in the happiness of securing the woman I love, of building a life and raising a family with her?"

Mr Garbrae gave a short, sharp laugh. "Do you still speak to me of love? Do not be so foolish. You are not some schoolboy; you were not raised to fall foul of such fancy. You have always known you were expected to advance the family name, and you must know you have to marry better than Miss Harrington to accomplish that."

"You expect me to marry for money?" replied the captain, all at once on his feet, taken aback by the calculating nature of his father's intentions.

"Lord, no, we have money enough, son – I expect you to marry a pedigree."

∽

"I take it, by the look on your face, that the discussion with your father did not go well," said James Garbrae's closest friend, Captain Michael Fitzgerald, as he entered their shared rooms with his usual swagger. "Well, fear not, you will work around him, as you always do, and I am sure sweet Miss Harrington will be yours in the fullness of time." Fitzgerald kicked free his boots. He reached across Garbrae for the nearest piece of meat on the table, and with a large slice of cold ham secured, he threw himself onto the couch, dangling his feet over the side.

"Miss Harrington and I are not to be married," replied Garbrae, his words clipped and his tone flat.

Fitzgerald turned to look at his friend and, on seeing his despondency, swallowed the mouthful of meat that remained, swung his feet around, and sat up to address Garbrae.

"Come now, it cannot be as bad as all that. Your father cannot object to her. She can be a little silly, but I am certain that, in spite of it all, she is a good sort of a girl."

"Father has no objection to her, but it seems I am to marry into a titled family, to further advance the Garbrae family line. It would be easier to accept if she were somehow unsuitable, but Lord, man! A title. What use have I for a woman with a title?"

Fitzgerald scratched his head, as though trying to root out a solution to his friend's problem.

"If I did not know your father, I might think you were joking, but Lord help me, I know you to be in earnest. Could you not defy him and marry the girl regardless?"

"If I marry her, he will disown me. I will lose everything."

On hearing that this was all that was amiss, Fitzgerald relaxed. Throwing his arms wide along the back of the couch, he suggested, "Well, you earn living enough in the King's navy. Withdraw the resignation of your commission, remain with us, and marry the girl."

"Do not think I had not considered it, but you know there

17

are things I wish to do which a commission in the navy will not allow. I have such plans for the mill—"

"Please, not another lecture. I swear I know your speech by heart," Fitzgerald interrupted, falling to his knees before his friend. "Heavens, I have never known a man to be so enthused about sanitation."

"No lecture, I promise you," said Garbrae, laughing at last, Fitzgerald's foolishness always sufficient to lift his spirits. "My heart has never truly been with the navy. I have done my duty and served my country, but the business has always been my passion. You know my father as well as anyone – do you believe him capable of cutting me off if I defy him?"

"You are his only child."

Garbrae pulled apart a slice of bread, dropping the torn pieces onto the empty plate in front of him. "But if I crossed him, would he punish me for it?" he asked.

"Yes, I believe he would."

"As do I, at least for a time. Oh, he would forgive me eventually, but forgiveness comes slowly to him, though he is quick enough to anger. My plans will not wait. Even if I were to sacrifice all I wanted, I do not believe Miss Harrington's father would consent to her marrying me under such conditions. He is a good man, but he seeks his daughter's advancement as much as my father seeks mine. Could I expect her to give up her family and all prospects of an advantageous marriage for a chance at happiness with me?"

"She is ridiculous and romantic enough to do it if you ask her," answered Fitzgerald.

"My friend, I know you never cared for Miss Harrington but must you, even now, speak so unkindly of her? Now that she is lost to me, at least leave me with an unblemished memory of the woman I love."

Fitzgerald, his usual exuberance subdued by this chastisement and the low spirits of his friend, could say nothing in reply. He smiled apologetically and offered comfort in the only way he knew how – by planting a heavy hand on Garbrae's shoulder and offering him the last of the ham.

∾

The captain, summoned to breakfast a few days later, made a conscious study of the filigree pattern on the curtains rather than look his father in the eyes as he asked, "Will I at least have some say in the woman I am to marry?" His first words to Mr Garbrae in days.

"Of course," his father reassured him. "Believe me, I have no intention of marrying you off where you cannot be happy. We need the marriage to be a success, the line of Garbrae must be secured, so we shall be looking for good breeding stock, as well as a title."

"Do you already have a lady in mind, or am I to be subjected to a run of uncomfortable dinners, impromptu introductions during parties, and evenings at cards?" the captain asked dryly, moving his attention to the patterned wall hangings, refusing to share in the joviality.

"There is no one in mind but do not be so downhearted. We shall find you a pretty wife with manners and grace, someone befitting the fortune you will bring to the marriage. With my wealth, I dare say we might procure the favour of the daughter of some hard-up baron or viscount."

"Good God, Father! You are not bartering for stock. We may succeed in buying the permission of her family, but I shudder at the thought that we would be buying the lady's affections along with it. What sort of a wife can I hope for if she is solely persuaded into marriage by coin?"

"Stuff and nonsense, son." Mr Garbrae leaned forward in his seat and took hold of the captain's forearm, squeezing it gently. His voice softened, as it always did, when he spoke of his wife. "Do you think your mother loved me when we married? Of course not, for we barely knew one another, but I could provide for her and that was enough to begin with. We were happy, you know that, until she was taken from us – Lord, rest her – and you will be the same. Trust me, you are making the right choice in forgoing your foolish attachment to Miss Harrington, for there is nothing like financial hardship to turn romantic love sour."

Captain Garbrae slumped back into his chair, drawing his arm out from under his father's touch, his misery with these plans increasing at every word. He had been to visit with Mr Harrington, and they had talked, in the most general terms, of the man's hopes for his daughter. When it was hinted that, in marrying Garbrae, she would secure a naval captain and not a captain of industry, Harrington moved quickly to thank the captain for calling and expressed his regret that they would not meet again under such intimate terms, there no longer being any reason for Garbrae to call alone at the house. Garbrae understood, of course. There must be no suggestion of an engagement between Miss Harrington and himself. He thanked Mr Harrington for his time and left, without so much as a parting glance at Anna being afforded to him.

"So, what do you say to it?" Mr Garbrae pressed of his son, eager for his ready acceptance.

"What?" the captain replied, having heard nothing his father had said.

"London, son. London. Shall we indulge in a season in town?"

CHAPTER 4

Grosvenor Square. April 1813

"And what do you say to our fine start here?" asked John Garbrae of his son over breakfast. "I knew this address would garner us attention, but such preference was unexpected. I received no less than three cards and two invitations to dine last night. We should have little trouble finding you a pretty wife of title and consequence."

"Not if the wife in mind is Lady Jane Montesque," said the captain.

"Oh," replied his father, a little disappointed, "I thought she was a wonderful young woman, an excellent match for you, and her father seemed inclined toward an offer. I had hoped to approach him."

The captain knocked eggs from one side of his plate to the other with his fork. "Oh, I am quite sure he would be delighted to secure an arrangement. For pity's sake, Father, the woman was a fool, and only another fool would tie himself to her. I doubt she has a thought in her head that was not drummed in by some governess whose sole ambition was to lessen the appearance of the girl as a dullard."

"Well, there is no need to be so critical; I thought she was charming," Mr Garbrae replied, taking up a large round of bread and slathering it with butter.

"Then you marry her!" shot back the captain before his father could say more.

The butter knife, now dripping with jam, paused in mid-air as Mr Garbrae cast a sharp eye across at his son. "I will overlook that outburst because not even your surliness can spoil the success of last night, but do not test my good graces, boy – you may not find me so forgiving a second time."

The captain pulled his arms tight across his chest, biting back the anger rising at the memory of the night before, and all the nights before that, holding on to his plans for the business and the hope this would all be over soon.

Since they had come to London, he had been subjected to introductions to a seemingly endless run of titled ladies, all of whom his father assured would make fine prospects, though he had yet to meet one woman who came close to his idea of a wife. Still, he would only need to meet his father's demands for a few more weeks, then he would make an excuse to return to Lancashire and the cotton mill, and be free of this silliness, at least for a short while.

His resolve to remain single, rather than settle for any of the women he had so far been introduced to, strengthened when his father asked, "Well, what of Lady Regina Cairnsworth? We met her on Tuesday – Lord Elderton's daughter. Now, she was a handsome creature, and she had breeding."

"We have wildly different opinions as to what makes a suitable wife if you think she and I could ever be happy," the captain said, staring open-mouthed at his father. "She talked of the colour of her dress for almost a quarter-hour, as though I had any interest in whether the shade perfectly matched the green of her eyes. And such false bashfulness, all half-smiles and darting glances, but when, on speaking of her eyes ... oh, the obvious flutter of her lashes. I could not ... I will not marry that woman."

He shoved back his chair and quit the table in search of hot tea. Finding the pot on the sideboard cool, he barked orders for a fresh brew.

"Do not shout at the servants. This is my house, not one of your ships," Mr Garbrae said, his patience with his son's frayed temper stretching beyond its limits. "Nothing seems to satisfy you – no one seems to satisfy you. You have resolutely declared you 'will not marry that woman' about every woman we have met, but I do not recall having met more obliging, pleasing ladies in my life, and you sit sulking, merely finding fault."

"But it is so easy to do; can you not see it?" the captain cut in, turning back to the table, his knuckles turning white as he gripped the back of the nearest chair. "Can you not see how interchangeable they are? Swap dresses and jewels, add or subtract a little height or girth, change hair colour ... They are all the same, all with the same agreeable manner, conversation, interests, charities, and ambitions. It is as though originality has been bred out of them. I get no sense that they hold any desires beyond preserving life as they have always known it. Is this truly the best you could have hoped for me?"

His father made no reply.

The two men stared at each other across a table and a now cold breakfast of ham and eggs. Neither was happy. Both felt misused, aware of the unfamiliar animosity that was creeping into their everyday conversations. Despite the recognition that something was amiss between them, neither was willing to be the first to back down by looking away; at least, not until the deadlock was broken by the interjection of a maid bringing hot tea.

～

"You know, as I stand here looking at you, I do not think I have ever seen a more pathetic prospect," announced Captain Fitzgerald on entering the breakfast room. He tipped his head to Mr Garbrae as the other strode out. "I see you have managed to upset your father already, and it is not yet ten."

"I am in no mood to be badgered, Fitzgerald, not even by you," responded the captain with unusual surliness.

"Surely London cannot be as bad as all that?" Fitzgerald continued, hoping to draw his friend out of his sour disposition. "Finding a suitable wife cannot be such an ordeal. I have only been here a night and have met several young ladies on whom I could happily settle the family fortune."

"Well, for pity's sake, do not tell my father that," said Garbrae, laughing, "or I shall never hear the end of it, for if the ladies in London can work their charms on even you, how am I to believably resist them?"

"That is a fine way to speak of a friend," Fitzgerald replied, feigning upset, as he lifted the closhes covering the dishes on the sideboard.

"I have said much worse about you and to you," hit back Garbrae, playfully punching his friend in the arm as he passed behind him.

"Come," Fitzgerald said, dropping the cover back on the last of the dishes and pulling his friend to the door. "This is only fit for the dogs. I will let you treat me to a bird and an ale and listen to all you have to say on the horrors of London and the trial of finding a wife."

"And so that was Lady Jane Montesque," finished Garbrae, leaning back into his seat in a secluded corner of The White Hart, having told his friend all about the disastrous dinner the night before.

Fitzgerald set down his tankard and stared at Garbrae. "You do not honestly expect me to believe she said that?" he asked, incredulous at the tale.

"As God is my witness, she overheard me speak of the Chesapeake Affair and asked me where Lord Chesapeake was from, for she was unfamiliar with the name. Before I could answer, she was speculating as to the possible woman in question. It seems dear Lady Jane has an appetite for social scandal."

"She had no notion that *Chesapeake* was a ship and the 'affair' concerned the execution of Royal Navy war deserters?"

"I doubt she is aware of anything that happens outside of her own social circle. If she is the sort of woman my father thinks a suitable match for me, is it any wonder I am so despairing?" Garbrae said, tipping his empty tankard at his companion.

Fitzgerald reached for the jug of ale he had requested be left with them and moved to refill the drink. "In this case, I agree with you. Lady Jane would not be a suitable wife, but I do not think your father completely to blame for his choice." He paused mid-thought and mid-pour.

Garbrae raised an eyebrow, daring him to finish.

Fitzgerald splashed a drop more ale into the tankard and said, "Well, consider the example you set him. Lady Jane sounds worryingly like someone you might be inclined to love."

"I suppose you mean to slight Miss Harrington with your comment," replied Garbrae, unimpressed, "but they are completely different. Miss Harrington is vivacious and spontaneous, where this woman is vapid and silly."

"My friend, you must remember that you view Miss Harrington through the eyes of one in love, one who has loved long and loved the youthful ideal more than the reality, I think. What you saw as lively and high-spirited in a girl of fifteen, I saw as childish and imprudent in a woman at twenty, but you loved the idea of loving her and could not see her faults. Those of us not so blinded saw a pleasing, pretty woman, who could be manipulative, impulsive, and petty when she did not get her way. Is it any wonder your father thought you would value a pretty face over a sharp mind, given your declared devotion to Miss Harrington?"

"You really thought that about her?" asked Garbrae, surprised by his friend's candour.

"What does it matter now? Cease this unhappiness and tell me more of the London women who have tormented you. Though I cannot imagine you will best Lady Jane, I am sure I will be entertained regardless."

Knowing there was nothing to be gained by dwelling on thoughts of what he had lost, Garbrae yielded to his friend's demands and launched into a spirited, if exaggerated, recounting of the other women he had been introduced to.

"I refuse to believe she had no teeth!" Fitzgerald exclaimed, when he could stop laughing. "Not even your worst enemy hates you enough to burden you with such a woman."

"Well, perhaps I take some licence with the truth," Garbrae replied, relaxed by the easy banter and companionship of his friend. "In truth, Lady Jane Montesque was the worst of them; her silliness was beyond measure. There was nothing particularly objectionable about the other women, but I found nothing compelling in them. I was drawn to Miss Harrington, consumed by her, and perhaps I was just caught in the flush of first love, but is it too much to expect some immediacy of feeling toward the woman I am going to marry?"

Garbrae stared into his drink, lost in the swirl of the pale golden ale, his amusement in sharing stories with his friend at an end. "They are so staid and proper, Fitzgerald. I feel no sense of spirit or desire for more than the life they already have – for parties and dinners, and evenings at the theatre. I want a woman who will be a partner in my life, not a shackle. Is it too much to ask for?"

His friend, aware of the seriousness in the question, took a moment before answering. "Perhaps it is simply too much to ask for in the first few minutes of meeting a woman. Have you ever considered this reserve you encounter is a consequence of the situation they find themselves in, being formally introduced to a potential husband and father-in-law? You complain of how awkward these evenings are for you; could it not be the same for the women?"

"But surely there should be some spark, some evidence of a passion for living."

"Give it time, my friend," Fitzgerald reassured. "Where do you dine tonight?"

"We are attending a private party. Our hosts are Lord and Lady Jenners. I am assured it will be an intimate affair with a select number of eligible ladies in attendance," Garbrae replied, mimicking his father as he described the evening.

"Well then," said Fitzgerald, choosing to ignore his friend's displeasure, "why not try enjoying yourself? No doubt it would make a change from how you usually spend these evenings. Stand back and observe the ladies a little before you suffer an introduction, try to find something in their face or their manner that is appealing, and hold on to that while they bore you with talk of their dresses. Then, for your sake, and the sake of your father, find the girl who is the most appealing and the least boring and give it a second meeting. You never know, she may just surprise you."

CHAPTER 5

Home of Lord and Lady Jenners, Grosvenor Square. April 1813

*L*ady Catherine managed to hold her smile through her introduction to Mr DeChancey, but on glancing around the large drawing room into which she had been led, she spied at least two other men of title and fortune to whom Lord and Lady Jenners could make no claim of acquaintance, and she knew at once what was at work. She took hold of her mother's arm before she could stray too far from her and, through gritted teeth, hissed, "Did you think I would be fooled?"

"I have no idea what you mean, Catherine, dear," Lady Westbury replied, trying not to wince as her daughter's grip tightened.

"You told me this was going to be a small evening party, but you and I both know Lord Jenners could no more have secured the attendance of the King as half the young men in here. This is your doing, Mother. Do they have any idea why they are here? Any notion as to your intentions? This is so humiliating."

"Collect yourself this instant." The countess turned to face her daughter, a forced slash of a smile set wide across her face, and with quiet, but unmistakable, sharpness said, "You need a husband, and this is how it is done. Any one of these young men would make a fine match."

"Any one of them is rich enough, you mean."

Her forced smile stretching even wider, the countess' eyes made a hurried study of who was about them. "Lower your voice. Do not embarrass your family, and do not embarrass our hosts. Smile and be pleasant and then, for God's sake, just pick a husband."

The two women stepped apart – the countess bearing a now rictus grin, her daughter glaring.

"Lord Jenners," the countess proclaimed to the room, "how good of you to invite us. Such a delightful idea – a private party with a select set is just what one needs …"

Catherine watched as her mother glided toward Lord and Lady Jenners, the silver brocade in her dress and the diamonds about her throat glittering under the light of half a dozen candelabras. She was resplendent, all ease and charm and witty conversation. There was not a single chink in the perfectly polished armour of her manner and appearance, nothing that would hint at the trouble behind the facade. Catherine touched the diamonds that circled her own throat. If she failed to marry, how long would it be before these too were sold to honour her father's debts? Her anger flared as she clenched at her necklace, the sharp points of the setting digging into her fingers.

A moment later, she released her grip, settled her jewellery, drew back her shoulders, and forced a smile to her lips. The evening had begun, though she was determined it would not end as her mother hoped; she would uncover the potential suitors who had been invited and dispatch them. She had promised she would marry, and she was determined to protect Rose, but she would not be auctioned off tonight.

~

From his seat across the room, James Garbrae's eyes were drawn from their examination of his fingernails to the main door by the rather loud speech of the latest arrival. His eyes rolled heavenward on seeing the woman and her daughter. Both were draped in the most expensive material and dripping with diamonds. Just as he was about to dismiss the young woman as yet another he would be at pains to avoid, a flash of disdain sharpened her features, and she gripped at her necklace as though she might rip it clean from her body. His gaze became fixed. This was interesting. She was interesting. The moment passed, and her face quickly settled into a wide smile, but Garbrae was certain he had seen anger. As he watched the lady draw back her shoulders, for the first time that evening, he found himself genuinely smiling at the unexpected sight of a woman preparing for battle.

~

"Mother, I have found you at last," Catherine said, approaching the countess who was enjoying a quiet, pleasant conversation with Lady Macklesford in one of the first-floor drawing rooms which had been set up for cards. "I have been searching you out for ten minutes at least."

"Catherine, dear," the countess replied, surprised her daughter was willing to talk to her so soon after their little disagreement, "is everything all right?"

"Of course, what could possibly be amiss? I was simply wondering if you could remember the name of the gentleman I was introduced to when we arrived. Lord, help me, but I cannot remember. Either the man is completely unremarkable, or I am as flighty as you so often say." Catherine laughed.

"Nonsense, I have never called you flighty; indeed, nothing could be further from the truth," interjected the countess, confused at the suggestion.

"Then I suppose the man in question is completely forgettable," was Catherine's deliberate response, given while she cast an eye to her mother's companion.

"I believe, Lady Catherine, from what your mother tells me, the man you now find so forgettable is Mr Robert DeChancey—"

"DeChancey, of course. The Earl of Mucklesford's son, I believe," interrupted Catherine, a slight smile pulling at the corner of her mouth.

"Macklesford, Lady Catherine; Macklesford," the woman managed, her voice shaking with indignation. "I do not believe we have met. Please allow me to introduce myself."

"Oh, Lord, then you must be Mr DeChancey's mother," Catherine said with contrived mortification as introductions were made. "Well, how terrible a first impression this is."

"Indeed, Lady Catherine, I am his mother. How unfortunate for your mother's ambitions that you find my son so entirely forgettable and that I place such stock in first impressions," replied Lady Macklesford, her discomfort at the slighting of her family plain. "If you will excuse me …"

The lady was gone in an instant, and Catherine could only smile as she walked away. The countess stood with her mouth slightly agape, shock preventing any objection being voiced. Indeed, she was so surprised by the suddenness of Catherine's attack and Lady Macklesford's departure that she did not even have the wherewithal to reproach her daughter before she too was gone.

~

Catherine entered the adjoining drawing room and cast her eyes about for any further prospects for disruption. The sight of two women engaged in a serious consideration of the drapes framing the two large windows that faced over Grosvenor Square brought a smile to her lips.

"Lady Wainwright, Lady Blakemore," Catherine said as she approached them. "How delightful to see you this evening. I did not realise you were friends of Lord and Lady Jenners."

"Why, Lady Catherine, how wonderful to see you again," Lady Wainwright replied, paying closer attention to Catherine's form and face than she had ever done before. "Indeed, I have only just met Lord and Lady Jenners; your mother was kind enough to secure Lord Wainwright and I an invitation."

"And you, Lady Blakemore, do you know the Jenners, or was my mother equally kind to you?" Catherine asked.

"No, I had not had the pleasure of knowing Lord and Lady Jenners until this evening. Still, one is always ready to expand one's circle in favour of the right people," the countess replied, paying as close attention to Lady Catherine's stance and manner of address as Lady Wainwright.

The ladies stood smiling at one another for a moment or two in silence.

Catherine, increasingly uncomfortable under their gaze, wished she had given more thought to how she would discourage these women, but knowing every word, every action was being scrutinised in their assessment of her suitability as a potential wife hoped an opportunity would reveal itself before long.

"And so how do you find London, Lady Catherine?" enquired Lady Wainwright.

"In truth, I do not find it suits at all," she replied honestly.

"You surprise me,' replied Lady Blakemore. 'I thought all young ladies were delighted by a season. Do not tell me you are one of those dour misses who takes no delight in amusement and prefers solitude to society."

"Oh, nothing of the sort, I can assure you. I live to be amused and find delight in many things, although I do find the constant commotion of London exhausting, and I do not think the air suits me quite as well as the country," Catherine replied, dropping her shoulders as though suddenly fatigued and adding a small cough at the end of her speech.

"Oh," Lady Wainwright said, alarmed that Lady Catherine might not be as robust as she appeared. "You are not unwell, I hope."

"It is nothing, please do not concern yourself. I suffer a little weakness about the lungs and find London air trying, but I manage quite well and only needed to lie down for a few hours this afternoon to be rested for this evening's exertions."

"A private party could hardly be considered an exertion, Lady Catherine," said Lady Blakemore. "Your 'little weakness' must be more considerable than you allow if you needed to rest in preparation for such an easy evening. That cough I hear; is it persistent?" she continued, her misgivings about Lady Catherine as a suitably healthy wife as plain to see as Lady Wainwright's.

"The cough? Well, I scarcely notice it now – we are such old friends," Catherine jested, as though trying to make light of it. "I am certain some honeyed tea will soothe my throat. If you will excuse me, I will just seek out a cup."

As she walked away, the two ladies shook their heads.

"Such a pity," announced Lady Wainwright.

"Indeed," agreed Lady Blakemore.

The two women regarded one another for a moment

longer before making their excuses and going in search of their sons.

"What are you about, sister?" Rose asked when she finally caught Catherine alone in a quiet corner of the dining room, gazing out over the paved courtyard to the stables beyond. "You look very pleased, very pleased indeed. If I did not know better, I might think you were enjoying this evening – but I do know better."

"Rose, such suspicion; it is most unlike you. I thought the point of a night such as this was enjoyment, with pleasant company and conversation," Catherine said, greeting her sister with a warm smile.

"And on any other evening I would agree, but I have seen the men invited here. I see Mama's hand in this, and I am certain you are not blind to it."

"No, and yet, I have enjoyed myself, though Mother will not be pleased when she learns just how I have managed it."

"Oh, good heavens. What have you done?"

Having finished her conversation with Rose and laughed at her sister's admonishment, Catherine went in search of the Baron of Chimsley, the last of her mother's potential suitors, more determined than ever that all matrimonial hopes would be dashed before the first hour had passed. Unlike the first three suitors, she knew the baron's mother did not wield enough influence with her son to make an approach through his matriarch worthwhile, so Catherine was forced to devise a means of discouraging the man himself.

She found him, at last, in the billiards rooms and

observed him for several minutes as he engaged in heated discussion with a handful of others. She drew close enough to discover that politics stirred him, and so she decided that would be her weapon.

"Gentlemen," she began, on approaching the small group, "what is it that so thoroughly occupies you? You seem quite passionate, and I must have my share of the discussion."

Chimsley gave a slight nod of his head to her before replying. "It is nothing, I assure you. Just dry matters of politics, nothing to interest a lady."

"But you spoke with such animation," persisted Catherine. "I cannot imagine it was as dry as you suggest. Please, continue as though I had not interrupted."

"I think not. The topic is one not properly discussed in delicate company, and I am quite sure it could hold no interest for you," Chimsley replied, his patronising tone infuriating Catherine.

"Oh, I am not so delicate and am rather more opinionated than you might suppose. Still, perhaps you are right, for I know little enough of politics, save two things ..." she replied, pausing just long enough to tease someone into asking her more.

"Oh really, Lady Catherine," one of the others said obligingly, his amusement at the idea of a woman having any opinion on politics plain. "I had not supposed women troubled themselves to think on such things, but you have my ear ... continue."

Catherine smiled her most willing and accommodating smile which, had they known her at all, would have warned of danger. "Firstly," she began, "Prinney is a fool, more likely to inspire contempt than respect. We simply cannot rely on him to ensure unity. So I say to you, secondly, we must look to France and take what lessons we can from there ... *Révolu-*

tion, gentlemen, *révolution*! We must watch our lower classes – and our heads!"

The men stood aghast.

"Lady Catherine!" objected the baron, his voice loud with horror that a woman would not only hold such opinions but also express them. "That is hardly fitting conversation … I cannot imagine where you came by such radical notions, but I dare say your parents would be appalled to hear you voice them – and in so public a setting. Your lack of decorum quite shocks me."

Catherine stepped back from the party and gave a slight nod of her head, attempting feebly to repress her smile. "Forgive me, Lord Chimsley," she chirped, in a manner that spoke little of repentance, "I cannot imagine what possessed me."

Garbrae, who had been hiding in a corner of the billiards room for the last fifteen minutes, shot a look across at Lord Chimsley's loud exclamation and was surprised to see the same lady as before at the heart of the commotion. What she had said to cause such a fuss was a matter of curiosity, although he noted that whatever it was, the lady appeared little concerned by the offence caused.

"It almost seems as though she were pleased," he mused aloud to himself, but before he could give the matter much more thought, the lady at the heart of it was gone.

CHAPTER 6

*H*aving dispensed with the most obvious suitors, Catherine sought out Rose and her mother, finally feeling easy in the hope that the evening would yet prove to be an enjoyable one. She found them both in the library where the countess had secured the companionship and consolation of the Viscountess of Dagmore, a woman as vexed as the countess with trying to secure an attachment for her eldest daughter, the Honourable Susan Dunne, who had attained the ghastly age of twenty-six without the merest suggestion of an offer of matrimony.

The countess shook her head in sympathy with Lady Dagmore and thought to offer hope on the possibility of finding just the right man but, upon meeting Miss Dunne, deemed it simply best to suggest, "Still, there is something to be said for having a daughter at home, to be a companion to you. You say you have another daughter, and a son; well, that must be of great comfort."

Catherine, having just joined them, burned with embarrassment for Miss Dunne who stood not a foot behind the women, appearing oblivious to, or at least unconcerned by, a conversation so obviously denigrating her.

The larger of the drawing rooms, the party learned, was to be set up for an impromptu dance. Rose was thrilled by the unexpected treat. Catherine grimaced at the thought and doubted there was any element of the evening that had not been meticulously planned. Within the first quarter-hour of their being gathered together, there were sufficient applications to dance for both Catherine and Rose to keep the countess delighted, Lady Dagmore envious, and Catherine dismayed. There had been no applications made for Miss Dunne's hand, and it appeared, as soon as the dancing commenced, she would be left, most markedly, surrounded by married women. That she could bear such humiliation with such grace was a wonder to Catherine.

"I do not interrupt, I hope, Miss Dunne, by begging the pleasure of your company," she asked, on drawing her aside.

"Lady Catherine, you are most kind. Indeed, I would be grateful for some pleasant conversation. My mother's agitation at my snubbing rises every minute, so I appreciate the welcome distraction from the most rueful of her glances." Susan laughed lightly.

The pair walked away from the group, and Catherine led them to a large table in the corner that had been laid out with bowls of punch and delicate glasses. "You are remarkably well humoured. I am certain I could not maintain such an unaffected air in the face of such treatment."

"Oh, I have had years to grow accustomed to evenings such as this. We are here, ostensibly, to find me a husband, but I know it is my sister's cause that will be promoted. I am an assured spinster; my mother knows it, though she refuses to admit it."

"Does it hurt?" Catherine blurted out, looking to the angry scar that ran the full length of Susan's face, curving from deep into her temple, cutting down through her cheek, and curling under her chin.

Susan coloured, and Catherine fearing she had been too blunt, turned away and busied herself with pouring them each a glass of punch. To her surprise, when Susan answered her, rather than being offended she seemed grateful for the question.

"Lady Catherine, you are the first to ask that in Lord knows how long. Most people stare, turn away, or try to ignore it. Some ask how it happened, but none ask if it hurts. But you know, save the constant wounding to my pride as a result of it, there is no pain now."

The women relaxed into an easy, interesting conversation that neither had expected to find that evening. Drinks in hand, they took a turn about the library and the adjoining dining room and were so happily engaged in one another's company that the announcement of the first dance came, for Catherine, as an interruption to the great pleasure of the evening rather than as the great pleasure in itself.

"If I could avoid the engagement I would," she assured Susan, on seeing the first of her dance partners approach, "but I have agreed and must at least honour my word or face the full wrath of my mother, and I am so weary of that."

"Do not concern yourself, Lady Catherine. I am accustomed to watching as others dance. Try to appear as though you are enjoying yourself, but if your partner proves less than appealing, I will welcome your company again."

"Oh, I am quite certain you will be seeing me as soon as civility permits my withdrawal," Catherine said, the two women having just time to share a smile and a warm handshake before Catherine was led away.

Garbrae had left the billiards room shortly after Lady Catherine and had gone in search of the woman. He found her in the library, surrounded by a group of ladies. He watched as she broke away from the group and took a turn with one of the other young women. There was a gentle sway to her walk where previously she had moved with a purposeful stride. He smiled for the second time that evening. Clearly the battle waged earlier, whatever it had been, had been won. Here was a woman at peace. He noted, taking in the swing of her hips, the triumphant elongation of her neck, and the slight shake of her dark brown hair, that victory suited the woman well. She talked with animation to the other women and seemed to laugh readily enough. The smile that settled on her face was soft and broad and genuine. He could hardly account for the difference in this woman to the one he had seen enter the drawing room not an hour ago. For the first time, he realised, he had found a woman he wanted to speak with, and she was one of the very few women at the party he had not managed to secure an introduction to.

"Excuse me," Garbrae began, on reaching the small group of ladies seated comfortably in a half circle at the far end of the drawing room, "you will forgive the boldness of my approach without previous introduction, but I find myself suddenly without a dance partner and unaccountably keen to be dancing. My name is Captain James Garbrae. Do I presume too much to ask for permission to dance with your daughter?" he said, finishing his little speech with a bow.

The three women stared at him. Lady Dagmore was scarcely more surprised than Susan by the application, but recovering admirably, she smiled and replied, "Well, we are all friends here, I am sure, so although a little unusual, I see no particular harm. I am quite certain she would be delighted."

Garbrae gave a second crisp bow and turned his attention to the young lady in question who, if he was any judge, was less than delighted. He hesitated for a moment, he had not thought to cause her discomfort, but the offer was made, and he could not walk away now. He raised his arm, and though she hesitated a moment, the lady did, at last, lay her hand atop his and allow herself to be led toward the far end of the room.

"How foolish of me, but I do not even know your name," he admitted as they moved to join the end of the line of dancers already waiting to begin.

"Is it a bet?" Susan replied coldly.

"What? Did you say Elizabeth?" Garbrae asked, straining to hear her quiet response over the noise of the room and the start of the music.

"I asked you if you were dancing with me to secure some wager. Do you have a bet with your friends – something to do with wooing the disfigured spinster?" she said, stopping their progress, refusing to move until he answered her.

Garbrae stood aghast. "Why would anyone be so cruel? Why would you even think that would be the reason I asked you to dance?" he replied, watching the sudden flash of an old pain flicker across his partner's face. "Lord! Someone has treated you so before … I …" He stumbled over his words. "I am sorry."

Susan watched him struggle. There was guilt at play about his features, but no cruelty, and he seemed surprised, even appalled, at the suggestion she had made.

"You are not, I see now, a man who would make such a wager," she admitted in response to his discomfort, "but there is something at work behind you asking for this dance, and I will know the truth, or I will not dance with you."

Garbrae stood, embarrassed by the rashness of his actions. "I can be such a fool. I should have waited and arranged a proper introduction. I am not normally so impatient."

"I await your answer, sir, and the first dance is about to begin."

"I wished to learn a little of your companion," Garbrae blurted, before sense could stop the words tumbling out.

Susan stared at him, a sudden burst of laughter from her catching Garbrae off guard.

"You wished to learn of Lady Catherine? Of course. Of course, you did." She smiled, all at once at ease. "Come, Captain Garbrae, we shall join the dancing after all, and I shall tell you what little I know of the lady – for we have only just met. Oh, and my name is Miss Dunne, Miss Susan Dunne."

"I apologise for the deception, Miss Dunne," Garbrae managed as they took up a spot on the floor. "I had not thought about the position I would be putting you in, but I did not think one dance could cause any harm."

"Captain, did you even see my disfigurement?"

"You will forgive me, but a scar that angry and on a face otherwise so pretty is not likely to be overlooked," he replied, before pausing for a beat. "Oh. I see now … I should have known. I should have guessed the scar …"

"It did not even occur to you that this would make me something of an outcast, did it?"

"It is an injury, unfortunate in its positioning, but just an injury. I have seen many more and many worse in my time in the navy," Garbrae answered, the genuineness of his reply warming Susan to him.

"Come, let us pay attention to the dancing for a little

while. It may be the last dance I have for some time, so I plan on fully enjoying it. Then perhaps, we can talk more of you and your interest in Lady Catherine Montgomery."

By the end of their dance, Garbrae had learned from Susan what little she knew of Lady Catherine and found he was disappointed to return her to her mother.

"I enjoyed our dance, Miss Dunne," he said, bowing politely. "If I were not already engaged for the next, nothing could stop me from asking for the honour of another."

"No, sir, such preference would be unsupportable," Susan jested. "You have done enough, and I would not wish to further encourage the hopes of my mother. Thank you; it has been a pleasure. I wish you luck with your next partner."

Despite Susan's best wishes, Garbrae found he could barely concentrate on his second partner. It was not merely that she was less witty and less engaging than his first, but that they took up a position across from Lady Catherine. He was distracted by the swirl of her dress and turned at hearing her voice, finding greater interest in trying to follow her conversation than his own partner's.

This preference did not go unobserved by the lady who ought to have captured his attention, and she was not pleased.

"You are distracted this evening, captain," she teased, drawing his attention back to her. "I begin to fear you asked me to dance out of duty and not preference."

Garbrae made no comment but looked guilty enough to tell the lady all she needed to know.

"Still, I suppose the woman you prefer is at least a worthy rival. Though, I warn you, she will not be an easy conquest."

"I cannot imagine who you are referring to," Garbrae replied with as much disinterest as he could muster.

"Oh, then it is not Lady Katerina who has you so distracted?" replied she, feigning as much disinterest as he.

"Lady Catherine, you say? Which one is she?"

"No, sir, I said 'Lady Katerina'," she replied, a wicked little smile at her jest breaking out upon her face, "but I believe you know the lady of whom I speak."

"Ah, well ... what of her? We have never met ... I have heard her name mentioned."

"Oh, I am quite sure you have. Her family are highly regarded, the estates extensive, and the coffers"—the lady paused to draw Garbrae in—"quite empty. It is whispered she will marry well this season, or her family will be ruined. So, I dare say you will have competition with any family wealthy enough to take on the debt in trade for the bloodline. Of course, she has already dispatched with a number of would-be suitors – not wealthy enough, I should not wonder—"

"My lady, I hardly think this an appropriate topic of conversation," cut in Garbrae, his heart sinking at her revelations. "I am not accustomed to giving credence to idle gossip, and I suggest you follow suit."

Garbrae's dance partner tried to look suitably chastened; she could see her little ruse had caused her to fall out of favour with the captain. Still, given his behaviour, she doubted she had ever had his favour. That he no longer appeared distracted by Lady Catherine, however, was a comfort at least.

It was a full two sets before Catherine could claim that fatigue prevented her from dancing further. Her next dance partner, disappointed but adamant she must not overexert herself, agreed to wait until Catherine had had the chance to take some rest and refreshment. His offers to secure her a seat and a glass of punch were refused with as much civility as Catherine could muster. Rather, she insisted, she would see him fully enjoying the evening, and so another dance partner must be secured.

Her first thought had been to join Miss Dunne again, but on finding her previous seat occupied by another and no sign of the woman, Catherine turned her attention to securing a seat of her own in a quiet corner.

Knowing she might find some peace from the clamour in the library, she headed there and almost as soon as she entered the room she noticed the man who had danced with Miss Dunne, the man who had put her friend at ease, and who had appeared charming, interested, and unconcerned by the stares of others in the line. In her weeks in London, he was the first man who had piqued her interest, and before she could call herself to account for her actions, she approached the couch where he had taken up residence.

"Excuse me, sir; may I—" she began, before being rudely interrupted.

"I am not a carcass, you know, waiting to be plundered," he said tersely. "Though of all the vultures encircling me this evening you might be the handsomest."

"Vultures?" responded Catherine in utter confusion at the man's meaning.

"Vultures, Miss Montgomery. It *is* Miss Montgomery, is it not?"

When she failed to respond immediately, Garbrae assumed he had the upper hand and continued. "I confess, I was prepared for an approach through some connected party – a mother or an aunt – but to approach me yourself … Well, I would not have expected such forthrightness. I suppose I should applaud your audacity at least."

There was a silent pause as each took the measure of the other.

Garbrae, still confident, added, "You continue in silence, Miss Montgomery, but it is too late for such coyness now. Or is there another explanation for your silence? Perhaps the comparison to a vulture offends you. Would you prefer something more genteel? A magpie perhaps? Yes, a charm of magpies describes you ladies perfectly, all grasping for a shiny treasure. I hear you are in need of a husband. Have you joined me in the hope of securing a fortune as well as a ring? I beg you will believe me when I say I am not inclined to be married and most certainly not to you or any of the other fine-feathered beauties being paraded about tonight – I ask you simply leave me alone."

Catherine listened in amazement to all Garbrae had to say, that she paid attention to his lecture evident from the slight flush in her cheeks and the raising of her eyebrows. She waited until he was completely through before replying, "Well, what a speech. Was it the work of studied practise, crafted and rehearsed as you sat here alone, or the work of the moment, inspired by my approach?"

Garbrae stood, perplexed by the response. This was not the hurried and embarrassed retreat he had anticipated. "You choose to mock me, Miss Montgomery, because I make my wishes clear?"

Catherine drew her shoulders back, a slight tilt of her head elongating her neck, causing a piece of hair to fall free of its pin and wind down onto her chest. Garbrae, his eyes drawn to her body by the falling curl, was momentarily transfixed by the swell of her breast and an unsought desire stirred within him. He fleetingly reconsidered his hasty dismissal of the woman standing her ground so self-assuredly. Perhaps his dance partner had been mistaken about this woman's situation, perhaps he no longer cared either way.

And then Catherine responded. "My name, sir, is Lady Catherine Eugenia Montgomery. I am the daughter of the seventh Earl and Countess of Westbury, and you will address me accordingly." Garbrae's attack had prompted the worst of her imperiousness. "As for my wishing to mock you, I can assure you that was not my intention. To mock you would suggest I am even slightly aware of who you are, and as it stands, I am not. It was simply that I had seen you dancing with my friend, Miss Dunne, and wished to commend you. I thought I had at last found a true gentleman in London, but I see that I was mistaken. Thank you for so quickly disabusing me of the notion. I am consoled at least in only having wasted a short time in thinking highly of you. Good evening, sir, I shall leave you at once," she snapped, "to the mercy of the rest of the magpies!"

~

"There you are, Catherine," Rose called out, on seeing her sister tucked away in a corner chair in the billiards room. "This is where you have been hiding."

"I am not hiding, Rose, merely resting. I am rallying myself to face a further set with a man likely to do more damage to my toes than I care to think."

"Then perhaps my news will be welcome – if nothing else, your toes might be spared. Papa wishes to introduce you to someone."

"Ah, there they are now ..." Catherine heard her father announce on their approach.

"Mr Garbrae, may I have the honour of introducing you to my daughters, Lady Catherine and Lady Rose Montgomery. Catherine, come meet Mr Garbrae and his son ..."

Catherine stared at the man her father was holding out as a potential suitor. It was the man from the library, the arrogant, insufferable, presumptuous man from the library.

"Oh, Mr Garbrae's son and I have already met," she replied, "though we were not formally introduced."

"How wonderful—"

"Wonderful indeed, for it will make this awkward introduction short," she continued, making no attempt to mask her displeasure. "You need not concern yourself with trying to arrange a match between us; the captain has no intention of being married, at least not to me."

She shot a sideways glance at Garbrae – new money, and he had the audacity to presume to turn her down. That someone of his standing should not only consider it a possibility she would make an approach to him but also that he should dare to refuse, rankled Catherine beyond measure. Her ire raised, and her high-handedness in full swing, she offered no quarter to the men standing dumbfounded before her.

"Now, if you will excuse me, gentlemen, I have a drawing room to parade around, and a dance partner I must not disappoint." She turned and walked away, dismissing all three with a sharp turn of her head before anyone could object.

Lord Westbury, embarrassed and furious at the unceremonious departure of his eldest daughter, turned to apologise to Mr Garbrae.

"Please, Lord Westbury, you need make no apology for your daughter," he replied. "I have no doubt my son will be able to explain why the lady was so obviously offended, and why exactly she should state he is not inclined toward finding a wife."

Mr Garbrae and the earl turned their attention to the captain to find him smiling in amusement.

CHAPTER 7

"*Y*ou will marry him, and that will be an end to it." Lord Westbury could be heard yelling from his study. "Would you see your mother destitute? Your sister penniless?" His voice quieter now, so no one outside the room would hear. "You know the peril we are in."

"Would *I*? I did not risk this family's fortune on the gamble of Argentine gold. I did not bring this judgement down upon us."

"Had the speculation been a success it would have righted our situation."

"But you failed, Father! And now I am being punished. I am responsible for saving us." Catherine spat the words at him. Her hands shook; she grabbed at the back of the chair in front of her and leaned heavily upon it. "You cannot mean to marry me to a tradesman," she said, her voice sharp, edged with disbelief.

They had been arguing back and forth in this manner for a quarter-hour, and the earl, his patience at an end, slammed his hands onto the table in between them and bellowed, "You will do as you are charged," with greater anger than his daughter deserved. Seeing her stiffen at his reply, he slid his hands back along the desk toward his body and lowered himself into his chair. Drawing a deep breath, he continued. "Captain Garbrae is hardly a tradesman, Catherine. The family business holdings, wealth, and connections are vast. There is no shame in the alliance, and the man is honourable – a good man. I have had him looked into; I do not enter into this proposal blindly."

"You do not enter into this proposal at all, Father; I do," Catherine replied tersely.

"What you see as sacrifice now might yet come to be something better. You will have a good life with him; he will provide for you."

"He will provide for you," she said, her patience with her father's attempted appeasement all but gone.

"The deal is done."

"Do I stand to change anything by appealing to you?" she asked, more subdued than she had been before.

The earl shook his head.

Catherine paled. She thought back to listening at the door of her father's study as he and Mr Garbrae discussed the possible match. She had not caught the whole of their conversation, but Mr Garbrae had spoken of risky plans and unnecessary expenditure, and her chest had tightened at his words. Mr Garbrae had promised all losses would be covered, that the earl need not worry for the future of his daughter, that the Garbrae fortune could withstand the follies of his son. But that had been cold comfort for Catherine.

"What if I were to accept one of the others?" Catherine begged, fearful for the first time. Dear God, if she married the captain would she simply be swapping one reckless man for another? "Mother was certain Lord Royston was inclined …" she added.

"A special licence has been applied for," her father said. "My debts are paid. My funds replenished."

Catherine stumbled back as though struck. "Then it is done, and it will not be undone."

"It will not."

She stared at her father, but he turned from her, busying himself with papers on his desk, refusing to meet her accusing gaze. "Then it is done," she said again, stepping further away, "so at least let it be done quietly, without celebration. Let there be none but family to witness my being sold."

"Catherine," the earl stood, his hand reaching out to her – no anger, only sadness in his voice. "Do not speak so. You are being wed into a good family. Please, you must see that."

"What I see is that what you want – what the Garbraes want – will be accomplished by this deal. What I want barely seems to matter. Your debts are paid; Rose is saved – in that, I must find some peace. You will grant me this one request: make my wedding day a quiet one. Promise me that at least."

Catherine did not wait for her father's reply. His low, "As you wish," barely audible over the sound of the closing door.

"You will marry her and that will be an end to it." John Garbrae could be heard yelling from the dining room.

"You promised me a say in who I would marry," countered his son.

"That was before," Mr Garbrae replied dismissively, opening the doors that led from the room and striding out into the paved court.

"Before what?"

The father spun about to glare at his stubborn excuse for a

son. "Before we had the chance to marry you to an earl's daughter, and before I knew what an ass you would be. The girl is not foolish, not ugly, not vapid, not too short nor too tall, not too large nor too small. In the name of all that is good, what is your objection?" he replied, his frustration plain.

Garbrae, who had followed his father out into the courtyard took a moment before replying. "Her ladyship is cold," he said.

"Cold?"

"As I say, she has no warmth to her. She is arrogant too. There is no life to her conversation. She is pretty, I suppose, in a hard way, and I have no doubt she functions well in the world, as a machine functions – mechanically."

Mr Garbrae turned away once more and resumed his journey to the stables, knowing his son would not relent and would no doubt follow him. "Lord, boy, you talk some rot. You met the girl twice, and if I recall, on one of those occasions you insulted her. Marry the woman. I am sure you will uncover feeling enough to see you through. The girl is as much flesh and blood as you are. She is bright and damned attractive. I do not care what you say, she had spark enough to cut you down on meeting you."

"I thought, on our first meeting, I had found someone interesting. I too mistook her disdain for passion. Our second encounter showed the lady's true colours. She cares only for our money."

"Her father cares for our money; the lady seemed little impressed to me," Mr Garbrae countered.

"But still you would have me marry her?"

"There is something in that girl, and it will be up to you to find it."

"And if I refuse?"

"Then you refuse, and the wedding will not go ahead."

The captain stopped at the stable door and stood silently, surprised at his father's response.

Mr Garbrae reached for the reins of his horse and drew her out into the yard. "Neither will your plans for improvements at the mill."

The captain stared at his father as the other man mounted his horse and wheeled it around to look down upon his son. This was what he had expected. "But you know those improvements to be a good thing," he argued.

"I know them to be an expense," Mr Garbrae said. "I know no other master is looking to lay out such costs and no other mill owner sees the expense necessary."

"The others are wrong, short-sighted, and greedy. They view their workers as nothing more than a commodity. Strip away the humanity and it is easy to talk of wasted profit versus potential return. My plans will benefit the workers, make conditions better for those we employ. At the very least, you gain a healthier, more stable workforce, able to work longer, willing to work harder, and that must be worth something."

"Then marry her ladyship and do what you will at the mill." Mr Garbrae, looking set to turn his horse and head out of the yard, paused a moment and stared at his son with a deeper concentration. "I will strike this deal with you: all that you want to accomplish is yours to accomplish. I will give you the mill, free and clear from any interference from me, signed over to you on your wedding day. I always told you there was a price to doing business, though you must admit accepting a pretty wife is not so great a price to pay."

"You would turn the mill completely over to me?"

"The mill and all the associated business interests," added his father, certain this incentive would ensure his son's compliance.

"The export and shipping companies? Our holdings in India?"

"All yours, if you marry this girl. I will maintain our other interests for now, but all our holdings in cotton will be handed over to you. So choose, son. I promised you a say; you have it. What will your answer be?"

CHAPTER 8

Manchester. May 1813

The couple were married by way of a small ceremony, attended only by family, and they decamped to Manchester as soon as the deed was done. No celebration followed their nuptials, for Catherine was determined to leave London at once and certainly before the announcement of her marriage could become common knowledge – worse yet, fodder for gossip.

Despite her husband's hopes, there was little opportunity for the pair to get to know one another as they travelled, for Catherine slept during most of the journey. When they stopped overnight, she kept solely to her room, even at mealtimes.

Thus it was that their first breakfast as husband and wife in their new home was not an easy one. Garbrae hoped their awkwardness around one another might be lessened by being in a room together, both awake, without the discomfort of a rocking carriage, with the buffer of servants and a full table between them, but Catherine was as ill at ease as ever. She barely looked at him for the first ten minutes of their meal. The only person to whom she paid any mind was Covington, their butler, and that was merely to provide instructions for changes to the breakfast.

"Lord, what a list of changes," Garbrae commented once she had finished, and Covington had stepped back from the table. "I am sure the breakfast is not as bad as all that. Should we start our stay here with such a list of demands for the servants?"

"If we do not tell them how things ought to be, how can they complete their duties in a satisfactory manner?" replied Catherine, reaching for her cup of chocolate and avoiding her husband's gaze.

"But can it matter what china is used? Or whether napkins are laid out? Or how many varieties of meat are provided?" Garbrae persisted, keen to take any opportunity to strike up a conversation with his wife.

"Of course it matters. It matters to me, so it matters to Covington. If I am not happy, Covington is not happy. If Covington is not happy, can anyone below stairs be?"

Garbrae laughed and threw his napkin across his now empty plate. "You cannot believe that."

Catherine, growing increasingly weary at her husband's lack of understanding of how things were done, was snappish in her reply.

"Of course I believe it, captain. The word servant comes from the French 'servir' – to serve," she said, looking at him for the first time that morning. "That is their purpose. To do so, and do it well, is to find fulfilment in their purpose."

"I know the meaning of the word," Garbrae answered tightly.

"And yet you find such difficulty in its proper application," Catherine countered, turning her attention from

Garbrae to the plate of rolls, her participation in the conversation at an end.

~

Alone in the dining room, waiting for luncheon to be served, Catherine had the opportunity to make a proper study of the room. It was set out beautifully. The walls, a pale green, were dotted with paintings of landscapes. The three large windows, surrounded by drapes of deep green and gold, framed the view of the lush landscape of their own gardens.

She did not turn on hearing the door open but continued to look out the window. "It is a pity you cannot see the lake from here," she mused aloud, more to herself than whoever was setting out her meal.

"You can if you stand at the furthest left corner."

She stiffened at the increasingly familiar strains of her husband's voice. "Captain," she said, without moving an inch, "I had not expected you."

Garbrae, determined to lessen the tension between them, replied with false levity, "No indeed, though I could not think to abandon you to your own company just yet. If we are to be companions, you and I, I think we ought to spend a little time together, getting to know one another. We are at our leisure for the next few weeks. I have ensured no work will call me away. I thought we might start with luncheon and plan how to spend the day?"

Catherine sighed; she had hoped business would immediately occupy her husband, leaving her to settle into her new home and local society with a degree of ease and decorum she doubted Garbrae could muster.

"Should we call upon our new neighbours, do you think?"

"Though your father spent time here, captain, we are new to the area, it is not our place to call. We must wait upon cards from our neighbours and then we may return their visit."

"Of course. Etiquette must be observed," teased Garbrae.

Catherine's head turned sharply in his direction. "Well, that is rather the point," she replied. "Would you prefer we throw out convention and let our whims govern us?"

Garbrae pulled out a seat and sat down, clearly intent on taking luncheon with her. "Nothing quite so radical, I assure you. I had simply thought to bend the rules that kept us from greeting our neighbours warmly and increasing our acquaintance."

"Although we have moved to Lancashire, I hope we have not moved beyond the realm of civilised society. Surely the same rules of civility apply here as in the rest of the country. I would not want your enthusiasm to be mistaken for brashness."

"If we are not to call on our neighbours, what do you say to a tour of the grounds, Catherine? No, not Catherine; may I call you Kitty now that we are married? A term of endearment for my new wife?"

"You may call me what you like," Catherine responded coolly, "although if you wish a response, I suggest you use something less likely to result in indifference, for I will not answer to Kitty."

Garbrae, still hoping to elicit some form of humour from her, continued. "So, a little less informal then – even when we are alone. Perhaps, 'your ladyship' or 'my lady' would be preferable?" he jested, anticipating a smile at least at the suggestion.

Catherine moved away from the window, her patience with the man at an end. In no mood for frivolity, she inclined her reply toward flippancy as she took up a seat at the table opposite his. "That would be less objectionable, certainly. When you feel the need to address me, either will suffice."

CHAPTER 9

"We have been invited to dine with our neighbours, the Nash's, this evening," Catherine announced at breakfast two days later. "Mrs Nash called on us yesterday."

The captain, pleased and surprised that his wife had opened a conversation without his prompting, engaged the topic with greater enthusiasm than was necessary, a barrage of questions all tumbling out at once.

"Did she? I would have liked to have met her. When did she call? Where was I? Why did you not call me?"

Catherine, who had taken to interpreting everything her husband said as a criticism was not pleased. "It was a little after eleven; I have no idea where you were, captain. I did not realise I needed to know where you were at every minute, and it did not occur to me to send someone to hunt for you. I was perfectly able to manage an introductory tea by myself."

"Of course you were, and I did not mean to suggest otherwise. I simply would have liked to meet our neighbour, is all."

"And you shall," she replied, giving Garbrae as little room for conversation as possible. "This evening at dinner."

Choosing to ignore Catherine's obvious attempt to end the dialogue between them, he continued. "And so, you must tell me all you know of the Nash's. What did you glean from your tea? Shall they be our sort of people, do you think?" he jested, ever hopeful of finally putting the lady at ease.

"Mrs Nash is charming and possesses a degree of refinement I had not expected to find among our neighbours. She is certainly my sort of person, someone I will be pleased to call a friend. Though whether she will suit you – well, I have no idea. I can scarcely imagine the sort of people you are accustomed to, the type of companions you secured in the factory and the galley." Catherine raised her coffee cup to her lips and stared across at the captain through upturned lashes.

Garbrae straightened in his seat, visibly bristling at the barb. "You really have no opinion of me, do you, my lady?" he said, displeased by Catherine's continued abrasiveness despite his efforts.

"On the contrary, I have a very strong opinion of you," she replied, laying down her cup, her mouth quirking briefly into a mirthless smile.

That the opinion in question was not a good one hung in the silence between them as each retuned their attention to breakfast and pretending the other was not there.

Settled into the carriage for the journey to the Nash's, Catherine sat across from her husband. The conversation, though stilted, was at least civil. The couple commented on the team of horses, the newly upholstered cushioned seats, and the unseasonably warm weather.

"And if this warm spell continues, captain, we should see

about organising a shooting party," suggested Catherine who, in an effort to fill the silence even she was growing weary of, had started outlining plans for their full introduction into Lancashire society.

"You know, you need not call me 'captain', for I have now given up my commission," replied Garbrae, seeking to change the topic of conversation. He had hoped to escape the worst of society when they left London and was exhausted at the list of parties being proposed by his wife.

"What should I call you then?"

"You could try 'James'; it is my name. Or perhaps 'husband', for it is what I am."

Catherine tensed; she could not imagine calling the man "James". It was too intimate a suggestion given their arrangement, and as for "husband" – the very word infuriated her.

"I could call you mill owner or tradesman, for you are those things too."

Garbrae stared at her, his jaw tight with tension. "Is that all you see me as? A tradesman?" he replied.

"Well, you bought me as if I were just another piece of chattel. You made your deal, and no doubt plied your trade well in striking the bargain."

"God, woman, but you are cold!" he exclaimed. "I have never treated you like chattel, and for you to suggest that is an insult beyond reckoning. I never presumed your affections could be bought."

"Just my father's approval," she snapped, tugging her cloak tightly about her.

"Am I to be blamed for providing a solution to a problem that was of your father's making? Is that my great sin, my lady?" the captain challenged. "Rescuing your family and securing your future? Do you punish me because my family's success in business allowed me to rise up in the world?"

Catherine's eyes narrowed as she glared at him. "While

my family's losses would have taken us lower, I suppose you mean."

"I never said that," replied Garbrae, his voice hardening. "Do not presume to speak for me; do not presume to know me."

"Oh, I believe I know you well enough. No doubt you viewed this marriage as quite a successful business proposal, and it appears you have everything you wanted out of the arrangement."

"Do you think I approached this marriage with nothing more than the transaction in mind?" Garbrae asked, wondering if she could possibly know about the deal he had struck with his father, wondering how much of what she accused him of was the truth.

"Do you profess to love me then?" Catherine retorted. A short humourless laugh following the suggestion.

"You know I do not, but do not judge me because I am willing to try. Although, Lord knows, you make it a hard enough prospect."

Catherine turned away and stared out of the carriage window, looking to the passing landscape for distraction. He was infuriating, and though he might play the innocent, she had listened as the deal was done; she had heard Mr Garbrae's insistence about what was due to his son. Despite her objections, the men had gotten what they wanted, and though he may protest now, she knew the captain was not innocent. She clutched the diamond-studded brooch at the collar of her cloak – a family heirloom her father had been able to buy back once her marriage was arranged. She wondered how long it would be before her future once more rested on the fickleness of fate and the gamble of a man's risky speculations.

Garbrae shifted his seat away from his wife, drawing into the furthest corner of the carriage, and sought a similar distraction in staring out of the window. Since this latest attempt at wooing Catherine had proved no more successful than the others, he was determined to exert no more effort in ensuring her ease. The woman wanted nothing more than civility from him, and though he doubted she was even deserving of that, he would see how happy she was when he complied with her obvious desire to be left alone.

Catherine wondered at his silence; it seemed his true nature was revealing itself at last. Still, that held no concern for her. She already knew Garbrae; she had taken his measure the first night they met – self-important and arrogant, the sort of man who believed money entitled him to standing. A new-moneyed master, married to a lineage to which he had no right by birth or breeding … Oh, she knew him. She could imagine how he must have rejoiced in securing the daughter of an earl, how he must have boasted. And now this taciturnity. Perhaps his inflated pride had been wounded by her refusal to be an easy conquest. He must have met other ladies in his quest for a wife: submissive, unquestioning, pleasing. Happy to be kept placated by a life of silk and trinkets. She would not be such a wife, and he would learn that. If he was determined to be silent, then she too could play that game.

CHAPTER 10

The Nash's home was a large stately manor nestled comfortably in the midst of a vast estate whose woods had been allowed to envelop the land right up to the boundary lawn of the main house. Catherine was about to make comment on the wildness of the property, when she recalled her resolution to be silent for as long as her husband managed to be, and so she waited until she met her hostess before saying, "Mrs Nash, what a surprise to find you so immersed in the woods – it is like something from a fairy tale."

"Captain Garbrae, Lady Garbrae," Mrs Nash called out in greeting, "Welcome, welcome, it is such a pleasure to have you here with us. What must you think of our little castle in the forest? I tell my dear husband almost daily we ought to cut back the woodland, but he loves the wildness of it. We compromise, I suppose, in that I have kept my lawns and rose garden. If I were not here, I swear he would allow the whole place to be overrun! Come, let me introduce you to the others here tonight. I hope you do not mind, but I invited some of our other neighbours to attend. I thought it might help you to settle more easily – new society can be so exhausting."

"Not at all," replied Catherine. "It will be a pleasure. I know my husband has been eager to expand his acquaintance in the area. I am sure he longs for some excuse to be out among other men for there must be plenty of sport to be had in such beautiful countryside. As you can imagine, the thrills of keeping house will not keep him entertained for long."

The two women laughed and continued their walk indoors, engaged in light-hearted teasing of Garbrae who, for his part, smiled in return, marvelling at his wife's capacity for duplicity. She hardly spoke to him when they were alone, could barely manage civility at home, yet here she stood in the home of another, playing the part of a new wife, all ease and enchantment, all charm and delight, with a light laugh and ready smile. *Lord! She should be on the stage*, he thought, such were her skills, for no one there would imagine her to be the cold, arrogant, and aloof woman he lived with.

But he knew her; he had taken her measure. She was a well bred society lady saved from the brink of ruin by his family yet still believing herself to be above him ... Oh, he knew her. How she must have felt demeaned by marrying him; how she must have considered it a degradation. And now this gaiety. No doubt her conceit had been wounded by his refusal to be impressed by her status. She must have met other men in her search for a husband, men slavish to her rank, captivated by her beauty – cold as it was – men willing to be subservient to her. Well, he would not be such a husband, and she would learn that. If she was determined to play the part of the happy couple for their hosts, then he too could play that game.

"Captain Garbrae, might I introduce you to my husband?" asked Mrs Nash.

"Of course, forgive me. My attention was taken by a painting of the naval fleet. I could not help but stop, though please, I resigned my commission so there is no need for—"

"Oh, captain, no, I must stop you, for I believe you are about to declare we must not call you captain, when in fact, we must. It was a rank well earned, I am sure, and the ladies will be disappointed at having another Mr in the fold. We need another seafaring man with tales of foreign lands and intrepid adventures, or we shall be disappointed."

"Well, I should hate to disappoint, though whether or not my poor tales will be enough to excite, I do not know." Garbrae laughed, happily taking up Mrs Nash's arm and allowing her to escort him to the drawing room where the rest of the guests were already assembled. "Another seafaring man, you said. Is there someone else from the navy here this evening?" he enquired as they approached the door.

"Indeed, my husband was a naval man."

Garbrae stopped her as she reached for the door handle, causing her to stay their entrance to the room a moment more. "Nash? Is Admiral Charles Nash your husband?" he asked, not quite believing it.

"Yes. You have heard of him then?"

"Heard of him," he replied, astounded the woman could talk so blithely about one of the navy's most celebrated admirals. "Your husband was an exemplary military man and strategist. I had no notion he was settled here. I thought, after retirement, he would have been called up in some advisory capacity."

"Oh, there were plenty of offers and more than a few demands, but he had already given a lifetime to the navy and was determined he would see our children grow – something he missed with his first two boys."

"You are the second Mrs Nash then?" asked Garbrae, who had been wondering at the age of his hostess, figuring she must be at least twenty years her husband's junior.

"Indeed, and twenty-five years his junior," she answered, in reply to the question he had not thought proper to ask, "but we are sinfully happy with one another and that is all that really matters, do you agree, captain?"

"I do." He smiled, giving her a short bow. "Now, if you please, it would be an honour to meet your husband," he said, turning the handle and following her into the room.

Catherine could not determine whether to be pleased or dismayed by the neighbours in attendance that evening. All were well-dressed, well-educated, well bred, and old money – these were her people. She had worried that Lancashire society would consist of well-to-do farmers, tradesmen, and their wives, for how could she spend her evenings making polite conversation with persons, however affable, of such low standing? How curious then, she thought, that she should find greater mortification in finding her neighbours her equal in birth and station, for in such company, the disparity between herself and her husband would be all too obvious. As in London, it would not be long before her situation was made fodder for gossips, or worse still, before she was made an object of pity.

It was with some relief that her husband did not immediately follow her into the drawing room. She could make introductions and establish connections free from the embarrassment of having to acknowledge her association with him. She talked of London, fashion, theatre, and charity, and while these things never held any real interest for her, the familiarity of the conversation was calming. These were conversations she had endured a hundred times in a hundred different drawing rooms. And where once she had complained of such banality, now she revelled in it, delighted in the consolation of it – the only misgiving being the wonder of how long such comfort would last once Garbrae made his entrance.

~

"There you are, darling," Garbrae announced a little too loudly upon approaching her.

Catherine baulked on hearing his voice, and on being addressed so familiarly. On turning, she noticed the flutter of fans, shared glances, and tittering from a group of women seated in a half circle in a far corner of the room. Four sets of eyes flitted between the captain and herself – already, they were an amusement. Still, refusing to appear in the least affected, she met the captain's full smile with one of equal brilliance.

"Here indeed … darling. Come, let me introduce you to some of our neighbours."

Catherine, subconsciously, had raised her arm in calling him closer. Refusing to let the opportunity to completely disquiet her pass him by, Garbrae took the proffered arm, laid it above his own, and secured it in place by putting his other hand atop hers. Catherine's reaction was just as Garbrae had hoped – he felt her body jolt as he touched her and watched the colour fade from her cheeks. Lord, she was incensed.

Indeed, the heat from Garbrae's body had certainly star-tled Catherine, as did his general closeness and the unques-tionable intimacy he was creating between them. However, if the shock of his presuming to touch her were not enough, Catherine paled upon being struck by the fear of what else he might do. Surely, not even he would be so brazen as to kiss her.

Regardless of how nervous her husband made her, a first round of introductions was managed without embarrassment, and Catherine began to relax. She begrudgingly admitted the man could almost be considered charming, and it seemed some of the ladies found him amusing, although the fact they were the source of much chatter among others in the room prevented her from feeling fully at ease.

"Has it occurred to you, my lady," enquired Garbrae, pulling her out of earshot of their companions, "that we are talked of for no other reason than because we are a novelty and not that we, or should I say, not that *I* am an embarrassment. It might actually be that the gossip is not disagreeable toward us at all. Even you must admit that we make a handsome couple."

"I have no idea what you mean, captain," replied Catherine, disturbed the man could so easily read her, concerned her fears might be as apparent to others.

"Oh, so I am 'captain' again – no longer, husband or darling?" he taunted. "Do not worry; I doubt anyone else has seen through your show You have quite the talent for acting; your skills are wasted here."

The couple stared at one another, uncomfortable moment following uncomfortable moment, neither willing to release their gaze, until Catherine realised how such behaviour must look.

"You seem to delight in my discomfort, captain," she said, turning her face away, forcing her attention to their neighbours, praying no one would see the falter in her smile.

～

Dinner was served just as Catherine feared she could no longer maintain her facade. She had, for half an hour, smiled, laughed, and even flirted a little with the captain. He insisted on touching her, and although there was nothing improper to it – her arm resting on his, or his hand at the small of her back – these were subtle gestures speaking of closeness and even possessiveness. She in return, so as not to appear ill-disposed toward the man, had responded in kind, never flinching from his touch and, once or twice, even reaching across to touch him, brushing his lapel or stroking his arm.

The captain, she thought, *was correct.* She was quite the skilled actress, and she was certain that no one there would have guessed their true feelings for one another. Nevertheless, the pretence was exhausting, and so she was grateful to Mrs Nash who insisted the newlyweds not be afforded the distraction of sitting too close to one another at dinner, not when her husband craved more of Garbrae's time. Thus it was, Catherine found herself seated with Mrs Nash at one end of the table, while the captain was seated with Admiral Nash at the other, a dozen other guests in between them. Catherine offered a silent prayer and spontaneous smile at the delight of a few hours respite from the great chore of the evening – pretending to be in love with her husband.

Garbrae's time with the admiral having been cut short by the necessity of making introductions to the rest of his neighbours, the captain was pleased to be seated so close to the man during dinner.

"I was an avid follower of your career, Admiral Nash," he said as he took his seat, "and was presumptuous enough to first model my command on the principles outlined in your treatise on discipline and order."

"Only at first, Garbrae?" Nash replied, finding his guest's enthusiasm refreshing after an evening of relatively staid conversation. "You did not continue to model your command after my good example?"

Garbrae took a sip of his wine as he considered how he ought to answer. "There were lessons I took to heart, but I thought it best to be guided by the principles rather than the letter of your treatise, incorporating elements that spoke most strongly to me into a style of command and discipline I knew to be my own," he said, hoping his honesty would not be viewed as insolence.

"Bravo, captain!" commended the admiral. "I am heartened to hear you say that. Too often men follow blindly the example of others, but one should always question and adapt. When one's actions come from who you are and not who you pretend to be, those who follow you learn to trust in them – in you. Consistency in praise and punishment is essential, and this will only come when the principles that govern you are truly your own. To be successful in command there must be trust. If a man is to follow his captain into battle, he must never waiver in his belief in the man – or in his understanding of the consequences should he fail to follow him."

A mutual appreciation established, the gentlemen settled happily into conversation to the exclusion of those around them, and this exclusion continued across the entire dinner service, much to the disappointment of the young woman who had been seated between them.

Miss Sutherland had expected to be the centre of attention for the admiral and the captain, or at least to be regaled with tales of seafaring adventures. Instead, she was largely ignored. Beyond some minor pleasantries and the customary praise for the table, the men spent their dinner locked in debates on duty, discipline, and strategy – issues in which she had neither interest nor knowledge. So it was, when the last course was served, Miss Sutherland, delighted by the sight of assorted nuts and sweetmeats, knew it would not be long before she could escape the tedium of the dinner table for the livelier entertainment of the drawing room.

The conversation that consumed Nash's and Garbrae's attention continued over port, and little changed when the whole party came together again in the drawing room.

"Will you join us at whist, husband?" enquired Catherine, hoping to encourage Garbrae to give attention to the others in attendance. "We are in need of a fourth."

"Thank you," he said, only just turning his head away from the admiral, "but I am no card player. I would be more of a hindrance than a help to my partner."

"Then I shall not insist, for I hate to lose, but you will not keep the admiral away from the rest of his guests the whole evening, I trust?" she continued, placing a hand on his shoulder and securing his attention.

"Have we been ignoring the others here? I suppose we have," Nash interjected. "I fear I have been the one who monopolised your husband this evening, and so I am to blame for any lack of attention to the rest of the company. It is rare for me to find someone as informed and opinionated as your husband to debate with, and I am afraid I let myself indulge a little."

"This is your dinner party, admiral, and so you are free to ignore whom you choose," said Catherine, laughing, "though I warn you, Mrs Nash may not feel the same."

"No, indeed, my lady, well mentioned. Come, sir, we shall

have to save this debate for another day. For now, let us forgo our own pleasure in the service of our wives!" Smiling at his own jest, he bowed to Catherine before taking his leave.

CHAPTER 11

Their goodbyes made, and their spirits high after a successful evening, Garbrae and Catherine sat back into their carriage seats and made for home. Each forgot their resolution to punish the other through silence, and they talked excitedly of the evening and of having such a fine introduction to their new neighbours.

Catherine's face still appeared flushed from the heat of the dining room and the effects of the wine, and her husband could not help but admire the look of the woman – her usual reserve having given way to enlivened animation. She was quite altered from the woman he had arrived with; he saw flashes of the woman who had so intrigued him from across the room at the Jenners'. While he knew his wife to be beautiful, the warmth visible in her smile and eyes captivated him. She was compellingly attractive now, and he found he could not take his eyes from her.

Catherine, oblivious to her husband's attentions, continued enthusiastically, recalling the various successes of the evening and more than once expressing her delight in

Mrs Nash as a new friend. She carried on in this manner until the shock of suddenly finding herself swept into the arms of her husband silenced her.

Before his wife could so much as catch her breath, Garbrae had taken her face in his hands and claimed her lips as his own – passion and brandy enflaming him, a sudden desire to fully enjoy his wife overriding every other good sense. As his lips crushed hers and his hands stroked the contours of her face, he revelled in the scent, the softness, and the taste of her, remaining oblivious to everything but this explosion of his senses … until an abrupt shove at his shoulders pushed him back, and the sharp sting of a slap brought his passion to heel.

He jerked further away. Falling back into the seat across from Catherine, his hand reached for his face, rubbing at the pain. "What was that?" he shouted.

"I might ask you the same," cried Catherine, anger flaring in her once warm eyes. "How dare you attack me."

"Attack you? Woman, I am your husband."

"And you believe that entitles you to behave like an animal?" she said, her voice shaking, but the disdain unmistakable.

"You know exactly what it entitles me to," Garbrae replied, his voice low and threatening.

Catherine stared at the man, unable to say a word, her breathing rapid, her eyes darting between him and the carriage door, her panic plain.

The terror on his wife's face was enough to cause Garbrae to fully recollect himself, the menace of his words now chillingly clear to him.

"My lady, I did not … would not … would never …" he spluttered, his mind addled by alcohol and desire. His ability to reason, to form thoughts and express them, apparently lost.

Catherine pulled her cloak tightly across, wrapping herself in her arms, and when the carriage finally stopped outside their house, she was gone before Garbrae could manage to say anything more.

CHAPTER 12

*G*arbrae, wishing to speak to his wife in private the next morning, paced the hallway outside her bedroom for half an hour before the woman emerged.

"My lady," he began, when she walked around him without acknowledgement, "with regards to last night—"

"I do not wish to speak of it," she interrupted, not breaking stride as she headed for the stairs. "I would prefer we never speak of it."

"We cannot simply pretend it did not happen," he said, following her. "My face still stings – that is reminder enough."

"If you think I want to be reminded about that disastrous evening, you are sorely mistaken; I would much rather forget."

Catherine reached the base of the stairs and paused, looking at one moment in the direction of the breakfast room and the next toward the library. She had no heart for letter writing this morning.

"Covington, I will eat early," she said to the man waiting at the foot of the staircase for her.

Garbrae held his tongue until the butler had withdrawn to make arrangements for their breakfast. "Disastrous? The evening was a complete success ... until the unfortunate—"

Swinging the door to the breakfast room open with unnecessary force, Catherine cut him off before he could say more. "A success, captain? What sort of a success is it when you ignore our neighbours so you can share stories with an old sea dog?" she said.

"An old sea dog?" cut in Garbrae, incensed at Catherine's lack of respect for Admiral Nash. "Have you any idea who that man is?"

"Have you any idea of how rude you were? Poor Miss Sutherland was terribly slighted by your ignoring her – she could talk of little else in the drawing room."

Garbrae jerked a chair free from under the table. "Perhaps that is because poor Miss Sutherland is a simpleton who had little else to talk of," he replied sharply, taking up a seat next to where his wife stood.

Her back to the table, Catherine leaned against the chair next to his and turned her head so she could stare down at him. "Even you could not have failed to notice we were a source of amusement for some of the ladies there. Did you not see how they gossiped behind their fans, laughing at us? Lord, we were the great joke of the evening. And you wish to call it a success."

Garbrae tilted his head to the side, so he could stare up at her. "You have no idea what those women were talking about. You were delighted last night by the reception we received. Why are you so determined now to declare the evening a failure? If this concerns what happened in the carriage, I can only apologise for my behaviour – what I did was unpardonable," he said, reaching out to touch her hand gripped tightly around the edge of the table.

"Unpardonable?" she replied, drawing her hand away the very instant his fingertips touched her skin.

The door opened, and she fell silent as a procession of plates and pots of tea, coffee, and chocolate were laid out on the table for them.

She moved behind the captain's seat on her way to the other side of the table but paused a beat and leaned on the back of the chair on his other side, bringing her face level with his. "You were monstrous," she hissed, dropping her voice so the servants would not hear. "What you threatened …"

"I would never have …" he replied, pleading with her. "You have to believe me; I would never hurt you in that way. The threat I made … if I could only take it back. The high spirits after the evening's success … the alcohol … the heat … It all acted upon me and caused a momentary lapse. But I have been patient with you, have I not? I have not made the sort of demands that are my right as a husband to make. You must know I would never … Lord, even you cannot think me capable of that!"

Catherine straightened and moved away from him, taking up her usual seat. "I scarcely know what to think," she replied, now sickened by the sight of the food on the table, anxious to be away from the room, from her husband, and the memories of the evening before. "If you say I had nothing to fear then I must take it to be true. You are my husband after all," she finished, but even from across the table, Garbrae could see a tremor in the hand she reached out to take up her cup.

Knowing his apology had not been sufficient, he moved around and sat next to her, taking a hold of the chocolate pot and pouring her a cup. "My lady, what can I do to prove to you the sincerity of my apology? It is foolish for us to remain on such bad terms. It was a misunderstanding, that is all. Tell me what I can do to fix this."

"Can you turn back time?" she replied, shoving the cup he had filled away from her, causing chocolate to race over the side of both cup and saucer and out across the table.

"Damn it, woman! I will not be your whipping boy," he spat back, his patience frayed. He grabbed at her arm, and his grip tightened as she struggled against him.

"I knew it. I knew you would show your true colours soon enough, captain, and here you are – a brute! But I warn you, this time you do not find me unprotected." She jabbed at his waistcoat with her breakfast fork.

Garbrae stared at his wife, wondering what he was doing. He hardly recognised himself. He released her arm at once and stood, stepped away from the table, and returned to his own seat.

Catherine drew her shoulders back as she rose from her chair. "I am no longer hungry," she said calmly, as she screwed together every ounce of her courage to ensure she managed to get out of the breakfast room without once betraying how unsteady she was. She walked toward the door, each step measured and controlled and then, pausing only for a brief exchange with Covington, she was gone.

Garbrae smashed his fist into the hard, polished wood of the table, causing the dishes to clatter and a knife to skitter off his plate.

Covington stepped forward to reclaim the knife and return it to its rightful place. As he did so, he also reached across the table and laid the mistress' fork back onto the plate opposite. On seeing this, Garbrae looked up to catch the butler's eye, and finding only accusation in the man's cold stare, he too gave up on breakfast and left the room.

CHAPTER 13

*I*t had been four days since Garbrae and Catherine had last breakfasted together. Every morning, Garbrae sat for as long as he could, hoping Catherine would join him. Her continued refusal to see him was beginning to grate. He was sorry for the threat he had made, and his actions the next morning had hardly helped, but even his patience was not without its limits, and she would not be allowed to sulk much longer.

"Covington, I spoke with Thomas yesterday," he said, seeking to distract himself from thoughts of his wife.

"Indeed, sir."

"He told me there is some silver missing."

"Did he, sir?" Covington replied, clearly unhappy. "If Thomas was concerned about the silver, he should have come to me and not bothered you. I shall speak to Thomas today."

"Very well, if you think it appropriate, but is there silver missing? Do we have a thief in the house?"

"I do think it appropriate, sir. You will appreciate there is a chain of command in this house, and Thomas knows better than to circumvent that chain. You should not be bothered by such matters unless I deem it necessary. As I say, I will have a word with Thomas."

Although Garbrae had only mentioned this incident to Covington so he could break up the silence and boredom of the breakfast room, it had not escaped his notice that the man failed to answer his direct question and in fact seemed deliberately evasive in his replies. Lowering his fork, and turning fully to address his butler, he asked again.

"But is there any silver missing?"

Covington stiffened. "There is not. If there were, I would have brought the matter to you myself."

"Then how is it Thomas claims one of the large serving forks is nowhere to be found?"

Covington lowered his eyes. "The fork is not in the set."

"Then is it missing?" badgered Garbrae, increasingly annoyed at the man's intentional obtuseness.

"It is not."

"Lord, man! I had not thought an inquisition would be necessary to get an answer to such a simple question. If the fork is not in the set but is not missing, where exactly is it?"

"Her ladyship has it," Covington replied, only just masking his disdain for his master. "She felt it necessary to have it, so I provided her with it."

Garbrae sighed and ran his hand roughly through his hair. "After breakfast on Monday?"

"Yes, sir – after breakfast on Monday."

"And I suppose you know why she felt she needed it?" Garbrae said, looking once more to his butler.

"Why her ladyship should want anything is not my concern; my only concern is to ensure she has what she wants." Covington returned his master's gaze.

They stared at one another.

Garbrae considered firing Covington, but what good

would that do? The man clearly disliked him; his preference for Lady Catherine was all too apparent. In this instance, the captain could scarcely blame him. The man did his job well, maintained order, and seemed to please his wife; now would not be the time to upset her further.

"Thank you, Covington, that will be all," he replied, determined that if he would not fire him, he could at least dismiss him. "You may have the breakfast things removed. Her ladyship will not be joining me today."

Once alone, Garbrae moved across the room to the spot where, if he stood right in the corner, almost behind the drapes, he was afforded a view of the lake. This vista always refreshed him, and this morning he needed to drink it in before he could face the day. He was quite hidden from view so that the young maid sent in to clear away the last of the breakfast things did not notice him and, thinking herself alone, hummed aloud, enjoying a few minutes of slow, easy work before she had to return to the main business of the day.

"What is that song?" Garbrae said, stepping out from his corner.

"Saints preserve me!" yelped the girl, startled by the unexpected interruption.

"Calm yourself," he said, moving toward her, fearing she might faint, for she was dreadfully pale and even shaking a little. "I did not mean to frighten you. Sit a minute; you have taken quite a turn. Come, there is warm tea in the pot, and a sweet cup would calm us both," Garbrae continued, oblivious to the impropriety of having tea with one of the servants.

"I ought to be getting back to my work, sir," she replied,

not oblivious to how the situation looked. "I am well and think it best I just go back about my work."

"Nonsense, I will not have it. You will sit and have tea," he ordered.

The girl threw her master a curious look. What was this man about? Why insist she stay? Why not have her return to the kitchen, or to her room? As she watched him pour out two cups, she wondered at his intentions. "I am not that sort of girl," she gasped aloud, the reason for his apparent kindness dawning on her.

"Not the sort of girl who takes sugar?" replied Garbrae, completely at a loss to understand her dramatic response to a rather simple question about how she took her tea.

"I realise, sir, that in some houses the master is free to take liberties where he may," she said, "but I will not be imposed upon, and if you try, I shall scream, so help me."

"What on earth are you talking about?" he said, "Liberties? Screaming? What is going on?"

The maid cast her eye at him. The expression he wore made it quite clear he had no idea what she was talking about. Ravishing her was not his objective. *Oh, Lord!* she thought. *The man just wanted to offer me tea.*

Garbrae, in the same instant, came to understand the wicked insinuation. "You thought I wanted …?" he began. "Is my reputation so far gone that I am believed a defiler? God, get out of my sight. Just get out!"

She drew out a chair and sat.

"I said, get out."

She stayed.

"Are you deaf?"

"No, sir, just sometimes a little dim-witted," she replied, still sitting.

Garbrae leaned forward in his seat. "You are not afraid of what I might do?"

"No, sir."

"And yet a moment ago …"

"A moment ago, I was still startled and not quite myself. Now, feeling much more like I ought to, I find I am glad to be in the company of a master who would be concerned about my well-being, and I am in desperate need of a sweet tea – two spoons if you please."

With the tea poured and half drunk in silence, the pair sat opposite one another.

"Did you honestly think yourself in danger from me?" Garbrae finally asked.

"I did for a moment, sir. It is not usual to be asked to take tea."

"No, I suppose not. I apologise; I will be more mindful in future."

She swirled the cup in her hand. "Why did you do it? You could have just sent me away."

Garbrae considered the question carefully and considered the truth of his answer. Dare he admit to a maid that he longed for a little easy conversation? Dare he openly admit to being so lonely? No.

"I scarcely know myself," he lied. "You looked undone, and I did not think."

The pair returned their attention to the tea.

"Why did you think me capable of imposing upon you?"

The maid considered the question carefully, and the truth of her answer. Dare she admit the staff knew some of what had happened in the carriage? Knew her ladyship kept a silver fork about her? That the below stairs gossip was the couple had not spent a night together since their arrival at the house? No.

"It was just a moment of silliness, nothing more. You will forgive me, sir; it will not hold against me?"

Garbrae leaned back in his seat, comfortable at last. "It will not hold against you."

Silence again.

"'Grog Time o'Day'," the maid offered, breaking the quiet once more.

"Excuse me?"

"The song, sir; you asked about the song. It is called 'Grog Time o'Day'."

CHAPTER 14

*A*lthough Catherine had, for several days, refused to entertain any thoughts on dinner at the Nash's. A note from her hostess, announcing her desire to call for luncheon, finally forced the issue upon her.

After some contemplation, now that coolness of mind prevailed, she conceded her husband was correct: the night, up until the incident in the carriage, had been a success. There was some snickering from behind fans – she supposed that was to be expected – but in the main, their neighbours were welcoming. Garbrae's attention to the admiral, while excessive, had allowed her to socialise comfortably without the strain of worrying about what he would do or say. Even in that dreadful moment when he had attacked her, when the threat in his voice and the wildness in his gaze had truly frightened her, she knew, in her heart, that he would not have hurt her.

He was many things, but that sort of man – no!

So it was, Catherine spoke of the evening with Mrs Nash in glowing terms as the pair sat in the small parlour room, enjoying tea, a selection of delicate sandwiches, miniature tarts, the sun, and a picture-perfect view of the lawns.

"I am pleased the evening went so well. I had my reservations about inviting such a large set, but my husband was certain a man accustomed to battle and a woman accustomed to London would scarce turn tail at the sight of a few new faces."

Catherine laughed. "No, indeed. The admiral was correct. Any concern I felt was simply due to the worry of not being well received."

"Not being well received? I cannot believe that was ever a concern. I do not imagine there is a dining room in all of England into which you would not be well received. As for the captain—"

"Yes, as for the captain …" Catherine sighed, rising from her seat and straightening out a small tug in the pale pink curtains, fully aware there were countless dining rooms into which he would never be admitted.

"Well, that man is sure to be popular wherever he goes," Mrs Nash continued, the disappointment in Catherine's sigh unnoticed, lost in the girlish giggle escaping her own lips. "My, but how your husband can set a fan aflutter."

"Whatever can you mean?" Catherine said, turning back to her guest, astounded by this enthusiastic endorsement of her husband.

"Oh, come now," Mrs Nash ribbed, "you were not immune to the man's obvious charms. Is it any wonder the other ladies were similarly swayed?"

Catherine blanched.

"Oh, I speak too plainly," Mrs Nash said on seeing the colour drain from her companion's cheeks. "I have been too long in the company of the admiral. Forgive me, I meant no disrespect."

Catherine relaxed, a sudden flush of heat returning the

colour to her face. "No, of course not," she said, seeming unperturbed as her fingers trailed across the trinkets on the small table by the window. "I am surprised, that is all, for I had not imagined my husband was viewed quite so … encouragingly."

Mrs Nash watched her and smiled at Catherine's practised disinterest. "And that surprises me – you had the good sense to marry the man, after all," she said.

"Yes, I suppose I did," replied Catherine, uncertain as to why her husband should be viewed so favourably and unwilling to ask.

"Handsome – well, was there ever anyone more so, save my own dear husband, of course – and wealthy," Mrs Nash continued. "Well, there are no doubts there. So sensible of you to look for a man outside the usual set."

"Sensible of me?" said Catherine, picking up a porcelain cat and twirling it between her fingers.

"Oh, absolutely. Too many young men these days are soft, spoiled by a life of privilege, rich food, and strong wines, but Captain Garbrae – well, there is nothing soft about him. Many of the husbands at the dinner suffered dreadfully by comparison." Catherine dropped the figurine, and Mrs Nash clasped her hand to her mouth. "There I go again, my mouth running away from me. What would the admiral say?"

Catherine retrieved the cat from the floor which, having landed on a rug, was no worse for being dropped. "I rather imagine he would say *Brava!*" Catherine said, laughing as she returned the cat to the table and took up her seat once more.

Mrs Nash smiled. "You may be correct. The man took an almost perverse pleasure in teaching me to swear like an old salt, and now I am completely ruined for decent society," she said, laughing at her half explanation, half apology.

"Well, I may be surprised, but how could any woman be offended by finding out her husband is so well favoured? I had not thought I would be the object of such jealousy," Catherine said, finding she enjoyed Mrs Nash's candour. It was so completely the opposite of the guardedness she encountered in London. "Although, I do not think I will let him learn of this favouritism. I should hate for the knowledge of such partiality to ruin him," she added, joining in her friend's amusement.

The luncheon was just what Catherine needed. Both women soon found themselves perfectly at ease with one another. Mrs Nash no longer constrained by the need to hide her predisposition for being outrageous, and Catherine no longer scandalised by it. They felt certain that in the other they had found a true friend, and at that moment, Catherine, still feeling the loss of Rose's company, could conceive of no greater prize.

That the captain had played a part in this acted to soften her opinion of him. He was perhaps not as flawed as she believed, and this marriage might not be the disaster she feared. Indeed, if she were to try to get to know her husband better, she might discover a way to help temper the worst of the fiscal recklessness she had overheard his father speak of. Her mother had been too blind, too trusting of her father. By the time the countess learned the full extent of the earl's secret dealings, nothing but Catherine's marriage could save them. Catherine was not so blind nor trusting. She would not be put in such danger again, and she would not be forced to rely on anyone else to save her. She would act now.

With a renewed sense of hope and possibility for the future giving greater vigour to her step, Catherine was determined to seek out the company of her husband. Once her guest had been seen to her carriage and knowing he often rode in the afternoon, she started out toward the stables.

"Barton, I believe it is time we went to look at that warm-blood cross you were telling me about," Garbrae announced as he strode into the stables.

"I had not thought you interested, master. I put no stay on the animal; it may already be gone," Barton replied.

"Well, no matter, we can enquire. If it is sold, it is sold. That will teach me to dilly-dally. Saddle up two horses, and you and I shall ride out at once."

"Could you saddle three horses, Barton?" enquired Catherine, having just reached the stable doors.

"You intend to go riding, my lady?" queried Garbrae, surprised to find her there and even more surprised to find her smiling most agreeably at him.

"Why, yes indeed, captain; I hoped to join you."

Garbrae stared, unnerved by this change in his wife's treatment of him. "I do not ride this afternoon," he ventured, regretting his turn of phrase as he saw the lady bristle.

"That is to say, I do ride, of course. You heard me order two horses be saddled," he said quickly, eager to correct the misunderstanding, "but it is just I do not ride out about the estate. I am going to a neighbouring estate to have sight of a horse that is up for sale."

"Well, I am certain I have skill enough with a horse to be trusted outside the estate," she answered, "but if you feel my joining you would be an imposition ..."

"No, of course not. Three horses, Barton, as her ladyship requests."

Mr Wellington's property was not as large as theirs, Catherine noted, as they rode up the winding tree-lined avenue toward the main house, but it was settled in a pleasant spot, and the gardens were beautifully maintained.

She spied a small rose garden in which the bushes had been planted to provide a brightly coloured border for a loveseat. She smiled at the sight, reminded of her favourite spot in Westbury – a small walled garden that she and Rose had claimed as their own when they were children. To this day, only she, Rose, and the gardeners who tended it were allowed access.

The family were not at home, but Mr O'Reilly, the stable-master, was happy to allow them into the stables to inspect the horse. The moment Garbrae saw Black Jack, he knew he would not be leaving without him; the animal was superb.

Walking around the horse, his hand tracing the long lines of the animal's flank, Garbrae said, "Well, Barton, for all I supposed it, you did not exaggerate the worth of this creature; he is quite exceptional. What is his line, O'Reilly?"

The stablemaster, clearly pleased by Garbrae's recognition of the quality of the animal in his care, stood straight-backed, chest puffed out. "On the thoroughbred side, the horse traces back to the Godolphin Arabian and Lady Roxana through the line of Lath, himself a nine times winner at Newmarket. As you can see, he does not favour the gold-touched bay or small build of Godolphin or Lath, though he has certainly been gifted their great speed and agility. The jet-black colouring and higher seat he gets from the shire-line bred in this stable."

"The Godolphin Arabian – that is a heritage to boast." Garbrae whistled, knowing his pocketbook would be heavily hit. "So, let us get to the matter: how much is being asked?"

Garbrae, not certain he had heard the man's response to the question correctly pulled Barton aside. "Surely, he did not say one thousand?"

"He did indeed, sir," Barton replied, as stunned by the price as his master.

Garbrae took the reins Barton had been holding and

pulled Black Jack's head to his. "There must be something wrong with the animal," he said, after a moment's more inspection. He tossed the reins back to Barton before turning to the stablemaster. "You seek to sell an injured or sick horse, O'Reilly?"

"I do no such thing," responded the man, affronted by the accusation and embarrassed it was made in the presence of Lady Catherine.

"This horse could go for twice what you ask; I can only conclude there is something wrong with him. I will not buy an animal that is ill, no matter what its bloodline."

The stablemaster twisted at the cap he was holding in his hands. He began to speak and then stopped, looking awkwardly at Lady Catherine, his eyes darting between her and her husband.

"Mr O'Reilly, while you discuss the particulars of this transaction, could I lead the horse out? Just a walk about the yard?" asked Catherine, aware of the man's desire to talk privately.

"Certainly, your ladyship," he replied, grateful for the opportunity her absence would provide to speak more openly with her husband.

Garbrae waited for Catherine to clear the stable door before turning to the stablemaster. "If there is something you wish, or ought, to say to explain the low price for an animal with this bloodline, then let us have it out. I will not stand here all day. I am trusting in your honour for the truth of the matter."

O'Reilly looked at the captain, hurt that his honour as a man of horses was being called into question, though understanding why with the animal being so undervalued at one thousand pounds. "If the horse was healthy, would you buy it, sir?"

"I would."

"There is nothing wrong with Black Jack. The price is forced by circumstance. My master finds himself in need of money. He asked the horse's true worth at first, and there was some interest, though it broke my heart to think of him sold. I showed the animal to those gentlemen who came to view him, but no offers were made." O'Reilly paused and looked about him, fearful he would be overheard speaking too plainly about his master's business.

"I am aware of Mr Wellington's current predicament," Garbrae said, "if that eases your concerns any."

O'Reilly nodded. "As my master's need worsened, he suggested the price be lowered to ensure a sale. I took it upon myself to seek out the stablemasters of some of those who expressed the keenest interest to see if lowering the price would entice them in, only to find this was the intention all along. Some of the masters were determined to have Back Jack but were equally determined not to pay his worth. They had worked it out among themselves to hold out and force the price down. They plan to use the horse to stud, ensuring each of them the opportunity to exploit the lineage."

"But Mr Wellington could sell the animal elsewhere," suggested Barton.

"I do not fully know my master's need, but his business does not fare well. He left the selling of the horses to the last, hoping some other way would be found, but the millworkers must be paid, and I heard him say to the mistress that he would not leave them with nothing when Black Jack could be sold. You caught me, sir, just as I was leaving to offer the horse to one of those men interested, but if Black Jack must be sold, I would rather sell him to you. If you will shake on one thousand, the horse will be yours."

"I will do no such thing," replied Garbrae, looking out into the yard to the sight of Catherine apparently engaged in an animated conversation with the horse as she fed him an apple. He smiled. His wife, it seemed, favoured the creature and that fact alone would make the purchase worthwhile.

Barton stared at him open-mouthed. To give up such a horse at such a price was madness.

"I will pay Mr Wellington what the animal is worth," said Garbrae, as he headed for the stable door and out into the yard. "Tell him to come by my house this evening. Bring the horse, and he will have his money – all two thousand pounds of it. That is a fair price; do you agree, Barton?"

Barton, following along behind his master and Mr O'Reilly, nodded.

"Then we have a deal. Will you shake on it?" Garbrae finished, holding his hand out to the stablemaster, who stood staring, as stunned by events as Barton.

"A deal? Yes. Of course," he managed at last, his senses returned. He grabbed Garbrae's hand and shook it vigorously. "We have a deal. I shall inform my master as soon as he returns and bring Black Jack to you this evening."

"Excellent. I shall await you with eagerness."

It was not until they left the yard that Catherine seized the opportunity to speak. "Why pay twice the asking price for the horse?"

Garbrae, happy at the thought of adding so fine an animal to his stables, turned to her, his smile irrepressible. "I knew what the animal was worth, and Barton agreed. I trust his judgement."

Catherine tapped at the flank of her horse with her boot, so that she caught up with her husband who rode slightly ahead. Drawing level with him she said, "Yes, but you could have paid what was being asked. I overheard a little of what was said. Wellington's need was great, his situation quite desperate."

"True," conceded Garbrae, "but what does it say of a man who would use the misfortune of another to such callous advantage? Wellington is a good man. I have heard of his cotton mill and his practices are fair. He was selling his most prized possessions to ensure his workers were paid. The man is honourable and deserves to be dealt with honourably. I could not, in good conscience, have paid one thousand pounds. I could never have enjoyed the animal, knowing the price at which it was bought."

Catherine regarded her husband as though seeing him for the first time. "No," she agreed. "No decent man could."

A compliment, if of an indirect sort. Garbrae held his tongue and his breath for a moment, determined to do nothing that would cause him to fall out of the good graces of his wife.

CHAPTER 15

The next morning, on finding herself alone, taking a walk about the gardens, Catherine replayed the events of the day before. The captain had once more been the charming man she had seen at the Nashes', and his honourable dealings with Wellington were certainly to his credit.

She began to wonder if his good nature was not the act she had presumed it to be. Perhaps she had simply married a decent, charming man, but if so, why had he kept that side of himself at bay? Giving thought to her own behaviour, she had to admit she had not been easy or pleasant, and she allowed that it was possible she had played some part in the trouble during their marriage. Still, if that were truly the case, she argued, what if she were to change? She could try to see her husband as more than a tradesman – that would certainly be a start – and she could try to spend a little time with him, maybe even dare to get to know him, for she realised she knew almost nothing of the man at all.

Resolved to do better and knowing the captain often took refreshment in the library at this time, she went in search of him, determined to begin improving their acquaintance at once.

As she entered the room with a lilting, "Captain, I ..." announcing her presence, Garbrae and a young maid stepped away from the fireplace. Her husband, with an unconcerned air, moved to take a seat behind his desk, and the maid, whose face reddened at their being caught in such compromising closeness, picked up the tray on the desk and bobbed a hurried curtsy to her mistress before leaving the room.

Catherine stared, all her high hopes, the built-up acclaim for the captain, her belief in his being decent, dashed in that instant. In that moment, she was cruelly confronted by the baseness of the man she had married. She stared at him, sitting behind the safety of his desk ... and smiling at her! How could she ever have thought him charming?

"Really, captain, if you must act in such a distasteful manner," she managed, once composed enough to draw breath to speak, determined to appear unaffected by the offensive scene she had walked in on, "I ask you to at least show me the courtesy of limiting your attention to those women not within our employ."

"Whatever do you mean, my lady?" he answered, his voice hardening in response to her obvious accusation.

"I am not completely naive. I am fully aware of what I interrupted, but there are women enough outside of this house who can meet your needs, and you can certainly afford them."

"Now I really cannot imagine what you mean," he replied glibly, refusing to show how insulted and disappointed he was. He had clearly misinterpreted the easing of tensions between them; her opinion of him had not altered. Lord! Her opinion was worse than he imagined.

Catherine leaned across his desk, her ire raised by the smirk on his face and the casual manner of his address. "You know full well what I mean. As long as there have been men like you," she snapped, "there have been whores enough to service them. I suggest you find yourself one and leave the maids be."

"Whores? Well, what fine language is this? And from a woman with your breeding, my lady. You quite shock me."

"And what fine behaviour is it from a man that would provoke such language from a lady? You are neither innocent nor honourable in this. If you find yourself wed to a shrew, give pause to think what has made her that way."

"Oh, yes, your ladyship's trials have been great indeed," spat back Garbrae, all the resentments formed early in their marriage resurfacing with astonishing force. "Saved from the ignominy of poverty and at what cost? What have you sacrificed? Fine surroundings, carriages, parties, and all the pleasures of the life you have always known have been maintained. What cause have you to be bitter? What has been lost to you?"

"What has been lost?" Catherine almost screamed in reply. "All that was ever worth having – my heart, captain, the freedom to give my heart. *Love* is lost to me!"

"Your heart? You have no heart and no feeling, madam; you are nothing but ice and stone," Garbrae said, laughing harshly at her suggestion.

Catherine staggered back from his desk, unsteady on her feet. "No heart? Oh, I am quite sure you think me heartless," she cried, hitting her fist hard to her breast. "But if I were to set free all that I feel, I could show passion enough to convince even you of the depth of my feeling. For I hate you, captain, with every beat of this heart and to the depth of my being. I hate you for all that you have taken from me, for every sting inflicted by the humiliation of being your wife. How I wish I were heartless," she said, emotion breaking her voice, strangling her breath. "I wish I were as hard as stone that I could suffer your company without feeling the indignity of our match, without the wretchedness of knowing exactly what I have sacrificed in marrying you. I have lost the hope of finding happiness, and for that, I hate you most of all!"

Stunned into silence by the outburst, Garbrae sat open-mouthed at the fierce, unbridled force of the woman standing opposite him. In a moment of unexpected tenderness, he reached toward her, a sudden desire to comfort her compelling him. "Catherine …"

She recoiled further from him. His addressing her in so intimate a manner caused her immediately to recollect herself. In the time it took to straighten her dress and smooth her hair, she stood poised and controlled, her breath measured, her tone even; she was "her ladyship" once more.

"Congratulations, captain, it appears you have managed to do what, until now, no one else has. For one moment, you broke me. You will, I am certain, take pleasure in the memory of my display, but let me assure you it will never happen again. You believe me to be stone? Well then, as you wish it."

"I had not intended—" Garbrae tried to interject.

"We are finished here. I bid you good day. I ask once more that you leave the maids alone, but beyond that, I want nothing from you."

In an instant, Catherine was gone, and the room that had been filled by her emotion, passion, and presence was suddenly empty. Garbrae collapsed back into his chair, shuddering in her wake.

Catherine stopped outside the room, uncertain her legs would carry her up the hallway and away from the library.

Her hand shook as she reached for the small table nearest to her, determined to steady herself in case her husband decided to follow her. She almost cried as she recalled the scene that had just played out – the captain's behaviour toward the maid more grotesque at every reimagining, her outburst more frantic and embarrassingly impassioned. To have exposed herself to him in such a manner was unpardonable. To have bared her soul in that way was failing enough but to have allowed him to see how capable he was of hurting her was the worst sin of all.

She pictured him sitting in his wing-back leather chair smiling at his victory. In the battle that had waged between them since the moment of their marriage, she had been the first to break. Catherine would not soon forgive herself that weakness.

It was not until she heard her husband's chair scrape, long and slow, across the library floor that she was able to move. The fear of being found, still trembling, outside the door was enough to force her into action. Catherine would not suffer the degradation of a further meeting, not while she remained so unprepared. She could not face him until she was truly composed and herself again.

Within the library, Garbrae moved from his chair to pour himself a drink. Though the glass was wide, designed to rest comfortably in the palm of a man's hand, he missed it entirely on two occasions, spilling brandy on the polished sideboard, watching as it dripped to the floor. In frustration, he hurled the glass at the wall, unconcerned as it shattered into pieces.

"What was that?" he demanded of the empty room, falling back down onto a couch. He ran his hands across his face and dragged them roughly through his hair, the painful tug assuring him he was awake, that the last quarter-hour had not been a dream. "Was that passionate creature truly my wife? How could I have been so blind to the nature of the woman I married?"

Thinking on the encounter, he recalled the flash in Catherine's eyes as she challenged him. He marvelled at her courage in confronting him so directly. Since their wedding, he had always believed that, as he controlled the purse, he had the upper hand. Title or no, he held the power in their relationship – but now he questioned that conviction. She believed herself somehow broken by him, even if for just a moment, but Garbrae knew better for he had seen a hint of what prevailed at the core of his wife – she was not broken, nor was she likely to be. This woman was not ice and stone, but fire and steel!

"Could it be that there is hope for us?" he asked aloud, allowing himself to believe for the first time since his wedding day that there was a future for him here after all.

CHAPTER 16

A week had passed since the scene in the library, and though Catherine's wretchedness at her outburst had all but relinquished, her anger toward her husband had not. Bitterness formed itself like a creature within her, burrowing deep, twisting and thrashing whenever she saw him. Though she knew that some form of accord with the captain would have to be reached, she could find no good reason for it.

He was not cruel in his treatment of her, but his indelicacy in his liaisons with the maid could scarcely be called kind.

He did not, even in the heat of argument, raise a hand to her, but he injured her in other ways.

At least, while he sought the comfort of other women, he left her alone, but how long could that last? He would want an heir.

As these thoughts played out in her head, Catherine knew she would not sit easy until she could rid herself of the demon gnawing away at the notion of finding peace in her marriage. Not wishing to satisfy the captain with another display of emotion, she knew she had to find some way of releasing the resentment festering inside her, or she would be consumed by it.

～

"Barton, I have decided to go riding today," Catherine announced on entering the stables. "Have one of the horses ready for me after breakfast."

Barton jumped up from his stool, gave a quick bow, and assured her two of the best would be saddled and ready for when she needed them.

"Two, Barton? I need only one horse."

"Beggin' your ladyship's pardon," Barton said with another short bow, "but the second horse is for the stable-hand who will accompany you. The master was quite strict that, should you ride, you would have someone with you, at least until you know the lay of the land and the horses a little better – it is for your own safety, my lady."

"Well, Barton," replied Catherine, pulling herself up to her full height and speaking to the man in a manner that assured him no argument would be brooked, "I have been riding almost as long as I have been walking and can handle any horse. As for the lay of the land, it is the English countryside not the plains of the desert or the wilds of the jungle; I am hardly likely to come to much danger out there! Have Black Jack saddled for me—"

"Black Jack is not yet tried, my lady," Barton interrupted. "The master has had no occasion to ride out, so we do not know how he will handle. A warmblood cross can be temperamental. The Quarter Horse or the bay mare would suit better – they stand a good sixteen hands as it is and have a broader seat. Black Jack is eighteen hands high and lean across the shoulders; I think I best saddle one of the others."

"You seem to be under the impression you have a choice in the matter, Barton. I have asked for Black Jack, and that is the horse you will have ready for me. If you value your position here, I suggest you learn to follow the instructions of those who employ you. Have the horse ready!" Catherine said, before turning on her heel and storming out.

Barton, stunned by the demand but determined not to lose a job that suited him, did as he was told. He thought to tell the master of her ladyship's orders, but the lady appeared in no mood to be crossed, and he knew only too well that if it came to it, a sensible man would choose his wife's happiness over a hired hand's employment.

The freedom of being on horseback was just what Catherine needed. Once safely away from the watchful eyes of the stable and the immediate surrounds of the house, she let the horse break out into a full gallop, the power of the animal surprising even her. His stride was magnificent and his speed unmatched by any horse she had ever ridden. She could not fault the captain's judgement in the purchase – the animal was exquisite.

For the first time in a week, Catherine noticed she had not flinched at the thought of her husband, her exhilaration overwhelming every bad feeling. She did not need to exorcise her demons, she realised; she simply needed to outrun them. Giving the horse a sharp kick to its flanks, she raced even harder.

Fields and meadows were crossed at speed and hedges cleared with ease. Catherine, heedless of the direction, was caught up in the freedom and excitement of the ride. She did not question the wisdom of running the horse flat out alongside the small woods at the far eastern boundary of their property, did not recall the captain telling her he would be shooting that morning, did not give care to the world around her ... until a game bird, startled by one of the captain's dogs, bolted out of the wood.

Black Jack, surprised by the sudden movement, reacted frantically, raising his front legs high and rearing up to his full height. Catherine, just as startled, could do nothing as she was thrown violently from the saddle. Landing heavily, she cried out once before everything went black.

"Well, I definitely heard something," said Garbrae. "We shall make our way to the boundary of the wood and make sure nothing is amiss."

Recalling the dogs from their duties, the handlers followed their master, sad to see a day's shooting interrupted and certain they would find nothing.

As the men emerged from the trees, they were surprised to see a riderless horse standing calmly in the meadow not fifteen feet from the edge of the wood.

"What the devil is Black Jack doing out here?" Garbrae asked aloud, annoyed someone had taken the horse out before him. "And where the devil is the rider?"

As though in answer to the question, Black Jack tilted his head toward an area of high grass and pawed at the ground. Garbrae moved toward the animal, gentle tones calling on the creature to hush and be still, his hands reaching out until they secured his reins.

With Black Jack quietened, and secured by one of the handlers, Garbrae moved around the horse to search the area behind him. He saw first a hand, draped awkwardly across a small tree stump. Guessing now that Black Jack's rider had been thrown, he picked up his pace and called out to the figure in the grass as he approached. It was not until he saw the full fan of a rider's skirt splayed out black against the green of the high grass that he considered the rider to be anyone but one of the stablehands.

"Catherine!" he cried out on finding his wife lying unresponsive, her body twisted awkwardly, her face deathly pale save for a stream of red blood that ran from an open gash on her temple, cutting through the pallor of her cheek.

His men were by him immediately on hearing the mistress' name and stood gaping at the body by their feet.

Garbrae, wrestling his gaze from the sight of his injured wife – and his mind from the fear that she would succumb to the wounds – snapped into action.

"Tomlinson, take Black Jack and ride into town, now. You know the surgeon on Wimpole Street?"

Tomlinson stood dumbfounded, never diverting his eyes from his mistress.

"Tomlinson!" barked Garbrae, forcing him to come to attention. "The surgeon on Wimpole Street!"

"Yes. Yes, of course, master," the man finally replied, reaching for the horse and pulling himself up into the saddle. "I'll call him to the house right away."

Turning his attention to Smith, Garbrae instructed the man to get to the house, to have preparations made there and to return to him with the means to carry her ladyship back. Smith, upon getting his orders, took to his heels without hesitation, leaving Garbrae alone with nothing to do but turn his attention back to Catherine.

Having seen enough men wounded in battle and knowing enough of a doctor's trade to make an initial assessment of her condition, Garbrae set about distracting himself from the horror of the situation by making a careful examination of his wife. He applied pressure to the gash on her head, stemming the bleeding, and secured a handkerchief over the wound. Once satisfied he had done all he could with her head, he continued to check for signs of other injury. With no obvious cuts or breaks, he began to hope that, serious as the wound to her head might be, at least it might be the only trauma from the fall.

He removed his coat and folded it as a makeshift pillow for Catherine, but when he lifted her head, he found her hair soaked. Touching the shoulders of her jacket, he realised those too were cold and damp to the touch. He knew he could not risk leaving her lying in wet grass – recovery from a head wound was one thing, but to battle a fever or chill while already weak was quite another. Placing his arms under her, with as much care as he could to keep her still, Garbrae lifted his wife and gently rested her body against his own. Knowing the way Smith would return with help, he walked toward the house, wishing with every step that Catherine would awaken.

"What would you say if you were to open your eyes now and find yourself in this position, I wonder?" he asked of the still pale, still silent Catherine. "I rather imagine you would have a great deal to accuse me of. I would give anything to be berated by you right now. Promise me," he whispered, leaning his face close to hers, "promise me you will make it through this to berate me once again."

"Doctor, how is she?" Garbrae was upon the man the moment he stepped outside Catherine's bedroom, his examination of her complete, his patient made comfortable.

"Your wife will be fine, Captain Garbrae," replied the doctor, reassuring him with a tight squeeze to his shoulder. "She had a bad fall, but you were correct in your assessment. There is nothing broken, and though unconscious when you found her, she is awake now. She knows who she is and where she is but is shaken and complains of a severe headache. A few days rest ought to see her well again. I will call again tomorrow. In the meantime, she should not be left alone – certainly not overnight – and you ought to try to keep her awake for now. If you have any concerns, or if there is any change, call for me at once, although I am certain she will recover admirably."

Garbrae, relieved, thanked the doctor, and after seeing him out, returned to his spot outside his wife's bedroom, taking a moment to steady his nerves before knocking.

Catherine had been settled comfortably into her room, a fire lit, a bank of pillows surrounding her, and a nurse at her side. She did not smile when her husband entered the room, nor did she order him out.

Taking that as permission enough, Garbrae approached her bedside, pulling a wing-back chair from beside the fire so he could take up a permanent seat next to her.

"I would not have thought a seat was necessary," began Catherine. "I do not imagine your stay will be long enough to require the luxury."

"You would have me stand all night, my lady?" replied Garbrae, for once pleased by his wife's disagreeableness; she was certainly acting like his Catherine.

"All night?" she queried, her eyes turning to meet his, her displeasure evident.

"Indeed, the doctor says you are not to be left alone, so I shall take up a post by you and stand guard as it were."

"I have a nurse who, I am sure, is more than capable of attending to me. You need not trouble yourself to stay."

Catherine, as she so often did, ended her part in the conversation with her arms folded tightly across her chest, her face turned away from her husband, staring into the nothingness of the far corner of the room.

When Garbrae failed to react in the way he so often did by huffing loudly and leaving the room, Catherine became unsettled. Her arms still crossed, her face still turned away, she allowed her eyes to drift back toward the bedside and the spot the captain had claimed as his. The man was smiling at her.

"You will not find me so easily chased away today," he teased, pleased his presence bristled her, relieved the fall had not knocked the fight out of her. The doctor was correct; there was no doubt she would make a full recovery – sheer stubbornness would see her through.

"I do not feel much up to having company. Perhaps it would be best if you left me to sleep; I am certain, after some rest, I shall be well enough," Catherine suggested, hoping this attempt at civility might be enough to rid her of him.

"On the contrary, the doctor insisted you be kept awake. We cannot expect the nurse to entertain you, therefore I shall play the fool for you and offer what amusement I can."

When Catherine failed to take up the obvious insult of his being a fool, Garbrae was convinced that, although she looked well enough, his wife was not yet fully herself. Hoping to keep her engaged, he jested, "Come now, you disappoint me. I offer to play the fool, and I get nothing in reply? I anticipated a volley of barbs across my bow; perhaps that blow to the head has done more damage than the doctor supposed."

Catherine turned her head slowly, the pain in the movement causing her to wince. "I am tired and in no mood to spar with you. I should have thought you might welcome respite from the worst lashings of my tongue. It must be quite a trial to be so consistently and completely whipped."

Garbrae, who had to fight to restrain himself from reaching out to help her on seeing her obvious discomfort, relaxed a little on this reply.

"Ah, now that is heartening. Before we know it, you will be back to haranguing me in true fashion, but until then, until your strength is recovered and your wounds healed, may we call a truce?"

Catherine, in too much pain and too exhausted to offer any resistance, provided her assent with a slight nod of her head.

It was at least an hour before she spoke again. Her attempt at conversation provoked chiefly by her amazement that the captain had remained so long at her bedside. Clearly, he seemed intent on staying there.

"Please tell me I did not injure Black Jack," she said, with sincere concern for the animal. "Please tell me I have wounded none but myself through this foolishness."

"Black Jack is well; he has been fully looked over by Deacon."

"Deacon?" questioned Catherine. "I would have expected you to trust such a duty to Barton. Why did he not see to the horse?"

"Barton no longer works here," answered Garbrae, his tone unusually hard, his jaw clenched and set into a grimace.

"But why?" continued Catherine, surprised by the news.

"It is quite simple: Barton was given clear orders you were not to ride out alone. No one was to ride Black Jack until I allowed it. He failed to follow those orders, and you were injured as a result. The man could not be trusted; he could not be relied upon, and he has taken his leave of us."

"But," she argued, "the fault was mine. I demanded Black Jack be saddled and that I ride out alone. Please, I will not have a man lose his livelihood and home due to my poor decisions."

"Barton had his orders."

"Captain, I am sure you cannot have failed to notice that I can be somewhat"—she paused for a moment, struggling to find a gentle word for her intransigence—"strong-willed. You must not blame Barton. I was quite insistent I have my way, and there are few who can stand up to me when I am at my most … determined."

Garbrae softened; it was entirely possible this was as close to an apology as his wife had ever been. That she took responsibility now for her actions, and in defence of a servant, was most unexpected.

"Surely, it is not too late," she continued, looking her husband square in the face for the first time since he had entered the room. "You could offer his position back to him."

That Catherine's tone was almost pleading took Garbrae further by surprise. For the first time since they had met, she had not demanded but asked something of him. He was not certain how to reply. His anger with Barton had been acute; he had cut the man down most publicly, his fear for Catherine increasing his ferocity. He was not at all certain the man would return or that he wanted to ask him.

"He failed to follow clear and simple orders, and there were consequences: you were injured. Do I simply ignore that? Do I act as though it had not happened? Do I leave it open for others to pick which of my orders they follow? It is no way to run this house; Barton will serve as an example to the rest of the staff."

Catherine was staggered by the captain's hard line toward a man she knew he greatly respected. Even in her weakened state, she was irritated by his mulishness.

"How often have I heard you praise Barton's way with the horses? Why do you continue to refuse to follow a course that will satisfy us all? You will have a stablemaster you respect and, barring this one small error of judgement, you know you can trust. Barton will have his position and home restored to him, and I will be free from the guilt that my pigheadedness has led to an unhappy state such as this! For pity's sake, captain, now is not the time for obstinacy."

Garbrae, amused by the anger with which Catherine spoke, her patience clearly tested by his immediate refusal to meet her demands, took a moment before responding. He allowed a short silence to fall between them, increasing the tension as they stared at one another. In deliberate response to her annoyance, he ensured his tone was playful.

"Are you bellicose by nature, my lady, or do I inspire it?"

"Am I what?"

"Bellicose: inclined to fight, ready to quarrel, from the Latin meaning 'war'."

"I know what the word means, captain," Catherine answered, almost smiling at him, remembering how she had taunted him similarly just a few weeks before.

"You seem ever at the ready to take up arms against me, even now when I thought we had agreed to a truce. I am lectured one minute on being too familiar with the staff and criticised another for being too severe. How is a man to know how to behave if you are so inconsistent?"

Though Garbrae had intended this to be but banter, his misstep was clear the moment the words were free from his lips. He noticed Catherine stiffen; her lips pursed and pulled tight, hardening her face, all earlier levity and childish pique replaced with cold fury. Lord, how could he be so foolish? Familiarity with staff, such an imprudent turn of phrase, given her belief that he was bedding the maids.

"Catherine I ..." he began, frantically searching for the words that would fix all that was so quickly going wrong.

"Get out of my room," Catherine snapped. "We are done here. Do what you will with Barton. What I want clearly matters little to you. Just leave me be. I have suffered enough today without the continued strain of your company."

Garbrae stumbled out a response, trying to claw back

some of the ease that had been growing between them, but Catherine was unwavering. Swinging his chair so that it skidded back into its position by the fireplace, he left the room, cursing his carelessness and fearing his wife was further from him than ever.

CHAPTER 17

Manchester. June 1813

"Catherine, you look dreadful!" were the first words from Rose's mouth as she entered her sister's bedchamber. She found her sitting in a chair by the fire with a large bandage about her head, her face pale, and her eyes dark and shadowed.

"Rose. What in Heaven? What are you doing here?" Catherine said, her sister's unexpected entrance taking her fully by surprise.

"Captain Garbrae arrived at Westbury with the news of your fall. Did he not mention he was coming? How did you account for his being gone? He was quite certain my being here would aid in your recovery and all but begged that I be allowed to return with him. Here I am, as you see, come to make you better, come to see you well again."

Catherine, overcome with joy at seeing Rose, seeing her so much her usual self and feeling at once happy to be with her, could do nothing but cry in reply.

This reaction, being so completely out of character for

her sister, alarmed Rose. There was something altered in her, and it was unsettling. But she brushed off all concerns, assuming any changes in Catherine would be accounted for by the shock of her injuries. She knelt beside Catherine, smoothed her hair, looked straight into her eyes and offered comfort. "Hush now, sister, do not cry; you will be well. I am here, and you will be restored. Come, let us lie down. You are clearly tired out by the surprise of having me here, and I am tired out from the trial of travelling here. Let us both rest. When you wake, I will be by your side, and all will be well. Hush now, Catherine, hush now."

Guided to bed by her sister's gentle hand and persuaded to rest by her soothing tone, Catherine succumbed to the first full and deep sleep she had had since moving to Lancashire. She slept as she had when they were children, her hand wrapped around her sister's, believing for the first time in many weeks that better days were to come.

It was dinnertime when Rose awoke, and finding Catherine still asleep, she judged it best to let her continue to rest and to join the captain in the dining room for something to eat. Not even delaying to change her dress, she entered the room to find him alone waiting on the first course to be served.

"You will forgive me, captain, for not dressing for dinner, but I awoke from sleep five minutes ago to find myself absolutely famished," she said on entering the room.

"My lady, such a surprise. I had not expected you to join me at all. Please take a seat. Do not concern yourself about dressing for dinner – I conform to such formalities solely for your sister's sake. Covington, have a place set for her ladyship," Garbrae said, standing to motion Rose to the empty chair to his right. "I left instructions for a tray to be delivered to your room; I hope all was in order."

"Oh, yes, everything was done as you directed, but I thought it silly to dine alone – for my sister is still asleep – when you were here. I also felt certain that after the recent trial of Catherine's injuries, company might be a welcome comfort."

"You are most kind," the captain said, smiling – this consideration as appreciated as it was unexpected. "Your company would, of course, be most welcome. I have spent too many dinners alone of late, and it does not suit me, as I am unaccustomed to it. So tell me, how did you find your sister? Was I right to pull you from the comfort of your home?"

"Oh, captain, you were certainly justified, for I find Catherine most altered. I had not expected the fall to affect her so. She cried on seeing me. Did you not tell her you were fetching me?"

"I could not be certain your father would agree to let you come and so did not wish to raise her hopes. She cried, you say," replied Garbrae, just as concerned by this reaction.

"Perhaps surprise accounts for it, and a lack of sleep. She seemed worn out. I fear the injury may have kept proper rest at bay. Still, I am certain I can remedy the situation. Though my sister was always the strong one, there were times when even she needed comforting, and I have learned some ways to console her: songs that soothe, warm milk and cinnamon, the scent of certain flowers. All these little tricks I have learned will be employed to ensure Catherine is returned to us."

"You cannot imagine what a relief your being here is," confessed Garbrae. "I was uncertain about going to Westbury but hoped you would be persuaded to return with me."

"Nonsense! There is little – indeed, nothing – that would

have prevented me from coming to Catherine's aid. I am simply pleased you had the good sense to ask for me."

With the serving of the first course, the pair settled into a comfortable silence, both solely concerned with ministering to the gnawing in their bellies. There was little thought given to conversation until the third course was being served. Now with the worst pangs of hunger subsiding, they turned their attention once more to the other and struck up a dialogue that was as easy and as comfortable as the silence had been.

"Captain, I have been thinking on Catherine's fall. When did you say it happened?"

"On Saturday just passed," he replied. "Why?"

"On Saturday? But how in Heaven did you get to West-bury so quickly?"

"I travelled on horseback, my lady, and arrived as quickly as the horse could get me there," he answered, not fully understanding the question put to him.

"No, of course, you did not take a carriage for we returned in Father's," Rose mused, as much to herself as to the captain, "but the horse could not have completed the journey from Lancashire to Westbury in such a time."

"No indeed, one horse could not. I stopped along the way to change horses. Four horses took me to Westbury – why should it matter?"

Rose's eyes widened on his reply. "But then it means you did not stop. It is the only way the journey could have been made in the time, or rather, it means you stopped only long enough to secure a new horse. You did not rest nor sleep."

"Your sister needed you; I saw no point in delaying the comfort you might bring to her so that I could sleep. I have been afforded sleep enough since reaching you at Westbury and am feeling no worse for the effort."

"But to travel through the night like that, the danger of it," continued Rose, her heart racing at the thought of the passion that would cause a man to act so rashly. "Lord, it is like something from a romance."

Garbrae laughed, amused by the excited look on Rose's face. "I think you might be overwrought from your journey here and the shock of seeing your sister. I hardly think my actions were the stuff of romance. Still, if it pleases you to think of my journey as such, by all means, continue."

"You were truly worried; there is no other explanation. I am glad my sister married a man who would take such pains to secure her comfort. We had no opportunity to get to know one another before you were married; I hope we can remedy that."

"I should like that," said Garbrae, happy to find Rose so eager to get to know him better and hopeful her attentions would soon see Catherine fully recovered.

CHAPTER 18

*C*atherine awoke late the following day, feeling immediately better after so full and deep a sleep. For a moment, she feared she had dreamed of her sister being there until Rose's, "Good morning," drew her attention to a large seat by the window.

"You *have* come," she said. "I thought you were a dream."

Rose was by her side immediately, fussing over her, checking her bandage, settling the pillows at her back, and admonishing her with as great a degree of severity as she could muster in the face of seeing her sister looking so much better than the day before.

"What in Heaven's name were you thinking, taking out a horse such as Black Jack and without having someone to ride out with you?"

"You have seen him then. Is he not magnificent?" Catherine replied, completely ignoring Rose's direct question.

"You deliberately do not answer me; do not think I will allow it. You are quite trapped here and quite at my mercy,"

Rose said, poking Catherine playfully in the arm. "I will not desist until I know the full details of your misadventure."

Catherine relaxed, knowing she would relent and tell Rose what had occurred, although she would never admit the reasons leading up to the fateful ride, for she would not suffer the humiliation of Rose knowing her husband bedded the servants.

"Well, you have seen the creature," Catherine offered at last, "could you have resisted the temptation of taking him out?"

"I could indeed," Rose replied. "The animal is magnificent, but he needs a far steadier and stronger hand than mine to control him. I would not have trusted my ability to master the creature."

"If only you could have felt his power; it was exhilarating."

"Until he threw you off – nearly killing you," Rose added.

"Lord, you are so fanciful." Catherine laughed. "I was hardly in danger of being killed. I simply forgot the captain was out shooting, and the horse was startled by a game bird. I am certain the fall was not half as serious as you imagine."

"You were unconscious for quite some time, and I can assure you the captain took your injury most seriously. If you could have seen his face when he told us what had happened. I swear I have never seen a countenance like it."

"Us? Then the captain went to Westbury … I had not imagined …" Catherine began, the rest of what she was to say lost as she bit into her lower lip, allowing herself to think for the first time on how her husband might have reacted to her fall.

Rose rang the bell and, once a light breakfast with tea and chocolate had been ordered, settled herself at the foot of Catherine's bed. "Yes, the captain came himself. I think he feared a delay or a refusal if he was not there, or perhaps he needed to be occupied, for there was a restlessness about him. I do not think he is a man who can easily sit by and wait. You know he travelled without rest, only stopping long enough to change horses," Rose added, certain Catherine had no notion as to her husband's efforts on her behalf.

A few moments of silence followed with each considering these revelations, only broken when Rose asked, "I hear you fell at a far boundary of the estate? How did you make it back to the house? Surely you could not ride?"

"No, I ..." began Catherine, before realising she had absolutely no idea how she had been found and returned.

The nurse, who had been sitting in a corner quietly busying herself, spoke up on realising the lady had no answer to the question at hand. "Pardon me, my lady, but the master carried you here."

"He carried me?" replied Catherine, uncertain she had heard correctly. "Surely he did not carry me all the way by himself?"

"Oh, yes, just so. There was two with him when you fell. One was sent to fetch the surgeon and one back to the house – he was to return with men and means to get you back. But the master would not wait. He picked you up and set off back here himself. Met Smith and the men as they was on the way to you—"

"Then they must have had a cart with them, or something to carry her ladyship," interrupted Rose, swept up in the tale.

"No. Smith – never been a clever man – he called out for four men in the yard, yelling only that the master needed 'em; he never had the good sense to order they bring a cart."

Catherine was horrified at the thought of being transported in this way, each man covering a leg of the journey, each having to hold her close against them. "You do not mean to say that I was handed over to these men and carried here?"

"No," the nurse continued. "When they reached the master, strong words was had with Smith, for a cart would have been the very thing they needed. But they reckoned instead they could stand close together with their arms raised so your ladyship could be laid out and carried by them all. Only, the master would not have it, refused to set you down. Carried you here himself. Held you to him the whole of the journey, till he laid you down upon this bed."

"Oh Lord! I might faint from the excitement," exclaimed Rose enthusiastically.

"Rose, collect yourself," admonished Catherine. "I doubt it was quite as dramatic as you imagine."

"The master was almost done in with it all," added the nurse. "The fright of you being injured, the distance of the walk, and the weight of your riding habit all acting against him. Still, he didn't step away from your door till the surgeon sured him you was safe." She was happy to be able to relate the tale, delighted on seeing Rose wide-eyed and gasping as the details became known to her.

"You cannot possibly know all of this," Catherine interjected.

"Well, I was here when the master brought you in," the nurse replied. "And I could hear him pacing outside the whole of the surgeon's visit."

"And how is it you know the rest?" asked Catherine, certain now the great romance of the tale would be undone.

"Smith is my brother, my lady, and told me all. He swore the master refused to let you go, said he was holding on to you as if for dear life." The nurse turned to Rose and added, "I did not think a man could cover half such a distance while carrying another and not in so quick a time, but my brother said the master never slowed, not till he had her ladyship safe and at rest in here." She finished with a self-satisfied smile to Catherine.

"Could you ever have imagined it?" sighed Rose, dropping back onto the bed. "I tell you I am in danger of swooning."

Not a quarter-hour after the nurse's revelations, Garbrae knocked at the door, begging admittance.

Rose, still under the influence of her romantic imaginings, blushed on hearing his steady knock and the deep rumble of his voice. "He has such a masculine knock," she whispered.

Catherine rolled her eyes to the ceiling. "Rose, I will ask you to leave if you insist on this foolishness. One knock is much the same as another." She signalled to the nurse to allow the captain in.

"But the knock was so bold in its striking – certain and self-assured, without hesitancy."

"He was seeking entrance to a room in his own house, to a lady's bedroom, not a nest of vipers. Why should he hesitate?" Catherine argued, increasingly concerned that her sister's love of romance might result in a permanent partiality for the captain which she simply could not allow.

"You are looking well, my lady," Garbrae said with a low bow. "I am pleased to see your sister has managed to be so positive an influence, even in so short a time."

"Yes, captain, Rose is indeed a great relief to me; I ought to have thanked you before now for thinking to bring her here," Catherine replied, genuinely grateful for the thoughtfulness he had shown.

"It was the only thing I could think to do," he replied

honestly, smiling at Rose as he spoke. "I could not bear to be idle and hoped only to be of some service."

"And so you were," Catherine conceded before addressing the other two in the room. "Might we have a moment alone?"

"Of course," answered Rose, as she and the nurse hastened for the door. "I shall have breakfast set up in the morning room. Join me when you are ready; you will not be interrupted before then."

On finding themselves alone, the couple tensed slightly – the comfort of having the diversion of company no longer afforded to them.

"Thank you for bringing Rose here," Catherine began.

"You have already thanked me, and as I said, I was glad of the distraction and for having something to do."

"How long do you propose she stay?" Catherine asked, cutting straight to the matter most dear to her.

"I had given no thought at all to the length of your sister's stay. In truth, I thought only of your well-being when I brought her here. It had not occurred to me that she might have plans of her own. She will stay, I suppose, as long as she is happy to stay."

"And what if she is content to stay until Christmas, or beyond? What if Rose is so pleased with being here that she does not wish to leave at all?"

Garbrae's shoulders relaxed, and the hands that had been clasped tightly behind his back came to rest loosely by his side. "If that be the case, my lady," responded Garbrae, "then your sister will stay for as long as you wish her to."

"For as long as I wish it?" said Catherine, surprised at having such freedom.

"As I say, your sister will remain with us until you send her home. We shall live here together, we three, until you are ready to be here alone with me, until you are ready to be my wife."

Catherine leaned into the pillows Rose had arranged at her back. She had been preparing for a fight and was so stunned by the captain's proposal that she could make no reply other than to stare at him.

Uncertain as to the meaning of his wife's silence, Garbrae grew uncomfortable and shifted from foot to foot where he stood, his hands going once more behind his back. "Well, if there is nothing else," he finally managed, unable to come up with any topic of conversation that would justify his being in his wife's room any longer, "I shall leave you to the company of your sister and be on my way."

"There is one more thing, if you are not in a hurry to be elsewhere."

"No, I have as much time as you need," he replied, eager for an excuse to prolong his visit.

Catherine, not content to stay in bed for the full course of this conversation, moved her legs to the side of the bed and readied herself to walk over to the chair by the fireplace, but as she stood, the room around her began to spin and bright spots of colour clouded her vision. Before she could fall, Catherine felt herself being swept up by a strong pair of arms. Garbrae had caught her and deftly pulled her up against his chest.

"My lady, are you all right?" he asked, his voice calm and steady, his arms holding firm, but his pounding heart betraying his concern.

"I am, captain," she assured him. "A slight dizzy spell, too long lying down. I am certain I can walk under my own power now."

"You will forgive me if I do not relinquish my hold just yet," he countered. "You do not see the paleness in your cheeks, nor did you see the unsteadiness in your stance. If you do not wish to lie down, I will take you to a chair, but I will not have you walking about as though nothing were amiss!"

"As you wish, captain," Catherine said; "you may take me to a seat by the fire."

With his wife settled in the larger of the chairs, Garbrae took a seat opposite and waited for her to continue with the matter that had stayed his departure.

"Yes, as to the reason I wished you to stay," Catherine said, on realising he was waiting for her to speak, "I have just been told how I was returned to the house. Is it true you carried me all the way from where I fell?"

Garbrae nodded.

"That is quite a distance. How is half of that to be managed while carrying another?" she asked.

"I do not know how to answer you; I needed to get you home. I could not leave you lying in wet grass with the threat of fever or chill increasing at every moment, so I did the only thing I could – I carried you."

Catherine's fingers worried at the button on a small velvet cushion she had pulled from the chair onto her lap and asked, "And you did not hand me over to the men who met you as you made your way back?"

"I did not think you would approve of being held in such a way by any of the servants. Do not tell my still aching arms that I was mistaken in that belief," he jested, leaning back into his seat and rubbing exaggeratedly at his left bicep, seeking to make light of the matter.

"No, you were quite right. It would not have been fitting for any of them to have had such an intimate hold of me," she replied, refusing to be dissuaded from her purpose by his off-handedness, "but they proposed a way of carrying me that would have been acceptable. Why did you not allow them all to carry me as though stretchered? There would have been no impropriety in that."

"I thought it best to continue as I was," he answered.

"But why?" she pestered, stubbornness refusing to let the matter lie.

"I just needed to carry you."

"Why?"

"Does it really matter now?" he asked, leaning forward in his seat, his shoulders rounded, his hands in front of him as though in prayer.

Catherine brushed the knuckles of his clasped hands with her fingertips. "It matters a great deal to me."

His fingers flexed outward in response to her feather-light touch, though she withdrew as he reached for her.

"I could not let you go, because I was afraid," he blurted out. "As long as I held you, I could feel your heart beating, could feel your breath against my neck, and these signs told me you were alive. I could not let you go lest I give in to the fear you would succumb to your injuries. I needed to feel you were alive with every step I took. Without it, I do not believe I would have had the strength to make it home."

Catherine stared. How was it that a man capable of such depth of feeling as he displayed to her at that moment could be so callous in other ways? He was so concerned for her safety that he suffered physical trial and brought Rose to stay, yet he fired Barton and sought the company of the maids. This incomprehensible opposition within his character stunned her, and she could offer nothing in reply.

On finding his honest admission greeted with silence, Garbrae pushed himself up from his seat to stand staring down at his wife. "If you require nothing else of me …" he said, noticing she had once more taken up her nervous worrying of the buttons on the cushion she clutched to her.

"Of course," Catherine replied, without looking up at the man, painfully aware of his discomfort but unable to think of how to lessen it. "Please do not let me detain you."

CHAPTER 19

"My lady, there is no need for you to disturb the routine of your day. I am certain there can be little to interest you at the mill," said Garbrae at breakfast, not for the first time since Lady Rose had announced her intention to join him on his visit.

"Nonsense, I have no experience of industry. I am quite sure every little thing will be of interest, unless of course, you think my joining you would be burdensome. I would not wish to impose."

Garbrae smiled at his sister-in-law, hopeful that if he could secure the good favour of one sister, she might exert some influence over the other. "I cannot imagine anyone considering time spent with you as burdensome. It would be an honour to have you accompany me. Can you be ready for nine?"

~

Though Rose had concerns there might be some awkwardness between them on the journey – their being alone for so long without a meal to comment on or the act of eating to explain away any periods of silence – she was surprised to find the time passed delightfully. The captain was an entertaining companion, and he talked with such openness that Rose could not help but feel at ease, enjoying his humour and even his talk of business. Indeed, such was her distraction that she paid little attention to the world outside of the carriage until it intruded noisily upon them.

"Lord! What is that?" she asked, a hiss and the screech of metal filling the carriage, making it almost impossible to hear anything else.

"Wait a moment or two," said Garbrae, raising his voice to be heard over the din, "and you will become accustomed to the sounds of the factory."

Rose looked out of the window and gasped as her eyes travelled up the sides of the building they were soon to enter. Stone and glass towered over them, at least seven, maybe eight, storeys of red brick. There was no character to the construction – brickwork without ornament, designed for practicality not beauty.

"What is it? What is the noise?" she asked again, covering her ears a little to keep out some of the sound.

Garbrae smiled in sympathy. He remembered his first visit to a mill – the place overwhelming, the activity and clamour almost frightening.

"The hiss you hear is from the steam engines, the screech and clatter just the noise of the machines. As for the rest, it is the general bustle of the factory, the people at work – those barking orders and maintaining control. Inside the workrooms, the sound of the shuttles being passed through the looms is just as loud. I swear I become a little more deaf each time I go in there."

"Shall I be going inside?" asked Rose, her eyes darting rapidly back and forth between the captain and the chaos in the yard just beyond the carriage door. She was beginning to regret her desire to accompany her brother-in-law.

"No, I do not think it wise. Aside from the noise, the heat and the cotton dust would not leave a favourable impression. I think it best if you wait in the office."

Rose readily agreed, thankful for the captain's good sense.

Garbrae escorted Rose to the main office, a small building with two rooms, attached to the factory, overlooking the main yard. Once she was settled, he left to conduct the business that had brought him there.

After only a few minutes, Rose had, as Garbrae said she would, grown accustomed to the noise and felt comfortable enough to take her hands from her ears, leaving her at liberty to explore the two rooms available to her. On her way through the first room, she had noticed a large square table covered with a scattering of plans and diagrams, so Rose left the captain's personal room to take a better look.

Rose examined the drawings. *Expansion!* she thought. *Heavens, is this place not monstrous enough?*

"These are not of the factory at all," she said aloud. "These are houses."

The only houses Rose could conceive of being favoured with attention were those of the workers, these she knew were provided by the captain. She was surprised by the notion that the improvements were for the benefit of the workers and not for the profitability of the factory and could not immediately account for her surprise. The captain had never given any indication he was an unfeeling man. Indeed, she knew him to be otherwise in his concern for Catherine and his treatment of herself. There was no reason to suppose he would not be a good master, and yet, here she was, surprised! She saw, on thinking on the matter, it was Catherine's influence at work, for there was little generosity to be found in her description of her husband. To Rose's shame, she realised she had allowed Catherine to manipulate her treatment of the captain.

Good Heavens, she thought, *he still calls me 'my lady'.*

There being nothing she could do, at that moment, to make amends for the failings in her treatment of her new brother, Rose continued her exploration, promising herself she would not forget what debt of duty and civility was owed him.

Her survey of one room complete, she moved back into the captain's personal office, guessing this was likely to be where he conducted his main business, hoping to uncover something of the man as well as the master. Much to her disappointment, she uncovered nothing of particular note. A large mahogany desk took centre stage in the room, the expected accoutrements of business cluttering it. There was a large leather chair behind the desk and two sturdy wooden seats in front. The small bookcase in the corner appeared to hold nothing but ledgers and legal texts. She took in the sum total of the room's contents at a glance and was disappointed by the lack of anything personal, such as might illuminate the man's character.

She had been determined her snooping would go no further than those items and objects left open and in plain view, but on being so cruelly disappointed by the findings, she decided more invasive measures were called for, and her inquisitiveness did not go unrewarded, for tucked at the back of the desk's top drawer, she found a small portrait.

Rose sat back in the chair, considering the painted image before her. The woman captured in oils was young and certainly beautiful, or at least, the artist represented her so. She wondered about the woman: who she was and what significance she had to Garbrae. On leaning forward to place the frame on the desk, she noticed it had two little feet and these dug slightly into the desk's leather top. She looked at the table with greater attention than before, and sure enough, there within arm's reach, for the captain at least, were two marks permanently imprinted into the leather.

Placing the picture frame in position, allowing the feet to sit neatly in the readymade grooves, Rose guessed some weight must have been exerted on the frame to create the impression in the leather, although she could not think how.

She had just leaned back into the chair to consider the portrait again when a noise from the other room startled her and caused her to recollect where she was. Not wishing to be found so obviously prying, she jumped up immediately and darted out from behind the desk.

Garbrae and another man entered the room to find Rose standing, looking out of the window, apparently enthralled by the comings and goings of the main yard.

"Your ladyship," Garbrae said, "my business here is almost concluded. Might I ask your indulgence for a few minutes more?"

"Of course." Rose smiled in reply. "I shall step outside and leave you to finish what you must."

Rose nodded at the other man who stood at the door, crushing the peak of the cap in his hand, as she moved around him to leave the room. She had just enough time to see the captain take a seat behind his desk, his brow creased in puzzlement.

Garbrae looked at the portrait on his desk. He was certain he had put it away, yet there it stood, its feet nestled in their usual position, the image of Anna Harrington gazing at him. It was strange – he had been consumed by the woman once, yet now, he could not remember the last time he had considered her at all. How could it be that the object of his passion had fallen so quickly from his mind and with so little exertion on his part? He had anticipated a great struggle to forget and yet …

The awkward shuffle of feet from across the room recalled Garbrae's attention to the matter at hand.

"So, Yarrow," he said, clearing his throat and focusing on the man before him, "what is it that so urgently calls for this meeting?"

Yarrow looked at his master and drew a long deep breath before replying: "I come to ask about getting a position for my boy, master ... something in the workroom. He can turn his hand to anything – a smart lad, you see – and I was hoping you might see your way to taking him on."

"Which boy is that?" asked Garbrae, trying to remember the man's family.

"My second, sir."

"That is young Robert, is it not?"

Yarrow nodded.

"The boy cannot be any more than eight years old."

"I know, master, and I know you is particular about them that work for you, but like I say, he is a good boy, and smart. His mother would train him up now, and when he gets a little older and stronger, he could haul with me."

"Yarrow, you know my feelings on hiring children. I have made my position on this quite clear, so why even ask me to take on your boy? You know what my answer will be. Why set yourself up for such disappointment? It does neither of us any good."

"It's the wife, master; she is in the way again, you see, and our wages just feeds and clothes the young'uns we got now. Won't hardly be enough when there's another one."

"Lord!" said Garbrae in amazement at the man. "How many is that now?"

"Number six, master."

"Six, so it will be eight in all and in that tiny house on the end."

"We make do just fine. Least, we will if I can get my boy

in here. I would rather he work for you than one of the other mills."

"Well, you know my feelings on this. I will not take on children younger than ten."

"I know, sir, I know, but the others will take 'em. I hoped, as me and the wife work here, you might see your way to letting him in."

"No," said Garbrae resolutely. "I will not rob the boy of what little childhood and education can be afforded him in his first ten years. He will stay in school and out of the mill for at least another two years. But," he continued before Yarrow had opportunity to respond, "there is something that might be done. I have, for several weeks, been thinking on your service to the mill. Johnson is set to leave at the end of the year, and I planned on asking you to take up his position."

Yarrow stood, dumbfounded.

"This would mean more responsibility for you, and I would expect you to learn about the business, at least in so far as your additional duties. There would, of course, be an increase in your wage which should see to your family's needs. I will require as part of the terms that Robert remain in school. Will you accept the offer?"

A quick nod of acknowledgement was all Yarrow could manage at first, followed by a sincere pledge he would not let Garbrae down.

"Then let us shake hands on the bargain, sir," said Garbrae cordially. "I will make arrangements with Johnson for you to be trained up, and for Heaven's sake, no more children, man."

Rose, who had made sure to take a seat that was as close as possible to the door of Garbrae's personal office, could not help but wonder at the exchange she had overheard. He was a generous master indeed, and his concern for the children of those he employed proved yet another surprise in his character.

She noticed the change in Yarrow as he strode out. The man looked a good foot taller and walked with his shoulders back and head held high. It was quite something to see a man leave an exchange with a master all the better for it!

The door had been left slightly ajar on Yarrow's leaving, and Rose peeked in to see Garbrae, expecting to see him smiling in satisfaction at what had passed, but he looked downcast. One hand rested on the sturdy portrait frame, his thumb tracing the image behind the glass. This, Rose guessed, explained the dents, the weight of Garbrae's hand pushing the feet into the leather. She had considered that the image was of his mother, but the sadness on the captain's face was not inflicted by the loss of a parent.

Rose considered her brother-in-law again. It had never occurred to her that Catherine was not the only party who had made sacrifices in agreeing to their marriage. She knew Catherine lamented the loss of the possibility of finding love, but here surely was proof of just such a love forfeited.

"Captain, I am so sorry," she whispered, knowing she would not be heard but needing to say the words, nonetheless.

"So how was your first visit to a cotton mill?" asked Garbrae as he escorted Rose back to their waiting carriage, his earlier sadness gone. "I trust you did not find the experience too unpleasant."

"Far from it. Thank you for the opportunity. Although I was almost overcome by the shock of the noise, I believe I recovered admirably, and there was much to enlighten me.

Indeed, I have one or two questions, if you have no objection to being interrogated on the journey home."

"Questions? Really?" he replied, his surprise evident. "I had not supposed there would be anything of sufficient interest to warrant questions but, please, by all means, interrogate away!" he said as he helped her into her seat.

"You may regret allowing me such free rein," she replied, "and please, we are brother and sister now, there can be no impropriety in you speaking my name."

"Then Lady Rose, it is," he said, clearly pleased, "and you must call me J—"

"I will call you 'captain', captain" interrupted Rose with a smile, "at least until my sister calls you otherwise, for she might never forgive any brazen display of preference for you, no matter how I might feel, not until she has seen the error of her ways!"

"Do you believe your sister is mistaken in her opinion of me, Lady Rose?"

"I do."

"And do you believe she might be persuaded to alter that opinion?"

"I do."

"And do you believe you might be of any service in that matter?" Garbrae asked, leaning forward in his seat.

Rose smiled. "You know, captain, I believe I do."

"So, let the interrogation begin," said Garbrae, as soon as they were far enough away from the mill to make conversation pleasant. "What is it you would like to know?"

"I could not help but notice the drawings on the table in the outer office. They looked to be for houses, not the factory itself, and I was wondering about your plans."

Garbrae was instantly enlivened, keen for any opportunity to discuss his ideas for the improvement of conditions at the works.

"The improvements are quite exciting. I am so glad you noticed them," he answered with animation. "Did you see the rows of cottages just as we left? The little village that seems to have grown up around the mill?"

Rose nodded.

"Well, there are to be a series of expansions to all living quarters, for families here tend to be large. We own the land around the mill, so there is nothing to stop us creating bigger, more suitable homes. There are to be at least two bedrooms, and a separate kitchen and parlour, but most exciting of all are the changes to be made to ..." Garbrae stopped, suddenly realising the topic he was about to hit upon.

"What? What is to be the most exciting change?" queried Rose, her enthusiasm for the project fired by Garbrae's obvious passion.

"Oh, it is nothing in particular; there are simply to be other improvements, that is all ... *other* improvements."

"You are hiding something from me," accused Rose. "What is it you were about to say? It is not something wicked!" she exclaimed, her imagination already running to the creation of public houses and gambling dens. "Lord, it is not something unchristian."

"Whatever do you suppose I am planning?" he replied, amused by the look on his sister-in-law's face and curious as to what she imagined. "It is simply not something that is generally discussed, and most certainly not with a lady."

Rose continued to regard him with the keenest interest, and he guessed that if he did not tell her it would not be a matter left to lie.

"Privies, Lady Rose; privies," he admitted finally, embarrassed by having such a conversation with a woman but determined not to appear so. "I am working with a brilliant young architect and engineer, and he is going to design a sanitation system. Not one in every house you understand – such an undertaking would be too great – but a number of shared facilities will be made available, with the … well, with the …" he stammered, "with safer and cleaner conditions for all those living at the cottages."

Rose had blushed at Garbrae practically yelling the word "privies", but her colour had returned to its usual pallor by the time the captain looked at her again. "I can see why you might take an interest in increasing the size of the houses – with large families, as you say – but whatever inspired you to consider sanitation? This must be a more complicated concern. Are the other mill owners doing the same?"

"Lord, no. I tried to convince some of them to join me, but they laughed at what they refer to as 'my folly'. They see the whole enterprise as a waste of profit and want nothing to do with it."

"Then why do it?" enquired Rose. "Why pursue such a course if it leaves you open to mockery among friends and peers?"

"Friends? I claim none of those men as friends. I pursue this course because it is the right thing. It will improve the lot of those who work for me and prevent illness. I owe them that at least for the hours they give to me, to the mill."

"Hours they are paid for," replied Rose, taken aback by the liberality of the man's sentiments.

"Indeed, hours they are paid for, but if I can provide more, do I not owe them more? I know the conditions they work in – thirteen-hour days in hot crowded rooms, breathing in cotton dust till their chests heave with it. Do I not owe them at least some comfort in the hours left to them outside of the mill?"

"You speak most familiarly of their hardships, but you cannot know what it is truly like. Perhaps it is not as pitiable as you imagine," Rose replied, increasingly surprised by her brother-in-law.

"As I imagine? I speak with such familiarity because I worked in those conditions, only for a month, but it was long enough to impress upon me the hardships my workers endure. Their situation is more pitiable, for after a month, I could walk away. They do not have such a luxury."

The pair of them sat silent for a time. Rose considered all the captain had related while Garbrae wondered if he had spoken too boldly.

"My father made his first fortune with the East India Company," Garbrae said at last, his tone gentler and less animated than before. "He and my mother lived for many years in India until his wealth was sufficient to bring them home to invest in business interests here. He had, over the years, fostered many friends and business connections in India, and when, through investment and speculation, he had increased his wealth even further he decided to turn his hand to the manufacture of cotton. He used his old connections in India, and the arrangement was incredibly profitable. As a reward for his success, he and my mother decided to tour, as they had always dreamed of doing, finally making their way back to India before returning home. I was sixteen and already in the navy so would not be joining them. I saw them off at the boat, and it was the last time I was to see my mother alive. She made it back to India, and there, cholera took her from us ..."

Garbrae paused, he had not often spoken of this, and he was not certain he should be doing so now, but it was important to him Rose understand his actions were not the result of folly. "Her death was needless. One of the doctors who tended her believed proper sanitation and cleaner conditions might have prevented the cholera outbreak that took her. When I saw the conditions here, at our own mill, I simply had to act. Perhaps I am wrong; it may be that such conditions have no part to play. I am certainly no doctor, but I feel it must be better, must be for the benefit and health of all concerned."

Rose said nothing.

"Am I a madman?" asked Garbrae in response to her silence. "Do you think me as foolish as the others do?"

Rose shook her head and smiled at the man. "I think quite the opposite. I think you quite wonderful," she answered candidly. "And I cannot fathom anyone thinking otherwise."

CHAPTER 20

"*W*as it torturous?" asked Catherine, as soon as her sister appeared in her bedroom, not five minutes after leaving the captain. "The journey to the mill must have felt interminable."

"On the contrary, the journey was most pleasant. I was so well engaged, I felt as though we were only minutes in the carriage."

Catherine, dismayed by so positive a response, continued in the hope her sister found less favour with the destination than she had the journey. "But the mill itself, that must have been frightful? Was it as hideous as I imagine?"

Rose removed her bonnet and set about fixing her hair. "The building was not pretty," she said, teasing the curls that surrounded her face back into place. "It is an imposing fortress of brick and glass – and the noise! I thought my head would burst at first, but I had cause to think, while I waited, on the purpose of the building. It was built not to give pleasure for the eyes but to fulfil a purpose, and there is some beauty in the notion that it does just that, and you should see the improvements the captain has planned …"

Rose continued to talk with eagerness on her day, but Catherine stopped paying any mind to the conversation, her vexation at her sister's all too obvious approval of her husband grating. Though one topic soon forced her notice. "He talked about what?" she asked, uncertain she had heard correctly.

Rose turned from the vanity table to look at Catherine. "Sanitation. I swear I blushed from head to toe when he said the word 'privies'. Lord! I am blushing again." She laughed, thinking the whole exchange now quite funny, completely unaware of her sister's outrage.

"Are there no limits to the vulgarity of the man?" exploded Catherine. "What possible reason could he have for engaging you in such a conversation? Every time I believe I have experienced his full unseemliness, he surprises me with new and abhorrent levels of coarseness."

Rose, in complete astonishment at her sister's reaction, could say nothing while Catherine vented every dreadful feeling she had for the captain, finishing her uninterrupted tirade with, "And though private impropriety is pain enough, he pains me more with embarrassing displays in public. Why, you know, once while we were at the theatre, he learned Earl Ballantyne was visiting an aunt in the area and would be attending. When the earl arrived, the captain took it upon himself to approach the man, without formal introduction, with an open hand, expecting the earl to … what? Simply take his hand? The man is a cretin."

"Catherine!" Rose said, shocked by her sister's language. "There is no need to be so disparaging of the captain. He made a mistake. Surely he can be forgiven for not knowing he ought to wait to be introduced."

"How is it a man can go so many years without knowing a simple matter such as that?" Catherine replied, unwilling to countenance any excuse that might lessen her indignation at her husband's behaviour.

"Well, do you know why he approached him? Did he have business with the earl? It may well be that in business such matters are more straightforward, and perhaps it is permissible to approach a man and offer an informal greeting and a handshake. If we do not appreciate the niceties of his world, is it any wonder he does not always appreciate the niceties of ours?"

"Please, do not remind me of the inferiority of the man I married," Catherine cut in, displeased that Rose was defending him, and with some spirit.

"Inferior? Good God. Who are you to judge him so? I have never heard you speak in such terms of another person, and I am appalled to hear you do it when speaking of your husband."

Catherine turned on her sister, her reply assuming a harshness usually reserved for the captain. "How dare you sit there and lecture me on how I may speak, not after the sacrifices I have made to secure your comfort."

Rose replied with an uncharacteristic steeliness in her voice. "Your sacrifice, as you put it, was of your own choosing; you cannot hold it now like a sword above my head. While I am grateful for the good that has been achieved through your marriage, I did not ask you to marry the man. You had a choice."

Catherine, scarcely able to contain her anger at her sister's censure flung open the door to her closet and pulled at the dresses stored neatly there. "Choice? What choice did I have with Father ruined, Mother making daily appeals for me to find a husband, and you in tears? There was little choice in the matter. I did what I had to so you would be protected. Tell me, is this all the thanks I can expect in return?" she blasted, pulling out her evening dress so forcefully she crushed its sleeve in her fist.

Rose, unimpressed by her sister's fury, continued, "Oh, I am sure you see yourself as quite the martyr, but do not forget you ensured your own protection through this bargain. I do not think you are any more suited to a life of poverty than I. While I am certain you thought of my interests, can you honestly tell me that you did not also act out of self-preservation? You could have married elsewhere, if you had made yourself less disagreeable to any of the men who first vied for your hand. You could have waited longer, for other offers would have come. But no. You chose to marry Captain Garbrae. If you regret that choice now, do not punish him for it."

Catherine had never seen her sister argue so vehemently about anything, and the shock of it silenced her.

Rose had never seen her sister so subdued and, assuming she would soon find herself removed from the house, continued with one final plea on the captain's behalf. "You have no idea of the measure and worth of the man you married. That you can even think him inferior shows just how little you truly know him. He is a good and decent man. He is honourable in his dealings and mindful in his treatment of others, which is more than can be said for you in this moment. Add to this his general good nature, sharp mind, and fine face, and I can scarcely understand your objections to him. If you find him lacking in the social graces you would have hoped for in a husband, I might ask exactly what it is you have done to polish his manners. Prior to this embarrassment with Ballantyne, had you even hinted at what would be expected of him? If the answer is no, then I suggest you look to yourself when apportioning blame for any misconduct. Lord, I never thought I should have cause to say this, but today, I am ashamed to call you sister."

~

The sisters avoided one another for the afternoon, each determined to allow the other time to see the error of her ways. It was not until Rose sent a polite decline to Catherine's suggestion of a walk before dinner that Catherine supposed she had been anything other than right during their earlier exchange.

"I was perhaps a little harsh in the tone of my address," she admitted to herself, taking a long hard look at her reflection in the mirror. "Mother warned I can be severe when goaded, and it seems nothing goads me more than Rose finding favour with a man I have decided to hate. Is it too much to expect her to hate him simply because I do?"

She picked up a brush and pulled at the curls pinned about her face and tried to distract herself from the look of guilt she was certain she had caught in her eyes. "And what might I have to feel guilty about?" she demanded of the face staring back at her, reading accusation in her frown and downturned mouth. "Do not stare at me so."

~

Catherine tapped lightly at her sister's door. "Rose, may I come in?" she called out, uncertain as to the reply she would receive, but hopeful Rose's good heart would not long bear a grudge against her.

Rose opened the door a little, and though Catherine could see no smile on her lips, there was a softness about her eyes that assured Catherine her sister was not fully resolved to remain unhappy with her.

"Will you forgive me, for all I said earlier? I will try to be better. I will try to see the captain as you do, to be gentler on him. Sometimes I think I might be able to and then quite unaccountably I find myself hardening toward him."

The door opened further. "I do not understand your insistence on finding fault with the man," replied Rose. "Quite frankly, your determination to dislike him staggers me."

"I was disappointed in my marriage," Catherine answered quietly, praying there were no servants to overhear her admission.

Rose opened the door fully to allow her sister inside.

"I was disappointed and angered," Catherine continued. "Whatever you might think about accepting the proposal being my choice, I can assure you the deal was struck without thought to what I might want. It was best for the family. Mr Garbrae was not only able to clear Father's debts but could also set aside a tidy sum for you, propose investments and lines of business that would be profitable, and ensure Westbury flourished. In my heart, I knew it was the best choice, but it was not a choice of my making, and I have – I see now – allowed the disappointment and anger I felt to cloud my judgement when it comes to my husband. I will try to do better – to *be* better."

"Is there anything else?" Rose urged, pleased by Catherine's openness. "Anything you are not admitting? Though I find favour with the captain, it is the favour of a sister not of a wife. Has he given reason to be a disappointment to you as a husband? Is he cruel to you, unkind to you in any way? Is he …?" She paused trying to think of how to broach a sensitive topic. "Is he forceful in his attentions?" she finally managed.

Catherine considered this. Though she thought herself free from the effect of finding her husband with the maid, she realised that since that day she had scarcely acted outside of the influence of it. Seeing him standing so close and sharing such intimacy with the girl had stirred a rage within her, which even now, she was swayed by. It was with surprise, she realised, his every word and action since then had been tainted by that rage, so she could only see, would only see, the worst in him. In thinking on his general treatment of her, she had to admit he had not been cruel, he had not been forceful in his attentions, and as he could not have expected her to come looking for him, he had not even flaunted his tryst with the maid. Indeed, he had shown her nothing but kindness, taking pains to see her comfortable, bringing Rose to be her companion, tolerating her sniping, and treating her with unwavering patience and good grace.

"I ... that is to say ... No. He is not unkind; he does not mistreat me," Catherine finally said while reaching for a chair, her legs suddenly incapable of keeping her standing.

"Sister, are you unwell?" Rose asked, taken aback by Catherine's sudden alteration.

"Oh, Lord! I have been so foolish," Catherine said, the shock of finally seeing the captain as anything other than unworthy undoing her. "He has been nothing but kind to me. I have attacked and accused the man beyond bearing, and still he takes pains to see me happy. How are we ever to be made whole after all that I have done?"

Rose knelt down, and taking her sister's face between her hands, she looked Catherine straight in the eyes. "Hush now, there is nothing here that cannot be fixed, no damage that cannot be undone. If you are willing to try, I am quite certain you can find peace in your marriage."

"And happiness, Rose?" asked Catherine, still a little uncertain.

"Assuredly, sister; on that, we may both rely."

CHAPTER 21

There was one purpose to the thoughts of the sisters the next day as they sat in the morning room – determining the manner in which Catherine could best make amends with her husband.

"Could you not simply apologise and promise to be better?" asked Rose, who saw little purpose in schemes when forthrightness could be employed. "The captain is not ill-favoured toward you."

"But is it enough to be a couple who are not ill-favoured toward one another?" asked Catherine. "Could I be content with such an approximation of regard?"

Rose closed her eyes and turned to the large windows in front of them, enjoying the warmth of the sun on her face. "Could you not be satisfied to begin with such preference? Love may grow from an easing of the tensions between the two of you."

"And how is it you know the captain is not ill-favoured toward me?" asked Catherine, paying mind to her sister's earlier assurance.

"He told me himself," Rose replied. "He was concerned

150

you had a poor opinion of him and was hopeful you might be brought to see the error of your ways."

"Yet that does not necessarily signify love. It could just as easily speak to a man who longs for a quiet life and a peaceful home. It is not proof of his regard," Catherine said, "although perhaps it is enough to build upon."

The sisters fell silent, each mulling over the problem before them – Rose, her eyes still closed, twisting and releasing an errant curl about her finger, and Catherine brushing imagined lint from her dress, the chair, and the small table beside her. The silence was interrupted by the entrance of a young maid who bobbed a greeting to her mistress and held out a long, thin, gold box before her.

"The master wanted you to have this, my lady," she offered, "and begged to know if you and the Lady Rose might ride with him this afternoon. He has a mind to order a picnic."

Catherine, taking the box, smiled at the young girl. "Please tell Captain Garbrae we would be delighted to join him."

As soon as the maid was gone, Rose spun about in her seat, all her attention on the gold box. "I so adore presents," she said, squealing with as much delight in Catherine's good fortune as if the gift were her own. "What do you suppose it is?"

Catherine moved to untie the ribbon before being unceremoniously stopped by a sharp slap across the back of the hand from her sister.

"Do not dare open that box before allowing us the thrill of trying to guess at its contents," Rose scolded.

"Do not try to prolong this. It is not your birthday, and I have no intention of spending the morning in one of your crazed guessing games."

"A little guessing then," Rose pleaded. "Is the box heavy? Does it rattle? Do not spoil my sport."

Catherine sighed but relented. "The box is not light; there is something with weight in it."

"So, it is not new gloves, and judging by its size, it is unlikely to be any other piece of clothing." Rose clapped her hands in excitement. "Go on, go on – what else?"

Shaking the box, Catherine could hear something solid hitting off the sides, though the sound was muffled, as if the object was wrapped in paper. "It sounds like there is one item within, not several, and I could not hear any rattling. May I open the thing now?"

"Oh, if you must, though I would have lasted much longer if the gift were mine."

Rose leaned forward to afford herself a better view of what was inside as Catherine undid the ribbon, removed the lid, and unfolded the neat layer of paper encasing the item. "Good heavens," she said in complete astonishment. "Whatever can the man have meant by giving you such a gift?"

Sitting back into her chair, she waited for an explanation from Catherine who, judging by the look on her face, was quite delighted by the offering.

"It is absolutely splendid." Catherine laughed as she lifted the dagger out of the box, removing it from the scabbard and turning the blade so it glinted in the morning light. Her examination of the dagger complete, she passed it to Rose and turned her attention to the neatly written note that had been included with the gift.

It is time the silverware was returned, and this is a far more fitting weapon.

Should you feel the need for protection – insert, twist, and drive upward for best effect.

Not a typical husband–wife gift, but I could think of nothing you would appreciate more.

"Splendid," Catherine said again, "absolutely splendid. Rose you were right. I believe I will find peace before we are done."

"And happiness too?" asked Rose, still puzzled by the gift and Catherine's favourable reaction to it, though pleased to see such favour, nonetheless.

"And happiness too," Catherine replied. "For the first time, I believe even *that* is not out of reach. Come, time marches on, and we have a ride this afternoon to get ready for."

~

At midday, Catherine and Rose made their way to the stables, meeting Garbrae – loaded down with a heavy basket – on the way.

"Good afternoon, ladies," he said, his pleasure at their decision to join him evident. "I do hope you will not mind, but I planned a day with as little fuss as possible. It is not my intention to have the servants join us, rather we shall saddle a spare horse to bring the food and blankets, so we may ride freely and set up the picnic ourselves whenever the fancy strikes us."

"What a wonderful suggestion," chimed Rose, "then we shall get the chance to ride after all. We were concerned a picnic would mean the carriage, forgoing the pleasure of being on horseback ourselves."

"No, indeed not; I know how much you both enjoy riding, and I would not deny you such a simple pleasure when it is within my power to bestow it." Bowing slightly, he turned his attentions to the stable. "Come, Barton has the horses saddled and ready."

"Barton?" said Catherine.

"Yes, Barton," Garbrae replied, a strong colour rushing to

his temples.

"Why such surprise?" asked Rose, completely unaware of the history there. "Barton has been stablemaster since you moved here, except for the week of your fall of course. I believe he said he was away then. Where was it he said he had gone to, captain? I have completely forgotten."

"Visiting his sister, I believe," he replied, unable to look at Catherine.

"Oh yes, of course, visiting his sister. She was unwell, or indisposed, or some such thing – so good of him to go to her when she needed him. Though we must be grateful he did not stay away too long for the man has a gift with those horses."

Rose rambled on distractedly, expressing her delight in Barton, in the stables, in the horses, but Garbrae and Catherine scarcely caught a word of what was being said.

"Gone just one week," she said to her husband, her voice low so as not to interrupt Rose and draw her into a conversation that Catherine wished to remain private.

"A week," replied he, finally looking her in the eye.

"You did not think to mention this to me?"

"At first, you were not well, and afterward, you did not seem inclined to hearing much I had to say."

"And now?" she queried.

"And now, you know," he answered. "Barton was gone a week and then he returned."

"You said you cut the man down in front of the others. It cannot have been easy to convince him to return."

"I made my apology as public as my firing. Barton is a proud man but a fair one. All in all, I am grateful it could be resolved as easily as it was."

"An apology in front of the staff must have been quite an embarrassment," said Catherine in disbelief at his easy dismissal of the whole affair.

"But it was necessary. Nothing else would suffice, and the man deserved no less."

"I am sorry for having been the cause of such awkwardness," she offered, reaching out and taking hold of his forearm to stay him a moment.

Garbrae stopped at her touch, turned toward her, and laid his hand atop hers. "Your apology, while appreciated, is unnecessary," he said. "I brought that grief upon myself, through my own foolishness, but see now, there is no harm done and all is forgiven. Barton is returned, so perhaps we might all start afresh."

His eyes locked with hers. Neither noticed that Rose had stopped talking and was staring at them both with giddy delight. When at last they turned their attention back to the yard, there was not another sole about them, everyone having disappeared into the house or stables.

Catherine coloured at finding they had been so obviously left alone and wondered whether Rose had shooed the servants out of sight. The pair finished crossing the yard in silence, but Catherine was pleased to find no uneasiness there, rather a curious sort of comfort in having him beside her, he apparently enjoying her company just as much.

"Barton, so good to see you," she announced, the moment they stepped inside the stables. "I am glad to have you back with us. I do hope your sister is fully recovered."

"My sister," Barton replied, stumbling at the subterfuge, "is most well, thank you, your ladyship. Though it is a relief to be back where I belong; the woman has five young'uns – these horses are not half so much bother."

Catherine looked to the horses that had been saddled and was surprised to see Black Jack among them. "You will ride out on Black Jack, captain?"

"No, my lady," replied he, "you will."

Catherine stared at her husband. "I do not know what to

say. After the disaster of that first ride, I am not certain I would be so trusting of another rider if the animal were mine."

"But he is not mine. Black Jack is yours. Do you imagine there is any horse within our stables that would suit you better? Though, perhaps we shall make it a gentler ride this afternoon," Garbrae said, teasing.

Catherine stared at her husband for a moment before burying her face and her brilliant smile in Black Jack's mane.

"And perhaps we ought to avoid getting too close to the woods," she said, happy to add a little light-hearted teasing of her own to the memory of her foolishness.

"A good plan, my lady. We shall ride out and return by the lake, where we may enjoy this fine day, our feast, and the safety of wide-open spaces."

"It has been a curious few weeks – would you agree, Rose?" Catherine said, stretching her legs out on the blanket they had laid down for their picnic.

"A remarkably curious few weeks. I had not hoped to see you happy so quickly. You were so resolved to be miserable when I first arrived. Had I realised a dagger, a horse, and a picnic were all that were required, I would have told the captain earlier and saved us all a great deal of trouble."

"I am not the only one in our little set to have changed,' replied Catherine; "you are now far too—"

"Much like you?" said Rose, smiling widely.

"Yes, exactly. You have become far too outspoken. Did I mention – opinionated and stubborn too? Mother will not be pleased. I believe one of her happiest days was the day I left to come here. She cried – for good show – but we were not suited to sharing a house, and now what will she do when I return you to her in such a state? You know I would feel sorry for her if I did not find the thought so amusing."

Rose rested back against the trunk of the oak they had found shade beneath and shook her head in mock disapprobation of her sister. "Lord, even at a distance you find delight in tormenting the woman. She was never half as bad to you as you made out, and you were twice as bad to her if you recollect. Though I grow a little more like you, I will remain gentler on Mama – if not only out of love then out of longing for a peaceful life," Rose said. "Do you want to send me home? Have I outstayed my welcome?"

"Heavens, no. You are free to stay here as long as you wish. I have no desire to send you home, and the captain assures me you may stay – forever, if you choose."

Rose smiled at the thought and asked, "And should I marry, could my husband stay too?"

"What a wonderful idea," replied Catherine. "What a happy foursome we would be. We could divide the house. I would take the east wing, for the view of the lake is far superior, and you and your husband could settle in the west wing to be that much closer to the stables for your early morning ride."

Rose reached for a strawberry and waggled it in warning at her sister. "You tease, but be careful, I may take your offer to heart. You know I have a terrible fondness for romance, and if I fall in love with a stableboy or penniless deckhand, we may indeed come for a visit and simply never leave."

"It would be just like you to do that. I shall have to hide those novels you read; they fill your head with such fanciful romantic notions."

The sisters laughed, enjoying the sun and their shared silliness.

"Whatever is it that so amuses you?" asked Garbrae,

drawn back from the edge of the lake by the women's laughter.

"Rose and I were discussing her marriage plans," replied Catherine. "She is trying to choose between a stableboy and a deckhand. I have offered her the west wing of the house as a wedding present."

"Well, those are certainly interesting options, Lady Rose. The west wing is yours if you marry the stableboy, though take the east wing if you marry the deckhand for it offers a much better view of the lake," Garbrae said, smiling wide before sauntering back to his fishing pole. "Oh, and I would recommend the deckhand as a husband if your nose is as sensitive as your sister's. You may find the salty smell of the sea far more pleasant than—"

"Enough," interrupted Catherine with a loud laugh, throwing an apple in the direction of her husband. "Let us cease this chatter before you finish that sentence."

Garbrae spun on his heel and bowed low to the ladies. "As you wish. Please call me back if you need help with any big decisions, especially if they concern wedding cake. I have a great expertise in cake."

Once Garbrae had moved far away enough to be out of earshot, Rose turned her attention back to her sister. "The captain has a fine sense of humour. I am pleased he makes you laugh. It has been too long."

"It had been far too long, and somehow, I find myself happier than I dared hope for."

Rose moved away from the tree and down the blanket until she sat facing Catherine. "Then perhaps it is time I was going home," she said. "Perhaps it is time for just you two to be here."

"No. You will not leave me," said Catherine, her voice suddenly fraught and tense, her hand flying out to grasp at

Rose's, clutching her tight. "I am not ready for you to leave me."

"But everything is going so well, Catherine; you are happy."

"That is just the thing, Rose – we are happy, we three. What if the captain and I cannot be happy alone?"

"Nonsense," Rose insisted. "I see you together, and you are happy. You will be happy, with or without me."

"Still, you will not leave, not until I am certain."

Rose, who had never seen Catherine so anxious, could do nothing but agree. "I will not leave until you ask me to," she said, stroking Catherine's clenched hands, feeling her fingers relax and release their grip on her. Then, to lighten the mood, "My husband, our five children, and our dog shall live here as long as you will have us."

Catherine laughed, her sudden rush of panic subsiding. "Five children. How wonderfully ambitious of you."

"Well, Ferdinando and I are very much in love."

"Ferdinando?"

"Yes, a deckhand – and Spanish."

"Mother will have a fit," squealed Catherine, before the pair descended into girlish laughter.

The sound lifted Garbrae, drawing a smile to his lips. "It is good to hear her laugh," he said quietly, offering thanks heavenward for the intervention of Rose. "Though, please Lord, no sailors."

CHAPTER 22

"Captain, we do not know one another as well as we ought to," Catherine said, following behind her husband who had steadfastly refused to tell her where they were going. "I concede, I bear some responsibility for that, so let me enlighten you. I do not like surprises."

Garbrae wheeled his horse around so he faced her. "That much I do know about you. Your sister was most insistent on the point."

"And still you wish to maintain your silence?"

"I do," he said. "Your sister was also insistent that you would like this surprise and that I must not spoil it by telling you anything in advance … regardless of how you might scowl at me."

Catherine, who feared her features had indeed taken on the aspects of a most severe scowl, tried to smile. "My sister has, of late, become very free with her opinions," she said. "My mother will not thank you for that."

"Me? I claim no credit for any boldness on the part of Lady Rose. I believe she looks to you as an example in that regard."

Garbrae brought his horse to a stop, dismounted, and was by his wife's side, offering her aid in her dismount before she could reply. Catherine stared at the small patch of woodland they had stopped in front of.

"I must have a word with my sister if she thinks an afternoon in a murky wood is likely to be a surprise I would enjoy," she muttered, as much to herself as to her husband.

The horses tied to a nearby branch, Garbrae ignored the complaints of his wife as he led her into the trees. Catherine was launching into her third complaint when the pair stepped out from under the dense canopy of leaves and branches into the open space of a natural clearing. She blinked as her eyes adjusted once more to the bright sunlight.

"Well, this is beautiful," she admitted, gazing about the open space, the land knee-deep in a blanket of wild grass and flowers, cut through by a small stream, and surrounded on all sides by the woods.

"I am pleased you think so."

Catherine leaned forward a little, trying to make out something in the heart of the clearing. "Is that a seat?" she asked, her eyebrows pulled together in confusion.

They walked across to the wooden seat standing out incongruously amid the trees, the grasses, and the wildflowers.

"Your sister told me of your garden at Westbury, the place you and she shared. I thought this might please you as somewhere you could call your own. You could have a wall built with an entry door for which only you and the gardener would have the key – just like at Westbury. You could have it cultivated and tended to as you see fit. I will have a path cleared – I doubt the gardener's barrow would fare too easily in the woods, and you may prefer to make your way here on horseback, rather than on foot. But what do say you, my lady? What do you say to my surprise?"

Catherine sat.

"Your sister was mistaken. You do not like it."

"No, captain," Catherine replied, looking up at the man who stood above her, his face bright with embarrassment.

"It was perhaps a foolish notion," he said.

"No, captain," Catherine repeated, reaching out and taking his hand. "My sister was not mistaken. This is wonderful."

Garbrae smiled. "Oh," he said, taking a seat beside her.

They sat a moment in companionable silence, and Garbrae did not fail to notice that his wife's gloved fingers remained wrapped around his own.

Catherine looked about them. "I would not dream of walling it off, or of cultivating it. We have gardens enough with tended beds and easy walks. We have enough trimmed and neatened nature."

"You like the wildness of it?" Garbrae asked. Turning his hand in hers so their palms faced one another, he slipped his fingers in between hers.

Catherine's face flushed. "I do," she said, pressing her fingers ever so gently against his.

Returning from their ride, the couple found Rose sitting in the garden next to a small table laden with cold meats, bread, and cheese, with two empty chairs across from her.

"You have returned from your adventure in the wild woods no worse for wear, I see," she called out, waving at them as they crossed the lawn. "I thought it best to have luncheon ready for you," she said to Catherine, "and set an extra chair in case you might care to join us, captain," she added.

Garbrae was not hungry, though he took up the proffered

seat with the eagerness of a man half-starved, happy for any excuse to spend more time in the company of his wife. "This looks delicious," he said, reaching for the wine and pouring each of them a glass. "The perfect refreshment after a morning's ride."

The ease that had so happily marked the start of the day continued when the pair joined Rose to enjoy shared food and company. As the captain and Catherine sat, engaged in friendly teasing of one another, Rose wondered if there were really any doubt in either's mind as to their being completely suited to one other. Surely, no two people could be so well matched and remain insensible to it for long. She had never known such freedom as she had experienced while staying with her sister, but she knew it must soon come to an end. Seeing the couple so comfortable with one another, she knew it could not be long before they would want to be alone. She would return to her parents' house, of that she was certain. A sigh escaped at the thought of being sent away.

"Even Lady Rose disagrees with you," Garbrae said, calling his sister-in-law's attention back to her companions. "That sigh was one rich with disapproval."

"You read a great deal into a sigh," Catherine said. "Am I to learn that among your many talents is a capacity for soothsaying? Do you also read palms or tea leaves? Or is it just the sigh?"

"I could read your future," he jested in return, taking hold of her hand and tracing his finger across her palm. His laughter caught in his throat. The softness of her skin and the heat from her hand distracted him from the tease he had been toying with. His lips were suddenly dry. As he licked them to offer some relief, he had a flash of how those lips would feel pressed onto Catherine's flesh, kissing her hand, his tongue tracing the lines of her palm, encircling her fingers, taking them into his mouth. Imagining Catherine responding to him, his breath quickened, and his colour raised. Garbrae sighed.

"Now that sigh even I can read," Catherine said, innocent of the thoughts at play in her husband's mind. "You are defeated. You can no more read my future than I can," she continued, her laughter ringing out.

"That is where you are mistaken," he said, dropping his voice low so she would have to lean in to hear. "I see your future all too clearly. Long life and happiness, long life—"

"And happiness," she cut in, her smile joining his.

It was not until the arrival of one of the footmen that any in the party gave a thought to the time.

"We have not stayed too late, I hope?" enquired Catherine, on seeing the boy approach. "You had business this afternoon in town, captain; you have not missed your appointment?"

Garbrae pulled out his watch. "No, I have more than an hour yet before business intrudes upon our pleasure."

The footman, having reached them at last, gave a swift bow. "A message for you, sir; the rider said it was urgent, and a reply is awaited."

Garbrae took the note, and his face paled on reading, all the levity of the afternoon evaporating in an instant.

"I must go," he said, jumping to his feet, ready to make off. "I do not know for how long, but I will send word as soon as I can."

Without offering any further explanation, he looked set to go before Catherine caught him by the arm.

"Captain, whatever is the matter? You cannot leave us without some explanation."

"It is my friend – Captain Fitzgerald."

"The man who stood with you at our wedding … He went to war just after?"

"Yes, the same man."

"Oh, Lord! He is not injured?" asked Catherine and Rose almost in unison.

"He is dying," replied Garbrae, shock and pain almost swallowing the words before they could make it out of his mouth. "Please, I must go; I cannot delay."

"No, of course not," she replied, releasing her hold on his arm. "Go to your friend, and Godspeed; I pray you reach him."

Before she could offer more, he was gone, racing toward the house, shouting orders at the footman for the carriage to be readied.

Catherine and Rose, watching after him, stood shivering.

"The day seems to have turned cold," Catherine said.

Rose could only nod in reply.

"Come, let us follow him in; it does us no good to stand here."

CHAPTER 23

Royal Hospital Haslar, Gosport, Hampshire. June 1813.

Save for the changing of horses, Garbrae did not allow his driver to slow the carriage's pace until Royal Hospital Haslar was almost within reach. Even then, it was only the imposing figure of a hollowed-out ship casting a pall over the port that caused him to shout to the driver to break the horse's stride. The sight of the vessel, jagged holes gouged out from its hull, startling.

He closed his eyes a moment, steadying his nerve, praying he was not too late, that his friend had not died – not here, and not alone. He turned away from the dock and, seeing the road that led from the port to the hospital, watched as the wounded were carted off the vessel in small barrows to be wheeled through the hospital's gates some short distance away. This then could not be Fitzgerald's ship, Garbrae reasoned, for the wounded could not still be pouring from its bowels. Surely to God, this wreckage was not his ship.

Garbrae exited the carriage on reaching the hospital gates. Leaving instructions for his driver to take care of the horses and return later, he walked onto the grounds. The sheer size of the place staggered him. He watched as men were wheeled in, orders given for them to be cleaned and their clothes changed before they could be taken inside.

"That one … it's too late," he heard a doctor say. "He will be buried this afternoon with the others. You know where to put him."

Garbrae cleared his throat to draw the man's attention, not wanting to step closer to the barrows, now three-deep in the yard.

On noticing the stranger, the doctor said, "You do not look unwell, nor do you look much like a sailor."

"I am … I was a naval captain," Garbrae said. "I received a message about a friend of mine. I was asked to come."

"Ah, then you have come in the wrong way, captain. This is the entrance from the ships. Cross the lawn," he pointed, "and look for a small office building on the left. There should be someone who can help you. As you can see, we are busy here."

"Of course, doctor, do not let me delay you; I shall look for the office, thank you."

"Good luck finding your friend," the man called out after him, though the captain was already striding across the grass and paid no mind.

"I am not too late?" Garbrae enquired of the man sitting opposite him who searched for Fitzgerald's name in the entry book.

"Too late? No, it is just … can you wait one moment, sir; I need to get one of the doctors."

The clerk, up and out of his seat before Garbrae could

protest, returned some minutes later, an older gentleman accompanying him.

"Captain Garbrae, thank you for coming so quickly. I had not imagined such expediency. I had not expected you for at least another day," the doctor said, extending his hand.

The two men exchanged a firm handshake. "I set off as soon as your message was received and have not stopped, save to change horses," Garbrae said, "fearing I would be too late otherwise. Tell me, doctor, is Captain Fitzgerald still alive?"

"Of course, he is alive. We have him restrained, so he cannot harm himself."

"Restrained? Harm himself? Why in Heaven's name would he harm himself?" asked Garbrae, astonished by the suggestion.

"What did the message you received say?"

"Simply that my friend was in a bad way and I should come straight away."

"Ah," the doctor replied, "I should have written the note myself and not delegated the task, but we are so busy – you have seen the warship in the port, no doubt. Heavy casualties. We have all been pressed upon, but no matter, you are here. Please, captain, join me in my office."

Garbrae, relieved to hear Fitzgerald was alive but disturbed by the suggestion he might injure himself, nodded in reply and followed the doctor inside, taking the seat and the brandy offered, without a word.

"You will have heard of Haslar Hospital, I am sure," the doctor began, when the pair were settled. "What you may not know is that it is not merely the physically sick who we attend to, but also those psychically afflicted."

"There is something wrong with his mind?" Garbrae said, his words barely audible. "This is an asylum?"

"There is a section of the hospital which acts as an

asylum, yes, and I am one of the doctors who oversees the welfare and treatment of patients in that section."

Garbrae paled, fear and fatigue acting against him. "What is the matter with my friend?"

"The last ship that Captain Fitzgerald sailed was heavily hit and badly damaged in battle. The destruction and loss of life the worst I have seen, and I worked the ships before coming here. It is as if the last battle broke something in your friend, something we cannot see to fix. Do you understand?"

Garbrae nodded. He had seen men driven mad by war, seen terror strip a man hollow until the shell that remained was good for nothing but the madhouse. But that could not be Fitzgerald.

"Are you certain it is Captain Michael Fitzgerald? I have known him for ten years. A braver, truer man you will not find anywhere in the navy. Are you sure the man you treat is indeed my friend and not some other?"

"I am certain, hard as that must be to hear. There is no doubt as to who he is."

Garbrae sat a moment, doubting the truth of what he had been told, hoping some mistake had been made, determined to hold on to the hope of that for as long as possible. "And what is the matter with him? You mentioned the possibility that he might hurt himself."

"The captain is lost in battle. The fighting rages on in his mind, and it is as though he were still there, as though he believes he may yet prevail and conquer."

"There are many of us similarly haunted, dreaming of better ends to battles than were actually afforded us. I have won skirmishes in my sleep that were lost in reality."

"But Captain Fitzgerald is not sleeping," the doctor added quietly.

Garbrae stared at him and swallowed hard. "But he

cannot be awake," he faltered, "because if he is awake then he is mad, and my friend is lost to me."

The doctor rose from his chair and moved toward the door. "Come, let me take you to him. I do not believe he is beyond being saved; that is why I asked for you to come here."

"Me? What can I do? I know nothing of curing madness."

"Fitzgerald does not need a doctor; he needs a lifeline, someone to ground him in the here and now, to draw him back from a past that threatens to consume him, and yours was the only name he would provide."

Garbrae, anxiety resulting in an unusual unsteadiness of nerves, took a moment to steel himself for what he had been warned might be a disturbing sight. Still, the spectacle of Fitzgerald strapped and bound to the bed hit him hard and, for the first few moments, left him staring horror-struck. How could a man so eager and full of life be reduced to this? How was he ever to be returned from such a pitiable state?

"Why is he bound?"

"He attacked some of the staff before turning his anger on himself. He broke his hand and almost knocked himself out by beating his head on the wall before falling into this cata-tonic state."

"Good God; why?"

"I can only think he saw an enemy there and believed himself to be fighting. He raged with such ferocity that it took four men to secure him. Though he appears quiet now, we could not risk him roaming free after that; he was too much of a danger – to himself and others. You see, captain, we are not trying to be cruel, however it must look to you."

"No, I can see that. You did what you believed to be right, but what is it you think that I can do?"

"Talk to him. Offer him something to strive for, coax him out of the battle," the doctor replied, moving a chair to Fitzgerald's bedside before heading for the door. "Someone will be nearby if you need anything. Good luck."

Garbrae took the seat and pulled it closer to the bed. "Hello, old friend," he began, struggling to think of what he should say. "What a mess you get yourself into when I am not there to watch out for you."

Garbrae took a room at the nearest inn, so he could be close to the hospital and visit every day. He arrived after breakfast, pulled his chair up close to Fitzgerald, and spoke to him for hours, leaving his friend's side only to eat and sleep. For three days, Garbrae repeated this routine, with Fitzgerald making no move to suggest that he was even aware his friend was there. Garbrae persisted nonetheless, talking at length on everything and anything he could think of – his life in Manchester, his wife, and Lady Rose, before, out of desperation, falling on the topic of the mill and the beginnings of his improvements there.

It was only then, on that third day, as he talked of building projects and difficulties with his architect, that there was any change in Fitzgerald.

His head slowly turned to face Garbrae for the first time. "Please!" Fitzgerald croaked, the hard and broken grating of his voice startling Garbrae. "Please, not another lecture. I swear I know your privy speech by heart!"

Garbrae smiled for the first time since receiving the message that had brought him to the hospital. "Then you must work on getting better, my friend, for you will hear it again and often, until you are well enough to make me quit."

~

It was a week before the doctor agreed to remove the restraints that bound Fitzgerald to his bed, although he remained confined to his room, seeing no one but the staff and Garbrae. It was two weeks before his improvement had been so steady that it was agreed he could be allowed out from his room accompanied.

"You are to be my nursemaid, Garbrae?" Fitzgerald said as his friend arranged for them to walk the grounds. "I believe I should have liked someone a little fairer."

"I am wounded, Fitzgerald. You do not think me pretty? And after all the effort I made this morning to get my hair just so."

"It looks like you raked your hand through it."

"Exactly – it is more effort than I normally afford when visiting you."

The men fell into an easy and comfortable banter as they left the hospital room. They headed out into the centre lawn, making their way to a small clump of trees.

"You seem much improved today," said Garbrae, the first reference he had made to Fitzgerald's illness since he had arrived.

"That was delicately put, old friend. You must think me sufficiently recovered if you feel comfortable enough to broach the topic of my being mad."

"You are as sane as I, and well you know it. You had some sort of fever or seizure of the brain, but I can see each day that you are righted a little bit more," replied Garbrae, hopeful his friend would be as convinced of the truth of this as he was.

"I still hear it," Fitzgerald said quietly, his voice falling to a whisper as though he feared being overheard, despite there being not a soul about them.

"What?"

"When I close my eyes, I hear it: cannon fire, the wrenching of wood, the sound of men screaming. I smell the gunpowder mixed with blood. I taste the acrid smoke belched from the bowels of my ship, and I see them dying, bodies ripped asunder, wooden splinters, large enough to impale a man, tearing limbs straight from bodies. My senses burn with it!"

"Why such a sickening defeat?"

"It was not my fault!" Fitzgerald snapped, all of his defences suddenly raised, anger bristling at this perceived accusation.

"I did not suggest it was; I simply asked why," Garbrae responded, his tone neutral, providing no more provocation.

Fitzgerald picked up a small fallen branch and began to strip away its bark, exposing the green beneath. "They gave me a ship half-manned by landlubbers. What the devil is a captain to do with such sailors? I thought we would have more time, but they were barely trained in the basic skills before we met the French. They were too green, too slow, too young ... God, Garbrae, too many of them were scarcely men at all, but boys grown tall across a good summer. They froze in the midst of battle, and they were slaughtered where they stood."

"But you know the battle is over. You know it cannot be relived, that those lives cannot be saved."

"Of course I know that."

"There are nights still when I wake startled from my sleep by a dream where I had been reliving lost battles, but those memories fade, and the worst of the horror falls away, as it must," admitted Garbrae.

Fitzgerald tossed the branch aside. "So you do not think me mad?"

"I think you are grieving, and I think it is time you were done with this place."

"I cannot return to London," Fitzgerald said, sounding panicked at the thought.

"Then what do you say to a stay in Manchester?"

"You might find me poor company, and how favourably do you think your new wife will view my intrusion?"

Garbrae planted a hand on his friend's shoulder and turned him about, leading them both in the direction of the main building. "I honestly cannot say what her reaction will be to my bringing you to stay, but regardless, it is what will be done."

"Consequences be damned? You are a brave man," Fitzgerald said, "or a foolish one."

During the journey back to Manchester, Garbrae watched his friend who slept at last, though the carriage rocked heavily over the rough surface of country lanes. This man was not the Fitzgerald he remembered. All joviality and light-heartedness had gone, replaced by a darkness and melancholy that would have been foreign to the man who had stood by Garbrae's side at his wedding just months before. His friend had always been so easy, so charming; people had always been drawn to him, but it was unlikely he would prove so popular now. There was a hardness to his tone and manner that surprised Garbrae. Refusing to sleep, refusing to relinquish his watch over Fitzgerald, Garbrae prayed for two things as they travelled – that the man he knew would be restored, and that, in helping Fitzgerald, he would not force Catherine further away.

CHAPTER 24

Manchester. July 1813

"How is Captain Fitzgerald?" inquired Catherine as soon as her husband entered the small sitting room where she and Rose were seated.

"He is resting," came the reply. "The journey was trying, and he is not at full strength."

"I was surprised on meeting him. He was not how I remembered, the change in him not what I had expected," Catherine continued, hoping to sensitively raise the issue of Fitzgerald's obvious brusqueness. "There was a coldness to him I did not anticipate."

"War changes a man, my lady," Garbrae said, easing himself into a chair, every muscle aching, fatigue draining the last of his reserves. "Do not judge him too harshly; he is not the same man I knew, but I hope that, given time, he may be healed."

"I did not see any wounds about him," piped up Rose. "No limp, or sign of injury."

"There are wounds which one might not see," replied

Catherine, before her husband could come to his friend's defence. "Wounds to the spirit can be as devastating to a man as any wound to his body."

"You speak as though from experience," Garbrae said, grateful for his wife's understanding.

"I believe I know a man so wounded," she said, thinking of her father, "whose spirit was not broken by the violence of war but rather the banality of life. Still, though the causes differ, the resulting rending of the spirit is the same. He became something different, something he ought not to have been, for how can a man – how can anyone – hope to be whole when their spirit is torn?"

Garbrae smiled briefly in appreciation of Catherine's sympathy for Fitzgerald. "I hope I can count on a continuation of such generosity of feeling in the coming weeks, for I fear my friend may not be easy to live with until he has had some time away from the recollections of battle."

"You do not think he could be violent?" Catherine asked, at once concerned, uncertain as to what a man damaged by the trial of war would be capable of.

"No, you need not fear that," Garbrae said reassuringly. "I would not have brought him here had I thought he would pose a threat to you. He will be harder than he ought, no doubt abrupt, and perhaps unfeeling, but the man would never harm you. Though his manner is altered; at his core, Captain Fitzgerald is decent and honourable – that has not changed. I wish you could have really known him before this … known him as he was," he continued, his attention given solely over to Catherine.

"Then tell me of him," she suggested. "Show me more of the man, so that I can understand him better."

"You would not be bored by such stories?"

"I cannot imagine how I would be," she replied.

And so they continued – Garbrae sharing tales of his long

friendship with Fitzgerald, and the adventures and mishaps that had so tightly bound them to one another, neither noticing as Rose quietly slipped away.

They saw little of Captain Fitzgerald in his first two weeks with them. He often slept through dinner and would only infrequently be come upon by the ladies, quite by accident, as they strolled one of the garden trails. On such occasions, he would give a low bow, refuse their offer to join them and then disappear back to the house.

It was not until the third week of his stay that Fitzgerald joined them for breakfast. Catherine observed him closely, trying to discern any hint of the man described to her by her husband, but she could find no trace of him. Her husband too, she noticed, struggled with the same realisation, and it pained her to see him brought low by this fact. Indeed, he looked quite worn out, and she wondered if, in an effort to ensure the comfort of his friend, he might have taken up their old habit of talking – and drinking – till dawn. Well, as that could do neither of them good, she was determined to catch them out that evening and guilt them both into getting a decent night's sleep.

Some hours after Catherine had, supposedly, retired for the night, she found herself wandering the halls of the house in search of her wayward husband and his friend. Surprised not to find them in the library or either of the drawing rooms, she was beginning to doubt her certainty that they were up and about when she heard a bellow and the sounds of a commotion coming from the direction of the guest rooms in the east wing.

Racing toward the sound, she opened the door to Fitzgerald's room. Garbrae sat at the bedside with his back to Catherine, holding his friend tightly. Although Fitzgerald slept, there was no doubt he was the source of the disturbance. He thrashed in her husband's grip, his eyes shut, his face contorted, and his hair soaked in sweat. Garbrae called on him to hush, assuring him he was safe.

It was not until Fitzgerald quietened down that Catherine found the nerve to speak.

"Has he been like this since he arrived? Lord, we had no idea!"

Garbrae turned sharply, seeing his wife standing at the door, its handle still gripped in one hand, her other hand up at her mouth, her eyes shot wide with fear and concern.

"He has had better nights, quieter nights ..."

"A quieter night hardly seems much comfort," Catherine said. "It is no wonder you have seemed so ragged lately. Have you watched over him like this every night?"

"I ..." Garbrae struggled to find a gentle way to end the conversation. If Fitzgerald awoke to find Catherine in his room, or worse, if he flew into one of his rages ... "I ..." he tried again, all fight drained from him. "It helps him to know I am here. Sometimes, when the nightmares start, I can calm him."

"He sleeps quietly enough now – more than I will, I fear."

"I am sorry," Garbrae said, covering Fitzgerald once more with the bed sheet, "I had not thought he would be heard so far from your rooms, but you have to understand, I will not ask him to leave."

"I had not thought to ask that of you, but something must be done."

"I will not have him tied down as they did in the hospital.

He is not to be bound," Garbrae continued, determined Catherine understand his intentions.

"Captain, you are exhausted. No one is asking you to do anything of the sort," she said reassuringly, and on seeing his distress, she went to him and took his hands in hers, unfurling his clenched fists, stroking from wrist to fingertip.

Garbrae sat, unable to respond. His fears calmed by the shushing of his wife, his troubled mind eased by the gentle play of her fingers across his skin.

"Fitzgerald is sleeping soundly now," she said, breaking the silence between them. "You should do the same."

"I …"

"Sleep, captain; we shall speak more of this tomorrow. For now, you will go to your room, and I do not expect to see you before noon."

"I cannot leave him."

"You can and you will. This is no longer a burden for you to bear alone. I shall summon Covington; he will have someone sit with Captain Fitzgerald. If he needs you, you shall be called, but he seems settled enough. Hopefully, he will see the night through without further incident."

"You are certain he will be watched."

"Fitzgerald will be kept safe; can you trust me?"

Garbrae rose from his seat, and locking his gaze with hers, he said, "I trust you, my lady, and I thank you for this service to my friend."

"You look better, captain," observed Catherine, as her husband entered the drawing room the next morning. "I see you managed to get some sleep after all, although it is only ten, and I believe I instructed that you were not to be seen before noon."

"You have not spoken of last night to anyone?" he replied, concerned his friend's night terrors would soon be the talk of the house; and worse, the town.

"Do not worry. I have not even spoken of it to Rose. Covington is far too discreet, and John – the young man we had sit with Fitzgerald – is receiving incentive enough to stay quiet. It is in hand; I see no reason why anyone should be made aware of your friend's predicament … unless you think we need some form of professional help?"

Garbrae sank into one of the large armchairs opposite Catherine. "No," he replied. "He speaks to me during the day; we are making progress. It is just these nightmares. When he sleeps, he is most vulnerable, but even his nights are getting better."

Catherine stood and rang the bell. "We will continue to help him," she said, once she had ordered a light breakfast for her husband. "But you must not do it alone anymore. You are worn thin with worry and lack of sleep, and I will not have it."

"But—" Garbrae attempted to interject.

"Do not 'but' me, I am quite determined."

"I will not have you sitting up with him; that is out of the question," Garbrae replied, astounded by the suggestion.

Catherine laughed. "I can assure you that was not my intention. I shall leave the night-time watch to you men, but we must try to encourage him back into the world, and that is where I may be of service."

"You have some manner of plan?"

Catherine gave a little smile. "Not yet, but I will think of something."

She crossed the room and stood next to her husband's chair, facing out the window at his back. She rested her hand lightly upon his shoulder. "We will help Fitzgerald, together, you and I."

Garbrae, worn out by the worry of the last few weeks breathed a sigh of relief that he need no longer bear this burden alone. "I shall never be able to thank you," he said as he raised his hand to rest atop hers.

Neither said another word, nor removed their hand from the touch of the other, until the arrival of the captain's breakfast forced them apart.

CHAPTER 25

*D*uring the week following the conversation with her husband, Catherine watched Captain Fitzgerald closely, looking for signs he might be ready to be tempted back into society. By Friday, he had not only been joining them for breakfast but also had finally started eating, so she decided the time had come.

"Mrs Nash has invited us to dine with her this week. Knowing you are staying, Captain Fitzgerald, the invitation has been extended to you. Do you feel you are sufficiently settled to join or should I decline?"

Fitzgerald's eyebrows knitted as he considered the proposition.

"You have already cancelled several engagements due to my being here," he replied. "It seems unfair you should miss another opportunity for a pleasant evening simply because I am … indisposed," he offered reluctantly. "I am sorry my being here has been such a burden."

"Nonsense, it is I who must apologise," Catherine said. "I was not aware you knew of our cancelled plans, for if I had, I would have taken time to explain. You see, you have been badly used by me, captain."

The gentle laugh in her voice was not lost on either her husband or his friend.

"Your being here has provided us a welcome excuse to avoid attending some of our more tedious engagements, those only accepted out of obligation in the first instance." Catherine, keeping her tone light, acting as though a decision one way or another mattered little, shrugged her shoulders and quirked an eyebrow. "I only mention this dinner now as I thought it might be an evening we could all enjoy, but it will be no hardship to us if you prefer to decline."

Fitzgerald smiled. "I am pleased to have been so useful to you. It certainly lessens some of the guilt that had been playing upon me."

Catherine refilled his teacup and said, "But now you see there was no cause for any guilt. Why, the mere suggestion of your being a burden is a ridiculous one, for what is the worth of friendship if it cannot be relied upon as a constant when all else shifts about us. You are family, and family will always be welcome here. Now, as to this dinner?"

"Ah ... the dinner ... You know, I believe I could manage a dinner."

Garbrae stared at his wife, amazed by her gentle manipulation of his friend.

Rose, who knew nothing of Fitzgerald's nightmares, but who understood that he struggled with some great pain, also sought to be of service.

"And you will not be alone," she said. "For we shall all be there, and you must sit by me if it would bring you comfort to have a friend close by."

"Thank you," responded Fitzgerald, "you are most kind. With the promise of such comfort and companionship, how could a man refuse?"

~

"Captain Garbrae, Lady Catherine, how wonderful to see you both. I am so glad you were able to come for it would have been a far duller evening if you had refused," enthused Mrs Nash on greeting her guests as they arrived.

"Your invitation was timed to perfection. We were just at that delicate stage when the introduction of fresh conversation and new amusement was becoming quite necessary lest we grow completely tired of one another and fall into bickering just to stave off boredom." Catherine laughed, her smile bright, and her manner easy, as she turned to introduce the others. "May I have the honour of introducing you to our dear friend, Captain Michael Fitzgerald."

"A delight I am sure, and another captain. Too wonderful. My husband will be spoiled for company this evening, and I know how it will be. You will be quite monopolised by him, gentlemen. We ought to determine some signal should you feel the need to be rescued," Mrs Nash jested. "Should I provide you with a flag to fly upside down to signal distress?"

"Mrs Nash, you tease as ever, but tonight, I fear it is your husband who will require rescue, outnumbered as he is," Garbrae said, on taking his hostess' hand.

"Well, I am determined there will be a little dancing this evening, captain, so you will have to abandon your tales of the sea for at least an hour or two, for I shall see your dear wife dancing – but beyond that, you gentlemen are free to monopolise one another quite unashamedly. I have been sensible enough to ensure poor Miss Sutherland is not trapped between you again at dinner," she continued, taking the captain by the arm and leading the party into the drawing room.

"Yes, by all accounts, we were most ungentlemanly in our

treatment of her when last I was here. She was, I believe, in her own estimation, cruelly ignored," Garbrae replied.

"Quite so. In order to avoid a repeat of such behaviour, I have resorted to a rather unconventional arrangement at dinner. You, Captain Fitzgerald, and my husband shall all be seated next to one another. I have abandoned the hope of introducing a civilised element by trapping some poor Miss between you."

"What would the ton say?" Garbrae teased.

"Oh, the ton. I am long past caring about that sort of nonsense. You know, it is such a joy to be free of all that silliness. I was never really one for it, you see, and was decidedly thankful when my marriage to the admiral afforded me an excuse to escape the worst of society and all its accompanying formality. Much like Lady Catherine, I imagine."

"Oh, you think so?" Garbrae replied, surprised by her opinion. "I fear my wife is more enamoured with the silliness than you suppose."

"No, I do not believe she is," Mrs Nash responded, "though perhaps as a young wife, with your marriage still in its infancy, she is not yet ready to release herself from being swayed by it. The certainty and stability provided by understanding the rules can be comforting in times of change, but given time and some leeway, I believe she may just surprise you."

Many of the guests for the evening's dinner were already assembled when the Garbrae party arrived. Mrs Nash was dutiful in her introductions to those not previously known and, being new to all there, gave much attention to Captain Fitzgerald and Lady Rose.

Catherine watched with trepidation as Fitzgerald was

introduced and then abandoned to a small circle of young women. She as much as held her breath until the little party erupted with laughter at some tale of the captain's.

Garbrae, standing on the other side of the room, witnessed the look of distress that flitted across his wife's face and scanned the room for the source of it. On tracking her gaze to his friend, he realised her discomfort was out of concern for him, and his heart swelled with emotion. How was it, he wondered, he could ever have thought this woman cold and arrogant? How could he ever have misjudged her so, and how would he ever make amends for it?

"Miss Sutherland," Garbrae said on approaching his wife and her companion, "I do hope you will do me the honour of a dance later this evening."

"A dance?" she replied in confusion.

"Indeed, Mrs Nash is determined that we are to make a gay a time of it, and dancing is to be among the entertainments. It would be my honour if you were to accept my request for the second dance of the set, for I believe civility requires the first dance go to my wife," he said, winking at Miss Sutherland and flashing a rakish smile at Catherine. This caused both women to blush and Miss Sutherland to titter nervously from behind her fan.

"Well, if Lady Catherine has no objection," Miss Sutherland managed, raising her eyes to look at her companion.

"Of course not," answered she, the colour still high in her cheeks, amazed the captain could have provoked such a reaction in herself with just a look, for she was most decidedly undone.

"Wonderful," said Garbrae, "I shall think of nothing else until then."

"My ... but the captain," began Miss Sutherland.

"My, but the captain what?" asked Catherine, noticing her young companion's high colour and rapid breath.

"Oh … well … you know," Miss Sutherland answered, suddenly uncomfortable.

"Yes, I certainly do." *Or at least I am beginning to,* Catherine thought, as both women watched the man retreat to the far side of the room, his presence commanding the attention of every woman he passed. *I am certainly beginning to.*

～

"You stare rather intently," Garbrae said, on finding his wife alone, her attention caught by something across the room. "I do hope it is not out of displeasure."

"Oh, you startled me!" Catherine gasped, jumping a little, feeling that same hot flush and sense of distraction that had unsettled her earlier. "Displeasure? No, indeed not. I was simply marvelling at my sister's ability to charm a room. She never fails to please; it is quite a talent."

"So I have noticed. Some women, your sister most assuredly included, possess such an easy manner and charm that they are sure of winning hearts wherever they go."

"Unfortunately, I never developed those particular talents."

Garbrae laughed. "No, indeed not." Seeing a hint of disappointment in his wife's face, he added, "You have far too much fire to ever be as easy as your sister, but do not think you are any less engaging. The gentleness she possesses is not always preferred. Some value spirit, however it may unsettle, over placidness."

"And you, captain? What do you prefer?"

"Me? I always enjoyed a stormy sea," he teased, taking his wife's arm. "Come, I believe you are mine for the first dance."

～

"Of course, I know her family," one of the ladies in attendance announced to the little group she had gathered about her. She tilted her head in the direction of Catherine and her husband as they danced across the floor.

"The Earl and Countess of Westbury were quite the couple. Why, before her first confinement, Lady Westbury was a highly sought-after guest, always so charming, a delight to be around – I see much of the same character in Lady Rose. I always thought it a shame that she remained in the country for so long afterward; she seemed quite to retire from society. And of course, you will all be aware of the earl's most recent financial difficulties," she continued, leaning in conspiratorially, drawing the group's undivided attention.

"I am not aware," replied one among them in a manner that begged the lady to continue.

"Oh yes, quite the scandal – lost the last of the family fortune on the speculation of a gold mine, I believe. Still, he was always careless with money, risky venture after risky venture. I believe the earl was but months away from losing it all."

The dramatic flair with which the lady delivered this last little titbit was greeted with a chorus of gasps from the group.

"A fortune was vital, and the captain's father, having a fortune the like of which is rarely found these days, even in the best and oldest of families, was just what was needed. Still, to be shackled to a tradesman," she sneered, making plain her aversion to the captain and the polluting of an old family line with new money. "He can never be one of us. Even she will suffer some exclusion now – such a shame. Makes his money trading cotton, you know."

"And remind me, Lady Beresford, just how your father made his money?" cut in a woman's voice from behind the group.

The women turned their attention to the speaker, horrified to find Captain Garbrae and Lady Catherine standing behind them.

"Slaves, I believe, if memory serves," Catherine continued, her face calm, as though unmoved, but her voice biting. "How much more civilised to earn your money trading people!" She arched an eyebrow, challenging the other woman to say something.

Lady Beresford, for her part, was so stunned by the attack that she could only open then close her mouth, not even uttering a word.

"Captain, I believe you promised the next dance to Miss Sutherland," Catherine said, her sport at an end, the woman sufficiently humiliated. "Come, it will do no good to keep her waiting. If you will excuse us," she finished, dismissing the group with a little nod of her head before allowing her husband to lead her away.

"You see how I am," she said to Garbrae, moments later. "Mother warned me about holding my tongue. I am no Rose; I do not have her ability to charm."

"No, it appears not," he replied, not attempting to mask his pleasure at her feisty defence of him. "The lady was quite unprepared for that. No time to batten down the hatches before that squall hit!"

"Stormy seas, captain?"

"Stormy seas, indeed."

CHAPTER 26

*C*atherine set down the vase of flowers she had taken from the hallway to the sunroom and turned to face her husband. "You bought Wellington's mill?" she said, amazed at her husband's revelation in response to what she thought had been a rather innocuous, "How was your morning?"

Garbrae peered at his wife over the edge of the paper and shook his head slightly. "No, the business remains his; I merely secured him an investor. Although I have agreed to help him handle some of the problems that have been plaguing his business of late."

"Why would you do that?"

"I believe it will prove to be a solid investment and will be profitable," he replied.

"But why get involved at all? He is your competitor. Why save his business at risk to your own?" Catherine continued, still at a loss to understand her husband's actions.

"There is plenty of opportunity in cotton. My business relations and connections are solid, and I have no fear from competition, certainly not from a man like Wellington; he is fair and trades honestly. Besides, what would become of his workers if the mill closed or was bought by one of the other owners? What then of Wellington and his family? No, I could not stand by and watch the man be brought down by others less worthy and far less scrupulous."

Rose, who had been sitting in the room with the captain for a quarter-hour, stared at her brother-in-law. He had said nothing of this to her when she enquired about the business that had kept him from breakfasting with them. "This was not about investment at all," she said, eyeing him suspiciously. "This was about saving the man. You could not let a good man fail."

Garbrae ducked back behind the pages of his broadsheet to avoid the sisters' stares. "There are a number of reasons I felt it necessary to intervene. I know for certain that the investment was a good one; it will bear a return. The decision was ultimately a business one, reasoned and sound."

"Nonsense," argued Rose. "The decision was all heart. It was a good thing you did. Do not try to pass it off as merely a solid business investment."

"Is that so?" asked Catherine. "You bought into the man's business to save him – to save his workers?"

Garbrae folded the paper in half and set it down. "No," he replied, a mischievous smile at play about his lips, "you did. The deal was struck by your father on your behalf; you are now part-owner of a cotton mill."

"The business is mine? This is … Why would he …?" Catherine stumbled, looking to Rose for some help, finding her sister just as dumbstruck.

Garbrae continued. "Your father has been greatly enjoying his new-found wealth and the freedom that wealth has secured him. It was suggested to him that some of his good fortune could be put to good use to secure you a similar measure of freedom."

"Why would I need an income?" replied Catherine, suddenly afraid of what her husband's answer might be.

"You do not need it," he said. "This money is simply yours – free and clear from me and your father. The investment is in your father's name, but the business interest is yours."

Rose, amused by the idea of her sister as a woman of business, left the pair to go in search of Captain Fitzgerald and a bottle of something to toast the good news with.

"Why would you suggest such a thing?" Catherine asked, once she and the captain were alone.

"It was because of something your sister said."

"Rose suggested it?"

Garbrae shook his head. "The day we visited the mill, on the carriage ride home, we talked of business."

"You talked of privies!" Catherine said. The comment accompanied by a slight smile.

"And other things!" Garbrae coloured; he had not realised Rose had shared that particular detail with her sister. "Lady Rose spoke of the pleasure that must be had in being master of one's own affairs. She spoke in general terms, of course, but I suspected she thought of her situation … your situation."

Catherine stared at him. She said nothing, though he saw how she paled.

"I cannot imagine the fear such a situation must inspire. I wanted to ensure you would never have to suffer such feelings again."

"My sister talks a great deal," Catherine said, finding her voice once more. "I do not think I have ever been more grateful for that than I am now … But I know nothing of business."

"I doubt there is anything you could not learn to do," replied Garbrae, "and should you wish it, I will happily teach you."

CHAPTER 27

"Good morning, Lady Rose," Garbrae announced on strolling into the breakfast room. "You look quite wonderful today. I believe that dress is new."

He gave his sister-in-law a slight bow before heading directly to the side table where breakfast had been laid out.

"How splendid of you to notice," Rose replied. "I did not think men noticed one gown over another."

"Well, it is not a colour you usually wear, which is why it caught my attention. Though in truth, my awareness of ladies' fashion was never quite so astute before my season in London. If I learned anything from my time there, it was the importance of fashion to ladies. Indeed, I discovered, quite early on, that a compliment or two on the cut or colour of a dress could extricate me from all manner of awkward situations."

"Such as?" Rose asked, pouring a coffee for the captain before refilling her own cup.

"Well, suppose there was a lapse in conversation, a comment on the colour of a dress as bringing out the shade of a lady's eyes was always sure to fill the silence admirably.

Or should my mind drift elsewhere during a less than scintillating conversation, any offence could be swept away by my confession that it was the lady herself and the tantalising cut of her dress that was the source of all distraction."

"Shocking, you are quite shocking!" Rose gasped in feigned disapproval.

"What is shocking?" queried Catherine, who entered at that moment and made her way to where her husband stood adding ham to the mountain of eggs on his plate.

"Your husband is sharing secrets about the motives of men in complimenting women; I am provoked into blushing by their calculating nature during a season."

"Oh, you do them little justice by suggesting they limit such calculation to the season, Rose," quipped Catherine before her husband could say a word.

Garbrae laughed. "Oh, how the lady judges. Do not try to pretend that women are any less calculating – your dresses chosen with deliberate care, your hair fixed just so, and jewels draped in a manner that most pleasingly draws the eye to …" He finished with a smile, allowing the last few words to fade away unspoken.

"Drawing the eye where exactly?" Catherine challenged, the innocence of her general expression betrayed by the slight arch in her eyebrow and the hint of a wicked smile tugging at the corner of her mouth.

"I am not certain I ought to finish that sentence, not with a maiden present," he responded, tilting his head in Rose's direction, his gaze never straying from Catherine. "Although, I would be happy to elaborate later, should we find ourselves alone," he whispered, his thigh lightly brushing hers as he moved around her.

A jolt shot through Catherine, igniting an unfamiliar heat. She blushed high and deep, a little dizzy at the closeness of the man, her senses overpowered by the heady scent of him.

"I ..." she said, so flustered she had to reach for the table to steady herself.

"Are you all right?" Garbrae asked. He took her plate for fear she would drop it and led her to a seat.

She burned at the touch of his arm across her back, his hand reaching around her waist to support her. *Lord, what is the matter with me?* she thought.

"I am well," she managed to say, once seated, her senses returning, her breathing slowing now that Garbrae no longer held her. "I must have a greater need for breakfast than I imagined."

"You see the effect you have?" Rose teased.

Catherine's eyes darted to her sister; she could not possibly know the reason for her turn.

"She is quite undone by your scandalous suggestions," Rose finished, then laughed as though nothing were amiss.

Catherine smiled weakly.

Garbrae regarded his wife, considering why his touch had caused such upset. Did he flatter himself to think he could inspire such a reaction? Heavens, what hope was there for them if he could? Lord, but such thoughts were making him uncomfortable, for standing there in the breakfast room was no place to dwell on the possible passions of his wife.

"Eggs?" he said, clearing his throat, looking for a distraction.

"What?" the sisters replied.

"Breakfast. You ought to eat something. Eggs?"

"Yes, thank you," Catherine answered, grateful for such ordinary conversation. *What silliness,* she thought. *What unaccountable silliness.* Perhaps I do just need to eat. She accepted the plate, certain that all would be righted by a hearty breakfast.

"I would like to visit the mill with you, captain," Catherine announced, her breakfast only half-eaten but two cups of hot chocolate finished. "When do you next go?"

"Today, although I would not recommend you join me, not after this morning."

"Nonsense, I am quite well; I just needed some breakfast."

Garbrae studied his wife with keen interest. She did appear to be recovered, quite wonderfully recovered. Her complexion bore its usual pink blush which deepened a little under his gaze – how he loved to watch that rising blush. As he stared more intently, he caught the slight increase in her breath, causing her breasts to catch at the scooped neck of her dress with greater urgency. What sweet agony it was to watch their rise and fall. He watched Catherine wipe at the corner of her mouth, drawing his attention to the luscious promise of her lips. This was insufferable. The woman was torturing him, without any knowledge of what she was doing, without arch or artifice. Her complete innocence of her power adding to its effect.

Rose, sitting silently across the table from her sister, could not help but smile at the pair. She had read enough romance novels to understand what she was seeing, even if Catherine did not. She ought to have encouraged her sister to read more, she admonished. Still, it was too late now. The captain was clearly in the sway of a grand passion, and Catherine was largely oblivious to her husband's feelings, but Rose sensed the beginning of a similar passion in her sister. That turn she had had before breakfast had been most illuminating.

There really is nothing quite as thrilling as romance, Rose mused, before glancing up once more to find both her brother-in-law and her sister staring at her.

"Are you even listening?" Catherine asked.

"I … um … no."

"I am to accompany the captain to the mill today. Will you join us?"

"Oh, I would be delighted, of course, on any other day. Sadly, Captain Fitzgerald and I already have plans for the morning. Is that not so, Captain Fitzgerald?" she asked, at his perfectly timed entrance into the room.

"Is what not so?" Fitzgerald asked.

"Our plans for this morning are quite fixed, so it will be impossible for me to join Catherine and the captain today."

"Quite fixed," he assured, having no knowledge of any plans but delighted at the thought of securing his friend some time alone with his wife. "You do not object?" he finished, turning his attention to Catherine.

"Of course not," she replied. "It will be just us two. I am certain we shall manage quite nicely."

Garbrae, hoping his countenance remained calm despite the rapid beating in his chest, replied, "No doubt we shall."

CHAPTER 28

Manchester. August 1813

"This was what your father spoke of, when he talked of covering your losses," Catherine said, staring at the plans for improvement Garbrae was talking her through.

"What?" Garbrae looked at her, his lips slightly parted, his forehead creased.

"I overheard him talking with my father before we were married; he spoke only of a risky venture you were engaged in. I feared ... well, no matter... It was these improvements he thought would lose money."

The captain's back straightened. "My father can be short-sighted. He sees no reason for the outlay of funds when others are not also making improvements. He is not unfeeling, but he is more guided by profit than I am, and there is no immediate profit in my plans."

Catherine stared again at the drawings and accounts scattered about the table. The man was not the reckless speculator she had feared. "The improvements are impressive," she said. "Have they already begun?"

Garbrae nodded. "Three of the houses are complete, the work continues on the others."

"The workers at Wellington's mill, I take it, do not live in such favourable conditions?"

"I am the only mill owner to have undertaken such improvements. Should you ever care to visit your mill, you will find Wellington does right by those he employs, though his resources would not allow him to undertake plans like mine."

Catherine plucked one of the plans out from the pile, one that detailed the extensions to the smaller houses. "What if we were to use my profits? Could work be undertaken then?"

"That money is yours," answered Garbrae, surprised by the suggestion.

"Yes, mine to do with as I please, so what if pleasing me means investing the money in improvements similar to the ones you are undertaking here? You make a compelling argument for the correctness of such a course of action; did you not anticipate I might be swayed into seeing things as you do?"

"I had not meant to influence you, I assure you."

"No, I am quite sure you did not mean to guilt me into improving conditions for my workers," Catherine replied, digging her husband gently with her elbow, "yet here I stand, sufficiently guilted."

"Guilted? Is that a word?" he jested in reply.

"Well, if not, it should be, for it is precisely how I am feeling. Guilted!" Catherine laughed. "Come, I believe I would like to see these improvements for myself, should there be a property I might take a tour about. And if it would not be too great an interruption to the working day, I thought I might speak with some of the workers before we are done."

Garbrae had thought their visit would not pass off as well as had been managed. That Catherine was keen to learn about the business and all of his improvements was surprise enough, but that she now expressed an interest in talking to the workers was really more than he had anticipated. He had, he realised, only just begun to explore the depths of the woman he had married. That he had remained oblivious to them for so long was a failing, and one he was determined to remedy.

Catherine sat in the carriage, waiting for Garbrae to finish up with the last of his appointments so they could set off for home. The day had been most revealing; she had not realised her husband possessed such a curious blend of business acumen and benevolence. He argued in favour of improvements on the grounds that they promoted the health and happiness of the workforce. A happy and healthy workforce was a stable one, unlikely to strike, willing to work longer and harder. Still, she was certain such concerns were not the reason for his actions. She was certain, rather, it was concern for those he employed. His refusal to employ children younger than ten was just as telling. "They ought to have a childhood," he had insisted, "and an education … for an educated workforce is a better workforce," he had added, in an attempt to hide his decency. Clearly, the man was uncomfortable with anything that would hint to his being influenced by compassion.

The pair were but minutes together in the carriage and headed home when a sharp, shrill scream cut short their conversation. Garbrae banged on the roof of the carriage and instructed the driver to halt. Once stopped, he jumped out to see what was amiss.

Catherine had just time enough to hear him yell, "Dear

God, no!" followed by, "Take her ladyship home!" before she caught a flash of his coat tails as he disappeared from view.

They took off at speed, and Catherine pummelled the roof with all her might, yelling at the driver to stop, threatening to leap from the moving carriage when he did not. The carriage finally stopped, and Catherine, shaking from the unexpected drama of the moment, stepped out and turned her gaze back to the factory, just in time to see one of the windows shatter as though punched out by the flames that now danced through the gaping hole.

Fire!

The mill was on fire.

Catherine took to her heels at once, ignoring the driver's pleas to stay with him, to return to the carriage. *The captain is in there*, was all she could think as she raced harder and faster than she had ever done in her life, her chest heaving with the effort by the time she made it back to the factory gates. With no time to waste on considering the burning of her lungs or the ache in her calves, she scanned the courtyard, desperate for a glimpse of her husband.

"You there … Yarrow," she cried out on seeing a man she had been introduced to earlier.

"My lady, get out!" Yarrow yelled, startled by seeing her in the yard. "This is no place for you. Get out. Get to safety."

"We must get everyone out," argued Catherine.

"No, the master will never forgive me if any harm comes to you, so out," he said, coming up on her and reinforcing his point by grabbing her by the arm and moving her around.

"Unhand me this instant. Remember your place," shouted Catherine with astonishing force. "I will not be bullied away like some child."

Open-mouthed, Yarrow stared at her.

"Where is the captain?"

"He has gone inside."

"So," Catherine began, willing herself to be calm, willing herself not to give in to the panic that struck at the thought of the captain inside the burning building; he needed her clear-headed not befuddled, "you must see to the organisation of the men out here, hauling water. Get them working together, three clear lines so they can work more efficiently. Have some order in place for when he returns. We must not fail him. I will see to getting the women and children outside. Do you hear me?"

Yarrow could only nod.

"Now, man. Now!" Catherine barked, sending the man about his task before turning to her own.

Once all the women and children who had been standing in the main yard were removed to greater safety outside the gates, Catherine set about trying to calm them, seeing to minor wounds, giving orders to the older boys to fetch help, blankets, water, tea – anything she could think of to aid or occupy those around her.

"William, William," she heard a young woman crying out, frantically running through the gathered crowd. "Has anyone seen my boy?"

Catherine was with her in an instant.

"My boy. I cannot find him," the woman gasped, terror causing her voice to catch. "He must be in there."

"Are you certain he is not here? I gave jobs to some of the older boys. Could your son be one of them?"

"He is but eleven, small for his age. You would not have mistaken him for older."

Catherine caught the woman as she made to run back into the factory yard. "Stay! You are no good to your boy in such a panic. I will go." Turning to one of the other women nearby, she instructed, "Hold on to her."

The scene inside the gates was beyond comprehension. She had never witnessed anything like it. Glass rained down as windows burst forth from their frames, small fires floated in the air as cotton caught alight and drifted about bobbing along the waves of smoke that bellowed from the factory. And at the centre of this madness stood her husband.

The man was in complete control. His decisive orders and clear commands rang out into the yard, inspiring order and efficiency among his men such as Catherine would not have imagined. They were frightened but did not falter in following him. He saw everything – small fires beaten out before they could spread, men moved back from windows before they shattered, water targeted where it would be most effective.

Catherine could not help but stare, but then he was staring straight at her – and furious!

"What the bloody hell are you doing here?" he blasted, striding over to her, practically lifting her off her feet as he spun her round. "Get out of here, woman!"

"There is a boy still inside," she pleaded, ignoring the fierceness of his command, and the rough manner in which he handled her.

"No, everyone is out," he barked.

"A boy named William. There is a boy named William still in there."

Garbrae spun Catherine on her heels once more, this time to face him. "Are you certain?" he demanded.

"His mother is," she replied.

"Damn it! Damn it all to hell!" he shouted furiously, dousing his coat in a nearby bucket of water and racing back into the burning building.

It seemed an eternity before Garbrae emerged again through the factory door. The fire was all but out, though thick smoke still filled the yard. It swirled about him, pooling about his frame, clinging to his face in great black streaks, staining his clothing, but letting him pass to the cleaner air beyond.

In his arms, he held the limp body of a boy whose face and clothes were blackened, his lungs no longer gasping for air.

Garbrae walked outside the main gates and lay the boy down on the wet ground. The world seemed to disappear from him for a moment as he stood gazing down at the lifeless body of the boy.

The boy's mother screamed and screamed.

She screamed until Garbrae thought he would hear nothing again but the sound of her screaming. Until a forceful tug on his sleeve brought him back to himself.

"Will you try it?" Catherine asked again.

"Try what?" He blinked, clearly unaware of what she had suggested.

"You must blow into his lungs, there is a contraption, but we do not have it, so you must just blow – your breath must do"

"You are not making any sense; my breath must do what?"

Catherine stopped and allowed him a moment to focus on what she was saying before she set about giving him instructions to resuscitate the boy.

"I know this technique, but he has not drowned," Garbrae said in confusion.

"You need to force the smoke from his body, just as you would water. It is as though the thing is trapped within his lungs, you need to breathe into the boy to replace the smoke with air then push upon his chest to expel the smoke itself. You must do it."

Garbrae stared at her. It seemed ridiculous, but she was in earnest. Before he was aware of having made up his mind to do as she suggested, he found his mouth pressed upon the boy's, forcing air as deep into his lungs as he could manage, pushing hard onto his chest.

The boy's mother stopped screaming.

Everything became silent, save for the order that sprung from the captain's lips. "Breathe!" he demanded.

"Breathe," Catherine added.

"Breathe," his mother implored.

Then the boy did.

Garbrae sat back on his heels, in utter shock at young William who now coughed and retched as he expelled the smoke from his lungs. The boy took in gasping gulps of clean air, crying at what was happening to him.

"Stand back, let me see the boy," a doctor yelled, having just arrived at the scene. "Stand back, I say."

CHAPTER 29

*N*either Garbrae nor Catherine could manage conversation on the journey home. The events of the day, the drama of the last moments, and the rescue of young William had taken everything they had, leaving them both feeling such exhaustion that a week in bed would scarcely be enough to recover.

Garbrae desperately wanted to talk to his wife, to praise her – Lord, just to thank her – but the day had hollowed him out, and the words would not come. He could not think how to start such a conversation – perhaps with an apology. He had raged at her in the main yard, and in front of the men – a woman as proud as Catherine would not soon forgive the embarrassment – but worse still was the manner in which he had attacked her. He was certain he had sworn, and he had grabbed her – unpardonable! Still she had not faltered, such bravery, such composure, and she had saved the boy. How could he begin to thank her?

Catherine continued to gaze at her hands; they had finally stopped shaking. Her heartbeat seemed to have slowed, and the rushing sound that had filled her head was dissipating.

She was beginning to feel like herself once more. The captain was quiet; she was waiting for something, some lecture from him, but so far, all she faced was silence – Lord, he must be furious. His anger at seeing her in the yard had been fierce. The coarseness of his language, the rough manner in which he had handled her … Well, he had been almost brutish. But his anger was preferable to his silence; his silence was unnerving. What had she been thinking? Removing herself from the carriage, believing it her place to order the men around, to order the captain around when it came to it. What an embarrassment for him, and in front of his men too. What had she been thinking?

The pair all but stumbled from the carriage – the last of Catherine's strength used in rising from her seat, the last of Garbrae's given over to helping her.

Rose, aware of some commotion, was immediately upon them, and almost fainted at the sight. Their clothes were blackened, their hair in disarray, and dark streaks of smoke covered their faces. Garbrae was coatless, his shirt torn.

"Good God in Heaven!" she gasped. "What happened?"

"There was a fire at the mill," Garbrae managed, passing Catherine to the arms of Rose. "Your sister needs a bath and some rest. Will you help her?"

"Of course," Rose assured, helping her inside before allowing two of the maids to take over. "Was Catherine hurt? She was not inside the mill? It is just that her clothes … her hair … She looks as though she were in the fire."

"She was too close to it for my liking," Garbrae replied.

Catherine, almost at the top of the stairs, caught his words. Lord, but he was furious.

"But she was amazing, simply amazing," he finished. He

looked up for one last look at his wife, but she was nowhere to be seen

～

The next morning, Catherine delayed coming down to breakfast for as long as possible, hoping to avoid her husband, supposing he would be keen to return to the factory, although not reckoning on how difficult it would be to keep her hunger at bay.

"I do not think I have ever been so hungry in my life, Mary," she said to the maid, who set about her with hair-brush and pins.

"That will be all the excitement of yesterday. Nothing like excitement to bring on a hunger. I would order a tray, but I think you would be better downstairs, my lady, for no doubt, you will need more than your usual this morning."

"I suppose you are right," answered Catherine, a little disappointed she could not hide out longer in her room, although the loud grumbling from her belly rather proved the maid's point. "I shall go down as soon as you are done. Do you know if the captain has left yet?" she finished, trying to sound as nonchalant as possible in her enquiry.

"I do not know; I could run down and see, if you wish?"

"No, no, I shall discover it myself soon enough," Catherine replied, knowing her husband must be faced at some point. Perhaps better now, before he had a chance to dwell on the events of the day before.

～

Garbrae rose from his seat on Catherine's entrance to the breakfast room and was by her side in an instant, helping her to a chair and pouring hot chocolate.

Catherine found his attentiveness even more unnerving than his silence the night before. Once settled, she looked up from her cup to see his face ashen, and his mouth agape. She could almost swear to there being tears in his eyes. "Whatever is the matter?"

"Did I do that? Did I do that to you?" he asked, his voice just a whisper.

Catherine looked down to see her shawl had slipped, exposing her right arm and the angry bruises that encircled it.

"Dear God, I did that to you."

Catherine fixed her shawl, covering the bruises. Her hand guided his face away from her arm so that he might look into her eyes and know the truthfulness of what she was about to say.

"It was in the heat of the moment, captain. I am certain you did not mean to hurt me. I am sure you felt justified, that yard being no place for a woman—"

"But—" he interrupted, his sentence in turn cut off by a wave of Catherine's hand.

"I will finish. I hold no anger for this. I understand why you reacted as you did. Last night, I was sorry for my interference, but this morning I am not inclined toward apologising for it. You may not have liked my interference, but I did what was right. I am sorry if I embarrassed you – if taking directions from a woman was degrading – but I helped save that boy. I will not feel bad about that."

"Have you quite finished?" Garbrae asked.

"I have, so you may lecture me now, but I warn you I will not be repentant, and should we ever face a similar trial, I will not act differently." She finished defiantly, the curt nod of her head assuring the captain of the seriousness of her speech.

"Lecture you? Have you act otherwise? Why in Heaven?

Look at me," Garbrae said, taking hold of Catherine's hand. "What you did amazed me."

Catherine blinked. Had she heard him correctly?

"There is no doubt you saved that boy's life. First by telling me of his being in the building – despite how angry I was at seeing you, an anger, I assure you, born out of fear for your safety and not some foolish notion of the inappropriateness of your presence because you are a woman. And second by telling me to resuscitate him."

"You knew what to do." Catherine said, "that much was clear once you started."

"I had learned to clear a man's lungs after downing. In the midst of the chaos, it did not occur to me that such a procedure would clear smoke. I shall forever be grateful for your help. You were extraordinary, quite simply extraordinary."

Catherine blinked again. This was bewildering.

"How could you think that I would berate you for your courage, your clarity of purpose and poise under conditions that would have broken many a man? How did you even know how to help the boy?"

"I … um … I attended a lecture on resuscitation given by the Royal Humane Society. I paid attention; I remembered what to do."

"I would not have imagined such a thing would be proposed by your parents – I must remember to congratulate them."

"Oh no, they would not thank you for the reminder. Mother was furious at the time, said such matters were not fit for a lady to pay mind to, and what if someone had seen me there – etcetera."

"If you were not encouraged to attend, then why did you?"

"A young boy from the estate drowned, and I felt someone from the house ought to attend the funeral. I overheard the reverend talking about the society and their work to save those feared dead from drowning. It intrigued me. When the opportunity came about to attend a lecture, I simply took it. They spoke mostly of removing water from the lungs but said the same procedure ought to work as well for smoke and noxious gases. I had no occasion to test their theory until yesterday."

"What a curious assortment of interests you have," Garbrae said, sitting back to observe the woman more fully. "I had not imagined I would ever encounter a woman with such diverse pursuits: needlework, painting, resuscitation of the dead.

"You mock me?"

"No, no," Garbrae said softly. "I tease, perhaps. I fall back on humour when in such unfamiliar territory. Still, there was little honour or indeed humour in my jibe. Forgive me. It is simply that the more I learn of you, the more I am undone by you. We have not understood one another up until now, I fear. It is a mistake I would take great pleasure in amending. Do you think it is too late for us to start afresh? To get to know one another, as we ought to have done long before now? Could you ever see me as anything other than a new-moneyed, brutish, ignorant tradesman?"

"Could you see me as anything other than an aristocratic, cold, arrogant elitist?"

"Have I ever accused you of such things?" Garbrae asked.

Catherine smiled at him. "That, and worse, I am quite sure."

"I cannot account for it," he said, taking up her hand and brushing her fingers with a light kiss.

"Then we are off to a splendid start. Indeed, it bodes well that we have been at least a quarter-hour together without a single snide remark between us."

"Let us see if we can last the afternoon, or might that be too much of a trial?"

"Well, if you can manage to keep the worst of your barbarism at bay, I might manage to curtail the worst of my tongue," Catherine said, enjoying the feeling of her hand still resting in his.

"Barbarism? Should I be insulted? Have we strayed so soon from the path to greater understanding?"

"Not at all. We are simply establishing the initial rules and running order of our little venture. For a brute, you really are quite sensitive. It is a flaw we shall have to remedy if we are ever to find peace with one another," she continued.

"Well, if peace is the prize, I shall shackle my inner brute." He laughed, standing up from the table and offering his wife a low bow and the crook of his arm. "Would you care to join me for a walk?"

"Are you not going to the factory today? I half expected you to be gone already."

"I will go there tomorrow. Today, I shall spend with you, if you have no other plans."

"None whatsoever. Indeed, it would be a pleasure. And what shall we do to pass the time? What shall we talk about as we walk?"

"I would like to hear more on this Humane Society lecture you attended. Did you go to others?"

"Heavens, no. There was commotion enough after the first one."

"Well, how foolish. That is something we shall have to see to."

"Really, you would let me attend further lectures of the kind?"

"Let you? I hardly think it is a question of letting you, though I would join you if you have no objection."

"I can think of no good reason to object," Catherine said with a smile, drawing his arm closer to her, "no good reason at all."

CHAPTER 30

arbrae, having spent every waking hour of the two weeks following the fire at the mill overseeing the repair works, was pleased to finally find himself at home and quite at his leisure. Having risen too late to join anyone for breakfast, he went in search of his wife, his sister-in-law, and his best friend but, on failing to find anyone other than the housemaids, went deeper into the house in search of an explanation.

"Covington," he called out, descending the stairs on his way to the butlery.

Despite the warning shout announcing his arrival, Covington, unaccustomed to the presence of his master in this part of the house, bore a look of anxious surprise when Garbrae strode into his room.

"Do not look so troubled man," Garbrae said; "I am simply looking for the others. I can find no sign of Lady Catherine, Lady Rose, or Captain Fitzgerald."

Covington, once again master of himself, set aside the cellar ledgers and rose to properly greet the captain. "The mistress," he said, "has gone riding. She and Lady Rose have been gone an hour and both are expected back for luncheon. The captain left just before the ladies, gone on an errand for Lady Rose."

"The captain is running errands? For the ladies?" Garbrae said, his voice edged with slight, but noticeable, disapproval.

Covington nodded but added nothing more.

Garbrae left without another word and headed straight for the stables.

"Captain, you have returned," Catherine said, on spying her husband striding across the lawn toward the table she and Rose occupied. "Will you join us for some light refreshment?"

"I had hoped to come across you on your ride," Garbrae said. "I rode out in search of you when I discovered all the members of the household were away before I had even had my morning coffee."

He sounded aggrieved, and Catherine could not readily account for it. "Had I known you would not be at the mill today, we would have waited for you," she said, wondering if that was the cause of his ill humour.

"And you did not think to ask Fitzgerald to join you?"

"Captain Fitzgerald was otherwise engaged."

"Yes, apparently in service of you, Lady Rose," Garbrae said, turning to her. "Fitzgerald has become some sort of errand boy, or so I hear. What is his service this morning? Collecting ribbons from the haberdashery?"

Rose blushed, discomforted by the captain's clear displeasure and the curt manner of his address. She looked across at her sister who was not blushing and appeared little upset by her husband's tantrum.

"He is collecting books," Catherine said, drawing her

husband's attention back to her. "A fact which, somewhat unaccountably, seems to have raised your ire, captain."

"He is a captain in the Royal Navy, and you are treating him like—"

"Like someone who needed a reason to get back into the world," interrupted Catherine.

"What?"

"For far too long Captain Fitzgerald has been locked away – first at the hospital, then here with us. I thought it high time he got back out into wider society."

"Nonsense, he has been twice to dinner at the Nash's."

"Where we were also in attendance, and where he scarcely spent ten minutes out of the sight or company of one of us. He has not been given the chance to be master of himself."

Garbrae stared at her. "And you think riding about the country on errands for you and your sister somehow accomplishes that?"

"I think it gives him a reason to go into town. I think it forces him to be among people, strangers, shopkeepers. It gives him the chance to step back into the world without the constant, watchful, fearful glances of those who profess to love him best."

"We are helping him," Garbrae argued.

Catherine locked eyes with her husband. "We are smothering him."

"He has been staying longer in town on each visit," Rose offered. "And he has seemed more at ease of late."

"He has also been sleeping," Catherine added. "When was the last time you had to be called to his room in the middle of the night."

Garbrae opened his mouth to argue, but no argument readily came to mind. "It has been some weeks," he admitted.

"I … I only want the best for him." He pulled out a chair but hesitated in sitting down.

"As do we," Catherine and Rose replied together.

"But there comes a time when our protection is not what serves him best," Catherine continued. "We must trust him to determine what he needs and hope that he will call upon us when we can be of service."

Garbrae finally took up the seat he had been holding on to. "I have been so distracted since the fire. You are right, Lady Rose; he has been more at ease. He has seemed more like my friend."

On spotting the footman approaching, a silver tray in hand, Rose left the table to intercept the man and give her sister and brother-in-law a moment or two alone.

"We truly meant no disrespect when we asked those little favours of him," Catherine said. "It was all we could think of."

"Of course you didn't," Garbrae replied, now feeling foolish. "I misunderstood your intentions. I …"

Catherine turned a smile to the man. "You thought your cold, elitist wife was using your friend as nothing more than a servant," she said, her tone light, without accusation.

Garbrae's cheeks and temples flushed, and Catherine, amused by the sight, could do nothing but laugh.

Rose retuned to the table, the small silver tray in hand. "Catherine, there are two letters from Mama," she said, passing out the letters that had been sorted into bundles before being placed on the tray. "Both are addressed to you. It seems she is not content to have me as her sole correspondent."

"Had that been your plan?" Garbrae asked, in mock astonishment. "Lady Rose, you have been sorely used …" He stopped mid-sentence, the sight of one of the letters causing him to pale.

"Are you all right?" Catherine asked.

"What? No … that is to say, yes, yes I am quite well," he replied, in a manner so distracted that neither lady was convinced of the truth of his statement. "I came here straight from the stable," he continued. "How unforgiveable – the smell of the horses is hardly conducive to easy digestion. Please ladies, do not interrupt your luncheon. If you will excuse me, I shall take a bath and return a new man."

~

"What are you doing here?" Garbrae asked when his wife followed him into his study not minutes after he had taken up residence there.

"I might ask you the same thing. You were, I believe, on your way to bathe."

"And yet you sought me out here?"

"Your first mistake was to suggest you were going to bathe. You have never been quite so diligent in matters of cleanliness. A basin wash I could have accepted, but a bath? No! A bath simply meant you were looking for an excuse to be away for a longer spell. So, tell me, what is amiss?"

"You really can be quite insufferable."

"So I believe," she replied, taking a chair opposite him and settling down for an explanation.

Garbrae dragged his hands through his hair and roughly across his face, breathing out loudly as he did so. Catherine remained unmoved, unwilling to leave.

"You will not be satisfied without some manner of expla-nation, I suppose?"

"I will not."

"Stubborn too, it seems."

"Yes, insufferable and stubborn describes me quite well," replied she. "Now, to the letter … from someone you know, for you paled before even opening it. I take it you recognised the handwriting."

Garbrae pulled out the letter he had slid in among the pile of papers on his desk. "Well observed. The letter is from a family friend who has fallen into some trouble in Italy. It is a request for help."

"And does this friend not have family of their own to whom they could turn?"

"A father, but the situation is delicate. There are concerns no help may be forthcoming."

"Lord, what has he done?"

"*She* has run away with a man."

Catherine's breath quickened. "She!"

"Yes. Someone I have known since childhood. She is in Rome – abandoned, without money, without protection, and without hope of return, unless I intervene."

Garbrae's words tumbled out of him in their rush to be told. Catherine observed him – his agitated speech, his still pale face, and the skewed cravat tugged loose about his neck.

"What do you propose to do?" she asked.

"I do not know, although I feel bound to offer help. I cannot leave her unaided in a foreign land. Who knows what might befall her?"

"You plan to send her money then, arrange passage back to England?"

Garbrae avoided his wife's eyes. "I will arrange for some lines of credit to be extended, but I think it would be prudent to travel there myself to ensure her safety in person. If the man she ran away with is still in Rome, I may be able to exert some influence, convince him of the necessity of seeing to his duty."

"This woman," Catherine said, her fingers strumming

restlessly on the arm of her chair. "This family friend you have known since childhood …"

She paused, willing the captain to look at her, refusing to continue speaking until his eyes met hers.

"Yes," he said at last, looking up at her, uncomfortable at the silence she had forced between them.

"Is there any reason she would call on you for aid. You, particularly."

Garbrae knew what Catherine was asking, and it gave him pause. Could he admit to his wife all that Anna Harrington had once meant to him? Would the delicate peace they had found with one another withstand the truth of why Anna was so sure he would come to her aid? No, he feared not.

"She knows I am wealthy enough to be able to help, and she likely believes I would not be dissuaded by concerns of what the ton might think," he said.

"And if you go, what of the mill and your responsibilities here?"

"The repairs at the mill are all but complete; I do not need to be here to oversee what remains to be done. Johnson and Yarrow can be trusted in my absence."

"Your father, he could oversee the running of the mill, surely?"

"I will not ask him to step in, for he will insist on knowing why I am leaving. If my father finds out where I am going, he will tell Mr Harrington, and Anna was most insistent that her father not discover where she is, not until she is ready."

Catherine's breath caught. *Anna*, she thought. *How decidedly familiar!* "We could go," she announced impetuously. "I have always wanted to travel; you could consider it a late wedding present."

"We could not possibly," said Garbrae.

"Why not? It is perfectly acceptable for newly married couples to undertake a tour after their wedding. That ours was delayed will be as unconventional as our rushed wedding. I doubt it will raise more than the briefest interest. On the return journey, the woman can be introduced as my companion – much more fitting than you travelling alone with her."

Garbrae strode back and forth across the room, seeking to walk out some of the agitation that would not allow him to sit. "And what of Lady Rose and Fitzgerald?" he asked, pausing mid-stride.

"I hardly think it necessary to take the entire household," said Catherine, who had been watching her husband's growing agitation with increasing disquiet of her own.

"Though he has made progress, I do not believe Fitzgerald is ready to be alone, and it is hardly proper to leave him with Lady Rose."

"No, indeed not," agreed Catherine. "What if we were to ask another to join them?"

"I take it you have someone in mind?"

Catherine leaned forward in her chair. "As it happens, I do. If we were all to travel to London, we could set Rose and Captain Fitzgerald up quite nicely at our house on Grosvenor Square. Rose loves London at any time of year, and Town should be quiet enough for the captain. I will ask my friend, Miss Dunne, to stay with them. I am certain she would be delighted with time away from her mother."

Without waiting for any sort of consent from her husband, Catherine stood, announcing, "It is settled. I will make the arrangements at once."

She turned from the captain and left the room before he had a chance to object, already planning what to pack and how best to break the news to Rose.

CHAPTER 31

Civitavecchia, Italy. September 1813

"You speak fluent Italian," said Catherine, when she heard Garbrae arranging their transport from the docks.

"You are surprised?"

"A little. I had not imagined you to be so well schooled."

"Some knowledge of other languages is always important for a life in trade, and as it turns out, I am quite proficient at it. I speak Italian, French, and Spanish with a degree of fluency, and have phrases enough in a few other tongues to either get myself into or out of trouble." Garbrae laughed and turned Catherine in the direction of the nearest osteria. "Come, we shall be collected here once all our baggage has been loaded."

"How on earth did you ever manage for years on the sea?" she said, taking up the arm her husband offered and following him toward a small tavern on a nearby corner. "I was sure at points on our journey I would succumb to that terrible sickness."

"Yet, you rallied; you did not allow yourself to be overwhelmed, and you followed instructions," he said, not caring to hide the surprise in his voice.

"Yes, for once I decided compliance was called for. I did not want to completely shame you. Imagine a naval captain with a wife who could not step on deck for seasickness." She gave a small laugh of embarrassment. "Your ginger tea rid me of the worst of the symptoms, and I forced myself to ignore the rest. How did you manage to find ginger on the ship?"

"I brought it with me, as a precaution. I remember all too well the curse of seasickness."

"I am certainly grateful for it, although I do think I was managing quite well toward the end."

"You certainly had your sea legs, my lady. A few more weeks, and you would have been climbing the rigging," Garbrae teased, showing Catherine to a chair outside the osteria before heading inside to order refreshments.

As he entered, a gentleman who sat close to the open door asked, "Excuse the interruption, but did I hear the welcome tones of a fellow countryman?"

"That you did, sir," replied Garbrae.

"A captain, I believe the lady said."

"Garbrae. James Garbrae, and the lady in question is my wife," he replied, aware of the gentleman staring at Catherine and displeased by his attentions.

"Your wife!" replied the gentleman, without sense enough to contain his surprise. He looked at the captain, the honesty of his response unmistakable. How curious, for the woman was most certainly a lady, with breeding, education, and rank, and the captain was most certainly – well, a captain. He smiled, hoping to cover any awkwardness. "Forgive me, captain; how rude of me to accost you in this manner and without so much as an introduction. I am Lord Wrexham."

"You are a long way from home, Lord Wrexham," replied

Garbrae, calling up an old recollection of George Endover, the Marquess of Wrexham, from newspaper reports, certain of some sort of scandal in relation to the man but uncertain of the details of it.

"Indeed, I am, which was why I was delighted when I overheard your conversation and was so brash as to force an introduction. It is always a pleasure to meet another English-man. At least, for a moment, it feels that home is not quite so far away."

Garbrae relaxed; the man was simply homesick. "Well, if a little conversation would be of service to you, would you care to join me and my wife for some lunch before we leave?"

"How wonderful of you to ask. It has been some years since I have been home and some months since I last shared a meal with a countryman. It would be a pleasure."

Lord Wrexham, Garbrae observed, was handsome, charming, and well bred. He was intelligent but never overbearingly so, witty but never indecorously so, and polite but never cloy-ingly so. Lord Wrexham was, all told, a man Garbrae found easy to dislike.

"What is it that brings you to Italy? Where is it you travel to? I do not imagine you propose staying in Civitavecchia."

"No. Pretty as the town is, we travel onward to Rome," Catherine replied.

"How wonderful," declared Wrexham, "for that is the very place I call home. Do I ask too much to claim your continued company as my guests during your stay?"

"We would not think to impose upon you in such a manner, Lord Wrexham," responded Garbrae a little too quickly.

"Imposition? Nonsense. But I am too forward – the joy of

having a little reminder of home overcoming both my manners and good sense."

"Not at all, Lord Wrexham," said Catherine, "it was generous of you to offer."

"If I cannot convince you to stay with me, you must at least allow me the pleasure of showing you the city, and I shall be hosting a ball in a matter of weeks – you must come."

Garbrae nodded his ascent, adding, "If we are still in Rome, we have not yet determined how long our stay might be."

Lord Wrexham, pleased with the promise of their continued company, talked on, describing the wonders of Rome and the delights that awaited them.

CHAPTER 32

Rome, Italy. October 1813.

"How was the search today?" Catherine enquired as Garbrae joined her for dinner, looking, she thought, increasingly worn by the continuing fruitless search for Miss Harrington.

"As unsuccessful as this morning. Two weeks – almost two weeks – we have been here. What was she thinking moving on, knowing I would come for her? Surely, her situation is not so bad that she could not have negotiated a longer stay. She must have known I would settle her account."

"And the line of credit you had extended?"

"She never used it." Garbrae shot an anxious look at his wife. "You do not think we are too late?"

Catherine shook her head. "She has moved on at least twice since her letter to you, perhaps she never received your letter, so she did not know. No doubt her landlord needed more than faith in her word that the debt would be paid," she replied.

"How dire must her situation be if she could not afford to

stay in that place. When I think of her being there – when I think of any lady staying there – my blood runs cold. Where is she? How in Heaven am I to find her now?"

A knot twisted in Catherine's gut. The captain's nerves were increasingly frayed by his failure to find Miss Harrington. She had enquired again about his connection to the family, and his brusque reply had not allayed her fears that there was more to the relationship than he admitted. She reached out and took his hand, moved to offer whatever comfort she could. They sat, holding hands, saying nothing until Catherine exclaimed, "Lord Wrexham! Could we ask for help there?"

"I do not think it would be appropriate to involve Wrexham."

"Oh, but he has been so good to us since we arrived. He must have connections, and we must use every advantage in our pursuit. Surely, the safe return of Miss Harrington is worth a little embarrassment. I am certain we can count on his discretion not to make the details of her situation known."

"You place a lot of stock in the man; you clearly trust him," replied Garbrae, only just managing to conceal his unhappiness at the fact.

"I do, and I believe we can trust him with this matter. He has been most attentive …"

I have no doubt he has, thought Garbrae, his initial dislike of the man having grown stronger during every moment spent with him, and stronger still during every moment Catherine spent with him. He was, Garbrae was certain, just the sort of man who Catherine would have married had circumstances not been as they were – had fate not forced her hand. He was quite the gentleman, and it irked.

"… and you must admit, that alone speaks volumes about

him," Catherine continued, looking at him for confirmation as to the truth of the matter.

Damn! He had not heard a word she had said. "If you think the man can be trusted, it is proof enough for me. You are a keen judge of character, my lady," he replied.

"I disliked and discounted you the moment I met you," she teased.

"As I said, a keen judge of character," he managed to say, his sour mood giving way to a short burst of laughter.

Catherine smiled. It was the first time in weeks she had seen her husband genuinely laugh. The moment of ease was a welcome sight, and she relaxed on seeing him less careworn – even for just as long as the laughter lasted. "You will talk to Lord Wrexham?"

"I will," Garbrae said, taking the opportunity to clasp her hands in his, delighting in their softness and the gentle heat he felt spreading through him on being able to touch her, allowing all thoughts of the troublesome Miss Harrington and the irksome Lord Wrexham to fade away.

"It is, as you can see, a delicate matter," Garbrae finished, having done as Catherine suggested and taken Lord Wrexham into his confidence. "I am at a loss as to where to turn next, and my wife thought, given your connections here, you might be able to assist me."

"Lady Catherine does me an honour, for she must trust in me a great deal to encourage you to tell me of poor Miss Harrington's circumstances. This is not news one would wish known; it would be ruinous."

"Ruinous, as you say, my lord," Garbrae replied, irritated that Wrexham considered his request for help as some sort of endorsement from Catherine.

"I am gratified by the faith she has in me," Wrexham continued, his smile broadening.

"My wife recognised the necessity of connections if we were to accomplish our task," Garbrae said, allowing a heavy emphasis to fall on his claim to Catherine.

"A clever woman, your wife," Wrexham replied, as deliberate in his emphasis as Garbrae.

The men regarded one another somewhat coolly, an uneasy and tacit understanding developing between them. There was little friendship, little respect, and little but Catherine to bind them.

"I will help however I can," Lord Wrexham offered at last, in his most infuriatingly pleasing manner. "I ask for only one thing in return."

"And that is?"

"That you and Lady Catherine join me at my villa. It will be a much simpler affair to deal with this business if it is run from my home. It removes the necessity of my man, Barnes, running halfway across the city every time he needs to speak with you."

"Your man, Barnes?"

"The soul of discretion, I assure you, and quite the best man for the job if you wish Miss Harrington found."

"Lord Wrexham," Garbrae managed through gritted teeth, "you are too kind."

CHAPTER 33

*L*ord Wrexham had set Barnes straight to the business of locating Miss Harrington. Garbrae was impressed by the efficiency of the man, for within two days, he had located a further address at which she had stayed and had leads to follow as to her more current whereabouts. That Barnes preferred to work alone until the woman was found was a great source of relief to Garbrae, as it meant he did not have to leave Catherine alone with their host – a man whose every word and action seemed to be an exercise in beguiling Garbrae's wife.

Despite the magnificence of their surroundings – Lord Wrexham's home and grounds could only be described as magnificent – Garbrae found no pleasure in his time there, until the fourth day when Lord Wrexham announced at breakfast that he would be gone for the day – last minute preparations for the ball that would likely not see him returned until well after dinner. Garbrae could not contain his smile.

"So you must entertain yourselves as best you can," Lord Wrexham continued, trying to ignore Grammar's obvious delight. "There are horses if you wish to ride about the estate; take a carriage out or explore the library if you prefer."

"You are, as ever, an attentive host," replied Garbrae. "With such choices open to us, we shall no doubt fill the day quite splendidly."

Garbrae watched their host closely; the man seemed prickled at the thought of leaving them alone together. The captain suspected Wrexham thought Garbrae unworthy of Catherine; the man had certainly been at pains to ensure he was always in their company. But – damn it! – no matter what his lordship might think, Catherine was Garbrae's wife.

∽

"My lady, it is sweltering. Do you honestly intend to go riding in that?" queried Garbrae on seeing Catherine enter the stables wearing her usual riding habit.

"You have seen me riding often enough; you know perfectly well this is what I always wear. What did you think I would change into on your suggestion of a ride?"

"The outfit is perfectly suitable when we are in England, but in this heat, under an Italian sun, you will not last long on horseback with yards of that heavy tweed wrapped about you."

Catherine raised an accusatory eyebrow at the man. "If you did not wish me to ride with you, you could have just said so."

"Quite the contrary, I am looking forward to our adventure. I simply do not wish to have it cut short because you have fainted in the midday sun."

"What do you propose?"

"I have one idea," Garbrae said with a broad smile as he

walked toward her, "though I am not certain you are going to like it."

~

"You cannot be serious!" exclaimed Catherine from behind the screen.

"Indeed, I am," Garbrae responded. "Can you think of a better plan?"

"What if anyone were to see me dressed like this?"

Garbrae tapped a riding crop against the side of his boot. "Who is here to see you? Lord Wrexham is away until this evening, and I doubt the servants care much about what you wear when riding. I hardly think it is likely to be the scandal you imagine. Now, come out from behind there, and let me see."

"But I look utterly ridiculous."

"I am sure that is not so. Come out from behind the screen; I promise I shall not laugh," he responded gently, his usual playfulness softening in response to her vulnerability.

Catherine stepped out from behind the screen, wearing the breeches and cotton shirt her husband had provided her.

Garbrae stood, staring and silent. His wife was exquisite. In recent weeks, he had spent considerable time pondering how she might look underneath the yards of fabric that usually swathed her, when shadows formed where sunlight hit cotton. The silhouette elicited from the twist and movement of her dresses had suggested she had a shapely figure, but seeing her standing before him, the shirt tucked in tightly, giving emphasis to the neatness of her waist and the full curve of her breast, breeches hugging to her hips and the long lean run of her legs, left him agog.

Catherine, embarrassed by the silence, and uncertain as

to the meaning of her husband's expression, assumed that she did – as she suspected – look ridiculous.

"I will not ride today," she said, flustered, breaking the silence between them to allow her an excuse to retreat behind the screen and put an end to the spectacle.

Garbrae collected himself immediately and cursed his foolish reaction. Of course, she would assume his silence to be an expression of disapproval.

"Nonsense," he replied as casually as he could manage, trying not to stare at the delicious curves of his wife's body, forcing away visions of her legs wrapped about him.

"You look splendid, but then true beauty and elegance will always shine through. We shall leave as soon as you are ready."

Catherine could not determine if the captain was in earnest or was mocking her. She knew her figure to be neat and her face to be pretty, though not classically so, not like Rose. Her biting tongue, her mother warned, often gave an unpleasant hardness to her features. Still, she found herself warmed by her husband's compliment. She chose to take him at his word and allow herself to be beautiful and elegant, even dressed as a boy, at least for that afternoon.

Before either of them could have expected it, noon was upon them. The heat, even allowing for the breeze, was becoming uncomfortable. Supposing that the horses would also be susceptible to the rigours of the midday sun, Garbrae determined it would be best to find a place for lunch, somewhere with water and shade. They followed the course of a stream that ran through the property and, upon rounding a small hill, found a perfect oasis in which to rest: a small clump of trees offering cover.

With the horses secured and watered, Garbrae turned his attentions back to their makeshift camp and lunch with Catherine. She was not in the shade as he had expected but had gone to the stream's edge. There, she splashed water across her face, wet a cloth, and held it to her neck to allow the cold water to trickle down her back. It was only when she turned that he noticed the water had also run down over her chest, soaking her shirt, and causing it to cling to her skin.

The sight of Catherine walking toward him – the rise and swell of her breast accentuated by the wet cotton, her face more carefree than he had ever seen it, her whole presence easy – was utterly captivating and gave rise to a startling circumstance.

Garbrae swallowed hard as realisation took hold within him. Something that had been infiltrating for some months suddenly pressed the centre of his consciousness. "Dear God," he muttered, "I am completely and whole-heartedly in love with my wife!"

The realisation was disquieting, and Garbrae stumbled a little under the weight of it. It could scarcely have come upon him at a worse moment – when he had travelled halfway across the world in search of another woman, and when his wife, by all appearances, was inordinately taken by the charm of another man. "Charm," he murmured. "Charm, indeed."

"What was that, captain?" asked Catherine, having just appeared by his side.

"What? Oh, nothing at all, just muttering to myself," he jested. "Must be the sun."

Catherine regarded the captain coolly. There was some-thing altered in his manner, but she could not quite make out what.

The pair sat for some time without conversation, simply enjoying the shade, their lunch, and the quiet company of the other. After eating, they finally succumbed to the tranquillity of their surroundings and the stillness of the day, sitting back on the blanket, both inexplicably at ease.

"It seems, captain, we find ourselves in the curious position of having come to some sort of peace after so many months of disquiet," Catherine said eventually.

"I am pleased you do not sound disappointed," he responded, happy for the opportunity to bring their relationship into conversation, hoping to learn the extent of any change in her feelings toward him. She had softened, it was true, but whether from tolerance or partiality was uncertain. "I have been hoping some form of accord might be reached between us."

"The hostility could not have continued, I suppose, for even I baulked at the thought of a lifelong conflict."

Her tone was light, playful, and Garbrae was encouraged by it. "There were many obstacles to be overcome in our marriage, though I fear our own stubbornness was principal among them," he said.

"That is certainly true, though honour must surely call you to claim the larger share of the stubbornness as your own," she said, teasing him.

"Honour, my lady? There have been times enough you have called my honour into question, so I shall not falter now at this opportunity for redemption. As you wish it, the stubbornness was all mine. I claim not a share but the whole of it and beg only your forgiveness for my foolishness."

With a light laugh in response from Catherine, Garbrae lay back, his body stretched to cover the length of the blanket, his hands tucked neatly behind his head as a makeshift pillow, pleased with the way the afternoon was unfolding. He thought his happiness complete when Catherine too lay back, taking the opportunity to fully relax.

"I warned my sister about you, captain."

"You did? Fearing what? That I was a bad influence perhaps?"

"I believe the word I used was 'pernicious'," she replied.

"Pernicious? Well, and what say you now?"

"The fact that I am lying here, the Italian sun beating down upon me, exhausted from a long ride, and dressed quite like a boy would rather point to my being right. You are a wicked influence, sir, though at this moment, I cannot seem to mind."

Catherine turned on her side to look at her husband for the first time in their conversation, resting her head atop her folded arm, only to find him also turned, gazing at her with the keenest interest. They regarded one another in this manner, until disconcerted by the directness of his gaze, Catherine dipped her chin and turned her face ever so slightly from his, praying the full effect of his regard was not hinted at by a blush.

Leaning across, Garbrae cupped her face in his hand and tilted her chin, turning her toward him once again.

"A man could become lost in your gaze," he whispered, noticing how she blinked, embarrassed at the compliment, delighted by the soft blush that spread across her cheeks. "You are exquisite."

Without saying more, Garbrae tentatively kissed her. It was a soft, short kiss, his lips pressed to hers for a moment before drawing back a hair's breadth, waiting for her reaction, half expecting to feel the sting of her palm across his face. But no, there was no sting, no retribution, and so he kissed her again, still softly, briefly, hoping for more.

From the first kiss, Catherine was lost. She had never supposed a simple kiss could caress so seductively or speak so intensely to the promise of what was to come. The gentle touch of his lips on hers called forth sensations she was unprepared for, leaving her body trembling in anticipation.

Garbrae could scarcely believe it when he found her receptive to his advances. That she had not flinched at his first kiss nor recoiled at his second was cause for amazement, but that he could feel a quickening to her breath and a slight tremble in her body was beyond expectation. He had always hoped she would respond to him physically, that he would have the opportunity to unearth the desire and passion he knew she was capable of, and here were signs of it surely.

He moved his body next to hers, pleased to feel her respond in kind, an almost imperceptible shift forward, but he had felt it. He took her face in both his hands and kissed her now with greater purpose than before. His lips pressed harder against hers, his mouth opened for just a moment allowing his tongue to softly touch her lips.

Catherine gasped at this but did not withdraw. Instead, to Garbrae's satisfaction, she allowed her tongue to search, delicately tracing the curve of his own lips before she drew back to look at him. He smiled at her hesitation, and there was such gentleness in his expression that for the first time, Catherine saw what Rose had assured her of all along: the captain really was a handsome man.

CHAPTER 34

*C*atherine stepped back from the wall mirror and wondered, not for the first time since putting the dress on, if she had made a mistake in picking this particular gown. "It is far more revealing than I imagined," she said to Mary, the young maid helping her prepare.

"That it is, my lady," Mary replied candidly. "You look quite wonderful if you don't mind me adding."

"Oh! You do not think it cut too low? I think perhaps it has been cut too low."

"Well, if we were in London, maybe. You'll not get much use of it there, but here, I think you can be more daring."

"I had not realised you were so opinionated."

"I have been watching you." Mary smiled.

"Well, such cheek! I cannot imagine what you mean," Catherine said, trying to sound offended or, at the least, severe but finding too much amusement in Mary's candour to truly manage either.

"I believe the captain will appreciate the gown," Mary ventured, Catherine's high spirits encouraging her to a forthrightness she would not previously have dared.

"Now, that really is quite enough!" Catherine cut in, unable to control the blush that spread right across her breast and upward. "I will have no further talk of that sort." *Though,* she granted, taking account of her reflection once more, *I daresay you are absolutely right.*

For all that he might dislike the man, Wrexham certainly knew how to entertain, admitted Garbrae as he stood in the centre of the grand ballroom admiring the handiwork of the last few days, exchanging pleasantries with the other guests, and enjoying the fine wine.

"From one of Lord Wrexham's own vineyards," his server had offered unbidden.

Of course the man has his own vineyard, thought Garbrae, *and damn him if it does not produce a fine wine.*

The ballroom was large, with a pretty little balcony offering a view of the grounds. The three wide double doors leading onto the balcony had been fully opened to allow in the evening air which carried with it the scent of the garden and the freshness of open spaces. The room itself shimmered in the glow of hundreds of candles, their flames dancing in the breeze or fluttering in the wake of a servant rushing by.

On the opposite side of the ballroom, and leading back into the entrance hall, were another two large doors, both also open. One afforded a perfect view of the hallway, and the other, Garbrae turned to observe, offered a perfect view of the main stairway … and his wife's appearance at the top.

Garbrae stared.

Catherine had stepped onto the stairs and paused as her young maid flitted about, making final adjustments to the dress. Catherine stood, oblivious to her husband's presence, smiling at the fuss, and by all accounts shushing her maid's concerns.

She was … Garbrae could not find the words. He was lost in the sight of her and could not take his eyes away as she descended the stairs, all fussing complete. Her smile as she spotted him adding to her radiance, the light from the ballroom and all eyes drawn to her as she walked in.

Catherine, unaware of the commotion her entrance had stirred, went straight to him.

"This dress is a little low cut, I fear," she whispered. "Do you think?"

"I do," Garbrae replied, still staggered. "I mean, that is, no, of course not. That is to say, it is … well, you can see …" *God, I sound like a fool*, he thought. *Stop babbling!* Garbrae took a deep breath. "The dress is exquisite, you are breathtaking, and I am quite undone."

Catherine blushed in response before saying, "I suppose anything is better than how I was dressed during our last little adventure."

Garbrae groaned. On that occasion, he had only just mastered himself enough to stop at kissing his wife. If she was capable of inspiring such passion dressed as a boy, think what she could do now, dressed unmistakably as a woman. She might just kill him.

"Come," he said, smiling, "let us show off that dress as it deserves. Will you walk with me?"

"Parade around the ballroom? Fine-feathered beauty that I am?" she teased.

"You have an exceptionally good memory." Garbrae laughed. "It is a flaw we shall have to remedy if we are ever to find peace with one another."

Garbrae could pay little attention to conversation and company as he and Catherine made their way around the ballroom. As if her easy charm and the cut of her dress were not distraction enough, he soon found a new and decidedly more unpleasant focus for his attentions: the other men in attendance. It did not escape him that his wife was noticed by others, and though the thinly veiled flirtations of some of the more daring men there did little but amuse him, when he saw one such man drop his gaze to his wife's bosom, allowing it to linger, it was all he could do not to call the scoundrel out.

"I'll have his bloody eyes," he muttered.

"What was that?" asked Catherine, turning to him, wondering at the expression he wore. "Are you quite all right?"

The man, who had allowed his gaze to linger, shot a brief look to the captain and, unlike Catherine, understood the expression immediately. "If you will excuse me," he managed, moving away from the little group, "I see someone I must …" The rest of his sentence was lost in the general clamour of the room.

"My lady," Garbrae said, relaxing upon the man's departure, "might we dance?"

"I can think of nothing I would enjoy more" she replied, nodding politely to their companions and taking her husband's arm.

Garbrae and Catherine reached the floor just as a waltz was struck up. Catherine faltered.

"Are you all right?" Garbrae asked.

"The waltz," she replied, as though those two words would somehow explain her hesitation.

"Yes?"

"They are playing a waltz."

"I know, which is rather a good stroke of luck, for I find it much easier to dance when there is music."

"But I have never waltzed."

"I thought all young ladies were schooled in dancing," he replied.

"We are, and I was taught it, but Mother was furious when she found out. She never thought the dance proper and refused to let us dance it in public. You know, once at a ball, she had a young man removed who dared to only *say* he longed to try a waltz."

Garbrae, who had been surprised by his wife's hesitation, could not resist a further tease. "Well, how perfectly correct of your mother. I must remember to thank her for her good sense, for I do not relish the thought of another man having placed his hands so intimately upon you. But we are in Italy, and we are married, and if a man as particular to reputation as Lord Wrexham can allow the waltz to be played, then surely, there can be no impropriety in our dancing to it."

"I doubt my mother would agree, about the waltz or Lord Wrexham."

"Though you find no fault with the man," Garbrae noted.

Catherine laughed lightly. Though they had not yet joined the others in the heart of the ballroom, she had relaxed, and her body swayed to the gentle strains of the music. "You sound jealous, captain."

"Jealous!" He barked a brash, unconvincing, laugh. "Jealous? Of a handsome, charming, intelligent, wealthy, titled man who appears to have fully secured the good grace and confidence of my wife – why the very notion is ridiculous."

Catherine looked at Garbrae. "Come," she whispered, leaning in to him, her lips brushing the side of his ear, her heat and her scent dizzying. "Waltz with me?"

Her breath caught as he clasped her hand in response and wound an arm about her waist. She offered no resistance, and as he moved her across the ballroom floor, every inch of her surrendered to him.

~

"I feel in need of some air," Catherine managed to say, once the waltz was done – her colour high, her breathing rapid. "Might we sit out the next set and take a turn on the balcony?"

"Certainly," Garbrae replied, grateful for the opportunity to cool down and release his hold of her, for if he did not, he doubted his ability to maintain his decorum.

The evening had turned cool, and both were glad of the breeze greeting them as they stepped outside. Spotting a small bench in the corner, away from the other couples and small parties that had gathered outside, Garbrae led them there. "Come, let us sit."

The pair were silent for several minutes. Something was altered between them.

"When do you hope to find Miss Harrington?" Catherine said at last; the silence between them agonising when she knew there were things that must be said.

"Any day, so Lord Wrexham's man assures me. He will send word to me the moment she is discovered. It will be dealt with without delay."

"And when everything is settled with Miss Harrington?"

"We shall return to London."

"And when we are returned to London?"

"Oh, I imagine, between you and Lady Rose, the matter of whether we stay in London a while or return to Manchester at once will be decided with little interference from me."

"And when we return home to Manchester?"

Garbrae covered her hand with his and slipped his fingers in between hers; they stilled at his touch, no longer agitating the small, embroidered flowers that decorated the waistband of her dress. "What is it you dance around? Is there something you specifically wish to discuss?" he asked.

Catherine faltered, the feeling of his hand on hers and the brush of his fingers against the silk of her dress adding to her distraction. "It is just I would rather not – that is to say, I would rather we … that I …"

"What in heavens is the matter?" he asked, concerned by the unusual turn in his wife.

"The maid!" she managed at last, the colour rushing to her cheeks.

"Ah, the maid."

"I cannot have her in the house, captain; I simply cannot. I hoped we were in a position where … where I could raise this matter with you without too much of a fuss."

His hand dropped from hers and fell stiffly by his side. "What do you think has been happening between that young girl and me?"

"Do not ask me to say it," she begged, her eyes glistening with tears.

"You think I have been bedding her," he replied, saddened by the pained expression she wore and angry that he had allowed the misunderstanding to go unchecked for so long.

Catherine nodded, averting her gaze from his face. "You are a man, and you have needs, and I have not been … dutiful."

Garbrae almost smiled at the absurdity of the moment. It was such a curious conversation for a man to have with his wife, but there was no real humour there, and he knew the topic was one Catherine should never have had to broach. "I am a man, and I do have needs, but please do not think that I am not master enough of my urges that I need to stoop to taking advantage of the staff."

"I doubt you would find many a man who would blame you," she said, glancing up at him, her eyes darting away again as though she were afraid of what she might read in his face if she were to look too long. "I need you to be honest with me. I think I might bear any pain so long as I am not kept ignorant of the truth."

"She has a brother in the navy. I told her tales of the islands and seas around which he sails. I gave her a shell from Antigua so that she might have a little part of the world he inhabits. We shared stories, nothing more. The girl is barely out of the schoolroom. I have never taken her to my bed, nor any of those we employ for that matter. Let me assure you, when I take a woman to my bed, I take a woman and not some slip of a girl."

Catherine did not know whether to be heartened or dismayed by this admission. He did not bed the servants, but there were women.

"Oh," she answered softly, her disappointment plain.

"And since the day of our wedding, none have shared my bed," he added.

"Oh!" she answered again, her eyes searching his face for the truth of the statement, finding nothing but honesty there. "But I do not understand."

"We are married, bound together in the eyes of God and man. I will not dishonour that bond with infidelity. You have had none to your bed during our marriage I take it?"

Catherine, missing the tease in his tone, responded in earnest. "Of course not!"

"And neither have I," Garbrae said gently, his fingers reaching out to stroke her arm. "I have made no greater sacrifice than you."

"But you are a man."

His mouth quirked into a curious half-smile. "My dear, I am not certain where you gained this notion that all men are slaves to uncontrollable urges. Perhaps among your set it is common for men to indulge all of their desires, but I was not raised that way. I learned discipline and respect at an early age – respect for myself and respect for others. My mother was quite clear in her instructions on the matter of how a woman – how a wife – should be treated. And by that I do not refer to the niceties and formalities of social custom – of which you are aware that I have a less than perfect grasp – but in all the ways that really matter. Encouraging freedom, creativity, and spirit, rather than suppressing it, allowing for mutual respect and for the hope that, in finding the right woman, I would find a partner to my life and not merely someone to be carried through it."

"And then you married me."

"I did," Garbrae answered, his face now alight with an amused smile.

"Your father, I take it, was more concerned about finding the right family than the right partner for you."

"Actually, I believe my father may have seen in you the best chance for both his needs and mine to be met."

"Oh," replied Catherine, a little surprised. "I cannot fathom how I would have made anything but the worst impression."

"He believed you had spirit and sense enough to challenge me and that would be a fine start."

"Have I been a frightful wife?" she asked, fully turning to him, her hand coming to rest on his chest at a spot above his heart.

"You have … never been boring, Catherine," Garbrae offered, reassuring her that whatever their history he bore her no ill will.

A delicious thrill ran through her; he had called her Catherine. Not my lady – as she had so ridiculously demanded – but Catherine, said while a smile played about his lips, and she thought she might burst with the joy of hearing it.

"I am trying to be better," she said.

"I see that," he replied, taking her hand in his and raising it briefly to his lips, refusing to release his hold once his kiss was complete.

Catherine turned his hand in hers and raised it, brushing her lips across his knuckles in a gentle kiss of her own. Garbrae reached for her with his other hand and drew her to him. His breath quickened as she leaned into him, her lips still sitting in the pout of a kiss.

"Catherine," he whispered, his lips brushing hers as he spoke her name.

She lifted her chin a fraction so that on speaking again he would kiss her. Garbrae, not oblivious to the subtle tilt, kissed her gently, feeling her mouth curve into a smile. He kissed her again with greater eagerness, drawing forth a gentle moan and the parting of her soft lips. He pressed his hand to her breast, aware of the pounding of her heart beneath, knowing every excited beat was matched by the beating of his own.

When at last they broke from their kiss, Garbrae rested his head lightly against hers. "I believe change was needed on both our parts, but tell me you believe there is hope for happiness between us now. Tell me I am not the only one who sees that, with a little compromise, we could be good together."

Catherine leaned back from him. "No, I see it too," she replied, and noting how his fingers and gaze lingered on the lace at the neckline of her dress, she added impishly, "and if I continue to wear gowns such as this, I believe I could induce such a state of distraction that the compromise need never be mine."

"Such wickedness!" Garbrae gasped with feigned horror.

With a smile, Catherine stood. She stepped back from her husband and, turning on her heel, allowed him the unabashed pleasure of watching her as she walked away.

CHAPTER 35

"You are certain we are in the right place" asked Garbrae as he stared in disbelief at the squalor of the streets through which they walked.

"I am. I was tasked with finding her, and I have, through various means, but there will be some expenses to be covered," replied Barnes, wishing to make certain as early as possible that the man understood money was required, for he had made promises that would best go unbroken.

"You will have your expenses paid, and your efforts will be rewarded," answered Garbrae. He cast a disapproving eye along the street. "I am simply appalled to learn she is here."

"It is not as grim as you think, for though the streets are crowded and the buildings sag from want of repair, this area is not so bad. There is no trouble here, families mostly, no dens of note where a man might scratch an itch, if you catch my meaning."

Garbrae, well aware of his meaning, did not care for the manner in which his companion licked his lips as he spoke of it. Barnes was a useful man, efficient and discreet, Garbrae could see that, but there was something unpleasant about him, something lascivious in his nature that was unsettling. The captain prayed that Barnes had not approached Anna himself, chilled at the thought of the man being alone with her.

"This is the building, sir," he said, interrupting the captain's thoughts. "I did not go in and look for her. Beyond seeing her enter and exit, I made no approach, not wishing to scare the lady."

"Very sensible of you, Barnes, I appreciate your discretion and good sense in the matter," Garbrae replied. "Now, could you see if the carriage will fit through the street here." He looked up the twisted side street, doubting there was room. "I wish to spare Miss Harrington being seen leaving this area on foot if I can." Tossing the man a purse, he made his way to the door.

"You came!" Anna Harrington squealed, rising from her chair and racing to meet Garbrae as he entered the room.

"Of course, surely there was never any doubt," he replied, thankful to find her looking so well, so like he remembered.

"You are married now, and I was afraid the promises you made to me might no longer hold any power," she replied quietly, her usual exuberance subdued momentarily.

"I told you once, I would be there should you need me, and I have always been a man of my word." Overcome by the joy of her being found safe and well, he drew Anna into an embrace. "What were you thinking?"

Anna pulled herself even closer to him, the comfort and feeling of safety she found in his arms easing every nerve that had been so rattled by recent events. She allowed his closeness and his heat to envelop her.

"Do you remember the last time we embraced like this?" she asked.

"Of course I remember," he replied, leaning his body away from her slightly, so he could see her face. "Your foolhardiness led you into danger on that occasion too."

"I could not resist the temptation of that wall. I admit the danger of falling into the sea on one side added to the excitement, but still, I did not honestly consider that I would fall. On losing my balance … Oh, Lord! If you had not been there, if you had not come now—"

"But I was there, and I have come, and you are safe," he soothed, brushing her cheek, his relief overwhelming every other feeling.

"I have often recalled the feeling of our bodies pressed together," Anna whispered, her hand lightly stroking his neck.

Garbrae, shocked by her remark and suddenly conscious of the unacceptability of their closeness, recollected himself. He released his hold and stepped back from her.

"Miss Harrington, that is hardly the sort of statement …" he began, struggling to find the words to respond to such impropriety. "You know perfectly well, you and I were never … that is to say, I never—"

"Oh no," she interrupted, a nervous laugh escaping her lips, "I did not mean to imply anything unseemly. That day by the shore when I lost my balance, you spun me toward you, caught me as I fell. You held me then as you held me just now. I never thought it possible to feel such safety in the arms of another. I felt as though nothing could harm me as long as you held me. I meant only I have often recalled that feeling of safety."

Garbrae considered the woman standing in front of him, uncertain of the truth of what she was saying, seeing for the first time something altered in the girl he once thought he knew so well.

"I hope it was not your belief that I would come to your rescue that allowed you to act so recklessly," he replied, motioning her to take a seat. "Tell me, Miss Harrington, what has led to this, to your being here?"

"Am I only Miss Harrington to you now? No longer your 'Anna Fair'?" she said, the pouted lip he once found so alluring now merely prompting annoyance.

"Miss Harrington," Garbrae said, sighing, "you know I am married."

"And yet you are here, and once, you promised your heart remained with me."

Garbrae coloured with embarrassment as he recalled the vows he had made in the last letter he sent her. How mawkish they seemed now, yet how heartfelt they had been.

"Please, I am here; is that not enough? Do not ask more of me than I am free to give."

Anna studied him a moment before surrendering to his wishes and pushing him no further. She took a seat in one of the chairs by the table.

"After it became clear to my father that you and I were not to be married, at least not under terms he found acceptable, it became his sole purpose to see me wed, as though I was somehow in danger of being left to spinsterhood," Anna said, clearly annoyed. "But his obsession with finding just the right man made every moment unbearable. I could have no fun, could not take pleasure in any of the outings or the parties we attended, always having to be proper and forced into conversation when I would much rather be dancing."

Garbrae's expression softened as he recalled how painful he had found it finding a spouse.

"Even when I could dance, he watched my every move, critical of every step. If a mistake was made, I spent the next day with a dance instructor, so the next time it would be perfect. It seemed he was determined to strangle any joy I might have. Do you remember our dance at the Brewster's ball? I was so free and happy, spinning with such wild abandon. Was a night ever so wonderful?"

"Miss Harrington, you were too young then to know better – barely more than a child. You could not have expected such a lack of inhibition to be tolerated in a woman."

"No, of course not, but I did not expect such complete restraint. I never felt so controlled when I was with you. I never felt as though you required more of me. You always made me feel as though I were perfect just as I was. Perhaps it was just that I was perfect for you," she added, the coyness of her tone and the manner of her gaze catching Garbrae by surprise.

Is she flirting with me? Deliberately, unashamedly flirting with me? he wondered. "I do not recall you being completely unconstrained when we walked out together."

"You do not recall our racing through Renton Woods, exploring the caves at Wey, or your stealing apples from Brewster's orchard, and what of our narrow escape from his man? I know you remember that."

"Yes, I had my first shore leave and was wild with the excitement of being home, of being free from duty. I allowed myself to roam unchecked, to behave without reservation."

"And it was wonderful," Anna said. "We were both so alive, so free."

"Yes, but that is not who we are now. We could never have continued in that way, with such disregard for responsibility and duty, being ruled by unfettered childish dreams."

The pair sat looking at one another without further conversation for a full five minutes. Anna had not recalled him being so proper. Garbrae had not recalled her being so imprudent. It was a surprising revelation.

"Your unhappiness in London does not account for your being here," he continued, aware of a growing unease at how her story would unfold.

"Yes, of course, you are owed that at least," she admitted, flashing him a half-smile and gently nodding her head. "My fortune was not large enough to secure my attendance at some of the grander events where I might draw the attention of a man who matched my father's idea of a suitable husband. His desperation at our being so cruelly on the out, led him to employ more subversive tactics. He encouraged me to ingratiate myself with other women in Town to ensure better access to their families, hoping my fair face might secure the interest and attachment of some younger brother or cousin."

"Lord! Is there anything more unseemly than the schemes even decent people will resort to when trying to secure a profitable marriage," cut in Garbrae, recalling the lengths his own father had gone to.

"Well, his scheming was not unrewarded, for in befriending a certain Miss Matthews, I was, in time, introduced to her brother, Mr Henry Matthews. He was so different from the others I had met, so full of enthusiasm, with such a passion for adventure. He reminded me of you, and I was at once filled with the hope that the life I dreamed of might not be denied me. I was under his spell almost from our first meeting. I was giddy and light-headed, captivated by his every word. I see now, I was completely in his thrall, though I am shocked to admit it and to you of all people. When he suggested we run away together, that I join him on his grand tour, it was not within my power to refuse him."

Garbrae, who had been silent throughout Anna's admission, sat in utter disbelief at her declaring she had been powerless to refuse this Mr Matthews. He brought his hands to his face, unable now to even look at her.

"You are not married?" he asked, the question muffled. He raked his hands up through his hair and forced his head up, forced himself to look at her.

Anna blushed. "I am not married."

Garbrae blanched. "Then you are ruined." His voice broke, choked and strained within his throat.

"No!" Anna blurted out. "He was a gentleman."

"A gentleman!" Garbrae exploded and shot up from his chair, sending it crashing onto the floor. He grabbed Anna roughly by the shoulders and forced her to her feet. "He took you from your family; he took you out of the country and left you alone and unmarried. What manner of gentlemen is he? What manner of man is he that he could act with such disregard for you and for your name and reputation? For God's sake, Miss Harrington, you were alone with this man for weeks. What you did or did not do hardly matters now," he continued, his incredulity plain. "Your ruin will be assumed; no decent man will ever consider you."

Anna, panicked by his anger and afraid he would not rescue her now, could only argue weakly. "You would forgive me; you would marry me still."

"Hell, woman, I am not free to marry you!" he yelled, releasing her from his hold, sweeping his hand across his mouth in exasperation, not allowing himself to add that even if he were free he would not likely be convinced into doing so now. Only the remnants of his boyhood affection held the expression of his disgust at bay. "God in Heaven, what have you done?"

"You will help me? You will not abandon me as Mr Matthews did?" she asked, her voice small and frightened.

"Of course I will help you, and I will make this right if I can," Garbrae replied, his anger toward her dissipating and switching to the cause of her ruin, settling heavily on the person of Henry Matthews, a man as yet unknown to him, but whose acquaintance would be made one way or another. "Come, it is time to go. I see Barnes has returned, though without the carriage. Can you walk as far as the piazza?"

"With you by my side, most assuredly," Anna replied, taking the captain's arm and fixing him with the same coquettish gaze as before.

She is flirting with me, even now, Garbrae thought as he led her to the door, *blatantly, brazenly flirting with me. Who is this woman? I scarcely recognise the girl I once adored. Lord, but what will my wife say?*

CHAPTER 36

Catherine had been able to concentrate on little since learning from Lord Wrexham that her husband had been summoned to Miss Harrington's residence that morning. She offered nothing to the conversation beyond nodding politely in response to everything said by her host and assuring the servants of her perfect comfort.

"In fairness to the staff," said Wrexham on her fifth and most forceful refusal of tea, "you do not look comfortable. I have never seen a person so on edge, and your testy replies hardly take from the general suspicion that you are most definitely not at ease."

The sound of a carriage approaching on the gravel swallowed up any argument Catherine might have made, and with a hurried, "Excuse me," she rose and was gone.

"Her husband returns," Wrexham said to his butler. "See to him, and if he has a woman with him, set her up in the blue room. I shall be gone for the rest of the day; please make my apologies."

Little had been said between Garbrae and Anna during the carriage ride back to Lord Wrexham's estate, although as they approached the property, he felt compelled to provide some account of their acquaintance with Lord Wrexham and the role he had played in finding her.

"You married the daughter of an earl?" she responded, the only point of interest from the history he provided her being in relation to his wife. "Your father must have been pleased. Does she suit you as well as she suited him?"

"I do not wish to talk of my wife," Garbrae interjected, uncomfortable at the thought of exposing his feelings for Catherine. "You will meet soon enough and will no doubt judge for yourself the suitability of the match."

"I did not mean to pry. I simply wished to know if she makes you as happy as you deserve to be, as happy as I once made you … as I always hoped to make you."

"Miss Harrington, please, there can be no further talk of that sort. I am married; it is done. I will help you back to England, but beyond that, I offer you nothing."

"Of course. Seeing you again … your coming to my rescue … well, it was overwhelming: relief, gratitude, the memory of feelings past. You need not be concerned."

Garbrae sat back and glanced at his watch – it was not yet nine. The message from Barnes with Anna's address had been delivered so early he had not wanted to disturb Catherine, but she would be out of bed now. Did she know that Anna had been found? He ought to have left her a note, some warning of what was coming. No doubt Wrexham had passed along the news – and perhaps taken some delight in doing so. Still, now that Miss Harrington had been found, he was hopeful this sorry affair would finally be brought to an end. His eyes were drawn to the front of the house as they rounded the final bend in the driveway, and his breath caught on seeing Catherine there waiting for him.

She stood, the very picture of calm, her hands resting comfortably at her side, no sign of agitation about her face. He glanced at Anna, who sat fidgeting in her seat, her eyes darting back and forth between the house and himself. The thought of Catherine having to pass this woman off as a companion for the return journey to England sickened him. He had no right to ask that of her. What had he been thinking when he agreed to her plan? How could he ask her to smile and introduce this chit as a friend? He could only hope Matthews would be found and a marriage arranged so Catherine might be spared any such mortification.

"That is the woman who stole you from me, I take it?" whispered Anna, leaning close to him as the carriage halted. "I grant she is handsome."

Garbrae, uncomfortable at her closeness, stiffened. As he exited the carriage, he glanced in the direction of his wife but found he was unable to meet her gaze. *You did not think this through, idiot,* he admonished silently. *What now? Do you casually introduce them and walk in for a late breakfast?*

Catherine spared him the trouble of deciding what would be done. She welcomed Miss Harrington, gave instructions to have her belongings taken in, and made an offer of refreshment, all with a softness of manner that bore no resentment or unease.

Garbrae took a deep breath, thanked God for the composure and cool-headedness displayed by his wife, and followed the pair into the house.

∽

Her husband did not seem comfortable, that much was plain, but how could he be: the situation between the three of them so decidedly complicated. Catherine had watched as the carriage pulled up and was displeased by the other woman's closeness to the captain, jealousy stirred by the sight of her leaning in to him, her lips a hair's breadth from his. He had stiffened and seemed to recoil from her – a good omen, surely, or was he merely uncomfortable at being observed?

The two women entered the small sunroom, a delightful space perfectly situated to capture the best of the morning sun and offer a fine view of the gardens. Catherine found amusement in considering that the room was perhaps a little too pleasant under the circumstances. Though what room would be suitable for entertaining a rival for your husband's affections, she wondered, allowing the image of a cold dungeon to linger momentarily.

Anna was at a loss to understand the woman opposite her, who stood politely offering her a seat, making arrangements for her comfort, and ordering light refreshments. A curious smile had drifted across her face, and when it vanished, what remained was a look she might consider almost serene – certainly unaffected. Perhaps this woman simply did not care. Perhaps she did not love her husband. Anna could only hope that was the case, for it would make stealing Garbrae from her so much easier.

"So, Miss Harrington," began Catherine, once tea had been poured, "you are a childhood friend of my husband's, I understand."

"Indeed, my lady, I can hardly recall a time in my life when he was not there. Our families have always been close. I cannot begin to express my relief on his being able to come to my aid, for my situation was quite perilous."

"Well, with a shared history, with bonds of friendship to consider, a man such as my husband could hardly have refused. Honour alone would have compelled him," Catherine said.

"I hope I do not only have honour to thank," Anna continued, "for given my current predicament, I have no reason to trust in the honour of men!"

"No, I am certain friendship played its part, though, in the honour of my husband you may trust – honour and loyalty being so much a part of who he is," Catherine insisted.

Anna smiled sweetly. Catherine's persistent use of the phrase, "my husband" was not lost on her. This woman might not be as easy to vanquish as she had hoped.

"Indeed, you are correct. I should have known to trust in him. He has been my saviour too many times for me to suppose he would fail me when my need was greatest," Anna said. Noting the slight arching of Catherine's eyebrow, she realised the lady had no real appreciation for their past. "He will, I am sure, have told you all of our little history? He would not have asked you to join him without appraising you of the circumstances of why he should feel so bound to come to my aid," she added, not daring to be so forthright as to admit to their being in love but hoping to suggest a deep attachment.

The smile on Catherine's face hardened, pulled so tight that it looked as though her jaw might snap. "I am aware that you grew up with one another, that your families have long been close."

"Indeed, it had been our hope to unite our families as one, but …" Anna raised her teacup to her lips and took a sip, knowing she did not need to finish her sentence.

Despite the situation, the look of discomfort on Catherine's face was not a source of satisfaction for Anna. She witnessed it, but she took no pleasure in it. In truth, Lady Catherine seemed a good woman, but she was titled with resources and connections enough to make it in the world.

She did not need a husband in the way Anna did. James Garbrae was all that stood between Anna and ruin. She could feel sorry for this woman, could regret all that needed to be done, and all the hurt that needed to be inflicted. She could try to make amends – after she was saved.

Catherine listened as Anna talked on. She sat and waited for the tremble in her hands to cease before she dared to reach out for her teacup.

Secrets and lies, she thought. *Is my happiness always doomed to be at the mercy of the secrets and lies of men?*

She had no right to him. As Anna continued, Catherine understood now why Garbrae had so forcefully declared on meeting her that he had no intention of being married. He had been devoted to Miss Harrington, had hoped to marry Miss Harrington, but had been forced to abandon her.

In the early days of their marriage, Catherine had assumed the captain had revelled in securing her father's permission for her hand. She suspected the agreement had been the source of much amusement among the captain and his friends. It never occurred to her that he might have been against the match. In a moment of painful clarity, Catherine realised her husband had settled for her, and that moment was almost her undoing.

Her heart broke.

She looked across the small table at the woman her husband loved. Anna Harrington, who was blonde and petite and who, despite the situation she found herself in, had an easy manner and ready smile. This woman was in every measure her opposite.

I have no right to him, she thought; *I never had.*

Catherine reached out for her cup of, now cold, tea and forced the smile back to her lips.

~

Garbrae stood in the doorway to the room, amazed to find the two women apparently engaged in pleasant conversation. Both were smiling and sipping at their tea as though they were indeed friends. It was not until he took a step closer that he spotted the disguised strain. Catherine's smile was frozen, forced into place, no hint around her eyes to suggest its genuineness, and Anna twisted her napkin between her fingers – this simple action shouting loud her unspoken discomfort. This was certainly not an easy scene, and he doubted his arrival would serve to make it any less awkward.

"I thought we had lost you," Anna teased, on spotting him lingering by the doorway. "Come, join us for tea. Your wife and I are just getting acquainted."

"Do you think Miss Harrington and I might be left alone?' Garbrae asked as he walked toward them. "We have much to discuss, and I do not wish to impose on you further."

"Oh, you need not leave us," Anna piped up. "I am certain there will be nothing said that you cannot hear."

Garbrae shot her a look. What was she thinking? How many people did she intend to expose the full extent of her disgrace to? Had she no shame?

"I know you were keen to ride this morning, my lady, and I do not see why you should have to forgo that pleasure."

"I do not feel up to riding today," Catherine replied, a desperate sadness welling up within her. "But I will leave you in peace. No doubt there is much you need to discuss. I will be in the library if you need me."

Garbrae marvelled at Catherine's self-possession, her composure never wavering. The woman had an undeniable dignity and grace even in the face of this horror. How would he ever make amends for putting her through this? He turned to Miss Harrington, finding her staring up at him, a curious smile playing on her lips. Well, he would start by removing this complication.

Catherine stopped at the door and glanced back to find her husband and Miss Harrington gazing at one another. Her sadness now threatened to engulf her. *He called me "my lady",* she realised, the thought crushing her. *I am Lady Catherine Eugenia Montgomery, and he settled for me.*

"Why did you ask your wife to leave?" Anna asked Garbrae as soon as Catherine had gone. "Given our history together, she might misconstrue your desire to be alone."

"Are you so eager to flaunt your shame?" he bit back, though admitting to himself the possible truth of her statement. "I will deal with my wife as I see fit. I will not have her scandalised by your presence any more than she must. If she is to smile and introduce you as a friend, she must know the full disastrousness of your situation, but I would rather be the one to tell her. I will not give you the opportunity to colour the truth to your own advantage."

Anna clasped a hand to her mouth, catching a cry that sought to escape, but unable to stop tears flowing. He had never spoken to her so harshly, and she could not risk his turning away from her now.

"It will do no good to cry," he said taking a seat. "Finish your tea."

"Please be kinder to me," she implored. "I fear I will not survive much more cruelty and certainly not from you – you who have been so dear to me for so long."

Garbrae surrendered. Nothing would be accomplished if Anna were further upset. "Drink your tea," he said quietly, all earlier recrimination gone. "You have much to tell me if I am to find Mr Henry Matthews."

"Find him?"

"The man was the cause of your ruin; we must try to

make him the source of your restoration. I aim to see you married before we leave Italy. Lord Wrexham has assured me he knows a man who will date the papers to our wishes. The wedding will have occurred after your decampment and journey here, but that cannot be helped now. In time, society may choose to forgive the indiscretion, though do not imagine for one moment they will ever forget it. His family, I am sure, and Lady Catherine and I will do what we can to ease your admission back into England, though you may have to stay in the country a while."

"You wish me to go into seclusion as though I had done something to be ashamed of?" she cried.

"And is that not the truth?" Garbrae countered, amazed she still refused to accept the magnitude of her wrongdoing.

"I have already told you we did not share a bed."

"It is not enough; your being here with him was all that was needed. You know how you will be judged. You will be snubbed by every house in London; there is no possibility of your being accepted back straight away, if at all. Could you not sit quietly in the country until some other scandal raises its head, providing distraction enough from your own?"

"And what am I to do there? Needlework? You know how insufferable such a small life would be for me. You know my spirit has always longed for greater adventure."

"I would think you have had enough adventure for one lifetime," he added, trying, though failing, to hold back the bitterness in his voice.

"Are you so disappointed in me that you cannot even look at me?"

Garbrae turned his eyes to meet hers. "I hardly know who you are now," he admitted. "You are not the girl I remember."

"No, I am not. I am the girl who was left behind, abandoned so you could inherit a business. I am the girl who was found lacking," she reproached.

"It was not like that. It was not done with the callousness you suggest. I spoke to your father; he would not have consented."

"You could have found a way."

"Miss Harrington—"

"If you had loved me, you could have found a way," Anna continued, refusing to allow him to brush their history aside so easily.

Garbrae stopped arguing, seeing the truth in all she said. He deserved her censure. He had not loved her. What he had felt had been but a pale imitation of love, one which his marriage to Catherine had all too easily erased.

They sat a minute or two, each lost to their own thoughts, before Anna spoke again.

"He favours gambling and has money enough to afford to lose heavily in the best dens," she said, seeking to dispel the angry accusations that hung between them.

"Matthews?"

"Yes. The gambling dens, that is where you will find him."

Garbrae pushed back his chair and stood to leave. "I will find him, and this will be righted."

She reached out and grasped for his hand. They locked eyes, and Garbrae read in her face, for the first time, her complete understanding of her predicament. "You will protect me? You will not abandon me again?" she entreated.

Garbrae, guilt stabbing at him, swallowed hard before assuring, "I will not fail you."

CHAPTER 37

$\mathcal{A}$rmed with as much information on Matthews as could be gleaned from his conversation with Anna, and provided most helpfully with a miniature she assured was a solid likeness of the man, Garbrae went in search of Barnes, knowing that if Matthews was to be found, and found quickly, then Barnes' services would once again be required. While the thought of spending more time in his company was not a pleasing one, Garbrae knew the man's discretion and silence were reasonably priced. He assumed that should Matthews require convincing to accept his duty to wed Miss Harrington, Barnes' muscle would be as cheaply bought.

"And so, you understand the delicacy of the situation, Barnes?" he asked on finishing recounting some of the tale of Anna Harrington and Henry Matthews.

"And if this man, Matthews, refuses to accept his obligations in respect of Miss Harrington?"

"Then he must be convinced to see the error of his ways."

"Well then, I understand you perfectly," Barnes replied,

his smile only half raising the corners of his mouth, giving a wickedness to his features. "I can be ready when needed."

"Then we go now. Arrange for the carriage to meet me outside," Garbrae said, turning away, unable to look at Barnes any longer. He did not like this man. He would be done with this business as swiftly as he could, and if fate were kind, he and Catherine would be gone within a week.

~

"You are leaving? But you only just returned," Catherine said, after Garbrae had found her in the library and let her know he had called for the carriage.

Garbrae stood in the open doorway as though he might dash away any second. "I know, and I am sorry for it, but I need to set about this now if it is to be accomplished."

"Set about what exactly? What is it you hope to accomplish?" Catherine asked, setting aside the book she had opened on her lap, so it would appear to anyone who should chance upon her that she was reading rather than simply sitting, staring into the emptiness of the room.

"The marriage of Miss Harrington and Mr Matthews. I intend to find the man and convince him to marry her."

"Oh!" she said, pleased for the first time that morning. She rose from her seat and crossed the room to stand next to him. This was good news. The captain was surely not in love with Miss Harrington if he sought to arrange her marriage.

"Miss Harrington must be saved, and this man provides the best hope. So, I must go. I am sorry, but I must go."

"Of course, of course, captain – go," she answered. She reached out to him, but he had already turned from her. As he stalked down the hallway, he tugged the hat he had been gripping onto his head. Catherine stared after him, taking note of his hurried stride.

She sat, dejected on his departure. *He wishes to see her married, and that stands in my favour, but he wishes it only so that her reputation might be saved. He does not seem happy about the task he undertakes; if anything, he seems angered by it, which must surely stand in her favour,* she reasoned, trying to determine the full extent of her husband's partiality for Anna Harrington before finally admitting, *He did not kiss me. He stood an inch away from me and made no move to kiss me.*

This was the heaviest blow, for despite the awkwardness of the situation, on finding herself alone with her husband when he stopped to take his leave, her thoughts had been consumed by their recent intimacy, her body had trembled at being so close to him, longing to feel him pressed against her, her colour rising on the remembrance of the night before, her lips slightly parting in anticipation of his kiss – a kiss that had not come.

He settled for me, she admitted once more, *but we can be happy together; he has admitted as much to me. I can love him better than that woman. I can be a better wife than some silly wisp who would run away with a man she barely knows, risking ruin and disgrace.*

Catherine stood, no longer dejected, feeling more like herself. "I am Lady Catherine Eugenia Montgomery … No, I am Lady Catherine Eugenia Garbrae, and he married me, regardless of the reason," she said aloud. "The man is my husband, and no slip of a childhood sweetheart is going to alter that. She will be married to another, and she will be forgotten."

~

Garbrae headed for the door with as much speed as possible, keen to be off and about his business.

"Is everything in order," asked Barnes as Garbrae approached the carriage, his eyes drawn to the man's hat, with its perfectly crushed brim.

"Everything is fine!" barked Garbrae, wrenching the hat from his head and tossing it into the carriage before following it inside and shouting orders that they be gone at once.

Garbrae sat back; his blood still racing. Dragging himself away from Catherine had been harder than he had expected. He had never imagined it possible to be so possessed by need and want and desire. He groaned softly thinking on desire. She had wanted him to kiss her – he knew that, could see the colour in her temples, the slight parting of her lips. How he had wanted to claim those lips again, to taste her kisses, and feel her yield to him as she had the night before. But he would have been lost to her if he had kissed her; all thoughts of Miss Harrington and Mr Matthews would have been forgotten. Catherine would have consumed him entirely and that he could not allow. Anna Harrington must be dealt with – that distraction removed. They must be free of Anna Harrington, Henry Matthews, and Lord Wrexham.

"Catherine is my wife," Garbrae muttered to himself. "Regardless of the reason for our marriage, she is mine now, and nothing will interfere with that. Miss Harrington will be married; we shall leave here, and all of this will be forgotten – I *will* see to it!"

It took several hours to uncover the lodging place of Henry Matthews, and Garbrae's mood was by no means improved by the delay. Barnes had offered to undertake the search himself and to send word to the captain when the man was found, but Garbrae needed to be occupied, and so they continued in their venture. It was not until they reached the third gambling house that any progress was made. Even then, the owner was reluctant to provide information until Garbrae greased his palm with enough coin to make the possible loss of Matthews' custom worth his while. It came to light that Matthews had been taken home, two, maybe three, nights ago by one of the owner's men after a particularly bad evening of losses and brandy. His lodgings were not far, and with the exchange of a purse for a set of directions, their business was concluded.

Garbrae stepped out onto the street feeling relieved that this adventure was finally drawing to an end. Matthews would be made to marry Miss Harrington, and this whole messy affair would be put behind them.

"Come, Barnes, we should not delay. You know the street we need?"

"I do; it is not far from here," the man replied, striding out. "If fortune favours us, we will be done with this business within the hour."

Garbrae knocked loudly on the door to the room occupied by Matthews and waited impatiently for the man to answer. He could hear a grunt from inside, the sound of someone shuffling about, a dull thud, and a swear, but finally, the door opened to reveal a sorry, and sore, looking Henry Matthews. He stood, blinking, pained by the sunlight streaming in from the hallway.

"What the devil do you want at this hour of the morning?" he asked. "And more to it, who the devil *are* you?"

"It is not morning, Mr Matthews; it is noon, so I hardly think the hour unsociable," replied Garbrae, shrinking back from the stench of the man, doubts about Matthews' suitability as a husband immediately weighing upon him. For Miss Harrington, a life of seclusion might be preferable to a life shackled to this wastrel. "May we come in? We have some business with you."

"An Englishman? Business you say, but I do not know you. What possible business could we have with one another?"

"We share a common interest, Mr Matthews: Miss Anna Harrington."

"Ah ..." Matthews stepped back and fully opened the door. "Well come in, if you will; I would rather not discuss this matter in the hallway. The gossips around here have quite enough to report back to my family as it is."

Garbrae and Barnes stepped inside the room, the door being closed behind them, cutting off the light from the hallway. They stood in almost complete darkness, the air heavy and cloying and filled with the same pungent stench that Garbrae had tried to avoid outside.

"I will open the shutters; stay a moment," Matthews said, making his way around the two men.

"And the windows, if you would be so kind," added Garbrae.

Matthews laughed at the request. "Oh, I am quite sure you have been to worse places than this, but as you wish. Lord knows, air might help cure the ache in my head."

Barnes stayed by the door as Garbrae took a seat opposite Matthews and allowed him a few moments to collect himself.

"I suppose you mean to ask me to marry the girl," Matthews said.

"I do."

"And, I suppose, if I refuse, your man here is prepared to

convince me," he continued, throwing a cursory glance at Barnes.

"He is not my man, although I believe he would be happy to put a more forceful argument to you, should you fail to be swayed by my reasoning."

Matthews smiled. "I cannot say this comes as a surprise. I had anticipated some such approach, though I expected her father. Who are you, by the way?"

"I am a friend," replied Garbrae, not wishing to elaborate further on his relationship with the woman. "I am concerned for Miss Harrington's well-being and would see this matter brought to the best conclusion possible. Will you marry her?"

Matthews let out a long sigh and sat looking Garbrae square in the eye.

"I will not," he replied, "and you need not set your dog on me, for not even he will provide cause enough for me to do it."

"May I ask why?" Garbrae said, bristling, anger pricking at the back of his neck.

"It is perfectly simple; I will be disowned. My family have no intention of me marrying down. A tradesman's daughter was certainly not what they hoped for me, and when they heard of our being here together, they made that perfectly plain. All letters of credit were withdrawn until I severed ties with her."

Garbrae exploded. His rage at the figure opposite him overcoming his aversion to the smell of the man. He pulled Matthews up by his collar and stood nose-to-nose with him.

"If you knew how your family would react and how you would bow to their wishes, why ask her here at all if your intention was never marriage?"

"I offered an adventure, and damn it, if she did not accept. I never actually thought she would, and when she did … well, her enthusiasm fuelled my own recklessness. And so, we find ourselves standing here at the end of it all, with Miss Harrington ruined. Her only hope for salvation being my own ruin. It is quite a quandary, but though I care for her, you must understand I care for my wealth much more. I will not forfeit the life I enjoy because of her foolish choices."

"Her choices!" Garbrae yelled, every ounce of his will engaged in resisting the temptation to pummel the man. "The choices were yours too. Why must she be the only one to pay the price for them?"

Matthews squirmed out from Garbrae's grip and slumped back into his chair. The wildness in the other man's eyes frightened Matthews and made the danger of his position increasingly apparent. He had assumed the man by the door was the threat; that he might stand to suffer a severe beating at his hands, but the man who glared down at him … his control strained to breaking … this man was the true threat, and he might not stop at a thrashing.

"You are not naive, sir, and I am not unreasonable. I am willing to pay for her upkeep and see she has a generous stipend. Neither of us benefits from the marriage – you must see that."

"Her reputation will not be saved by a stipend," Garbrae countered.

"Her reputation was ruined the moment she left her father's home to join me, nothing can save that now. There is no good name to be salvaged, and if I lose the backing of my family, and my wealth, I have nothing of value to offer her."

"Her father can settle a dowry on her, and as he has no son, you could inherit."

"And what? Become a tradesman? No, you had better just kill me now, for that kind of life would surely render me dead – though more slowly."

"It is no more than you deserve," said Garbrae, leaning

down over Matthews, his hand clamped around the man's throat.

"It is quite obvious you care for the girl," Matthews croaked, his mind racing to find reasons for the man to release his hold. "Do you honestly consider our marriage the best possible hope for her? Do you honestly consider I will be anything other than a failure as a husband?"

Garbrae stepped back. For all that he might hate to admit it, Matthews was right – losing his wealth and the life he was accustomed to would be a heavy blow, and who knew what sort of bitterness might grow in a man such as Matthews under those conditions? Could he really trap Miss Harrington in such a marriage?

"I will pay any price for my part in this, so long as that price be pecuniary," offered Matthews.

Barnes stepped forward, but Garbrae halted his advance, his hand raised to stay him. "You are certainly not the best that could be hoped for Miss Harrington, I grant you, and I am surprised you see it so plainly."

"I am aware of what I am. I see my failings and my addictions, and I do not hide from them."

"On the contrary, you rather seem to embrace them, Mr Matthews."

"I like money, women, alcohol, and gambling. I make no apologies for being true to my nature and for accepting myself for who I am. My family was grateful that I waited until my grand tour to fully indulge the worst of my debauchery, their tolerance only tested by tales of my being in the company of a tradesman's daughter. It seems they preferred I return from my adventures with rumours of a series of whores rather than an actual wife."

Garbrae's fists clenched as he struggled to bite back the rage threatening to overcome him at the man's coarseness.

"You will not marry Miss Harrington, but you will pay for

your mistakes. I will have the terms sent to you once arrangements are made … and Matthews … you will not fail in this undertaking. Is that quite understood?"

Matthews could only nod, relieved the encounter was coming to a close and on such favourable terms. He scarcely dared to draw breath until the men were gone, the door firmly closed, and his room his own once more.

CHAPTER 38

Catherine had not settled since her husband's second departure. She flitted from room to room and, finding a comfortable seat in none, began to walk the garden trails, only to turn back minutes later. She picked up and returned to the shelf at least half a dozen books that on any other day would have entertained her for an afternoon. She was not at ease, and left alone, she took no pains to hide it. Had Anna been with her – had she not taken to her bed – Catherine would have forced a greater degree of composure. She would not allow herself to appear vulnerable in front of that woman. But she was alone. She was unsettled, and nothing but the speedy return of the captain, dragging Miss Harrington's betrothed in tow, could possibly soothe her.

Though she had been praying for her husband's return, the sound of the carriage as it approached the house nevertheless startled her, causing a sudden flush and rush of her heartbeat as she bolted from the front parlour. She ignored the raised eyebrow of the butler as she reached the entrance door before him, swinging it forcefully back on its hinges.

"Captain," she began, barely waiting for the carriage to come to a stop, "how went your business?"

As he stepped out to meet her, she could see he was unhappy, though she could not determine if his distress stemmed from having failed or succeeded in his venture.

"I found Mr Matthews. He and Miss Harrington will not be married. The man is a wastrel, the worst kind of a rogue. I will not see her bound to him. We shall find another way to fix this. Have you eaten?"

Catherine, suddenly exhausted by the thought that no speedy resolution to the problem of Miss Harrington would be forthcoming, shook her head and followed him into the house. Neither said a word as they made their way to the dining room. Her husband only spoke to order luncheon to be served and to ask that Miss Harrington be called from her room.

Catherine had never known such dejection of spirits, and as she sat opposite the captain, silent, with a table and the imminent arrival of Anna Harrington looming large between them, she wondered how she was to rally once more. The realisation that she did not know her husband's heart well enough to understand his feelings for her or for Miss Harrington was a cruel blow. The thought that she would always be second in his affections taunted her. The sight then of Anna Harrington entering the room, with her hair set prettily about her glowing face, and her dress accentuating her classic form, enraged Catherine. She was more than a little surprised by the vehemence of her emotion. She seethed! She smiled outwardly, of course, but inside, she actually seethed. She had never been stirred in such a manner. That it was the captain who had evoked such passion from her was as staggering as the passion itself.

The man is still my husband, and so I must ask myself: Will I lose him to this little Miss? she thought, watching as Anna took a seat close by her husband. *No, she will see me dead and buried first.*

"How went your mission?" Anna blurted out before she was even seated.

"You will not marry Mr Matthews," Garbrae replied, without providing any further details. "Although, he has agreed to look after you and award you a stipend – the terms of which I shall draft."

"But I will be alone and unmarried."

"You did not seem overly concerned by that fact earlier," Garbrae said.

"I thought perhaps he would marry me."

"We shall find another way, Miss Harrington. We shall return to England, as there seems little point in delaying our departure, and once home, we shall find a way to remedy this."

CHAPTER 39

Civitavecchia, Italy. November 1813.

"Lady Catherine, might I have a moment of your time?" Lord Wrexham asked, coming up to the lady and Miss Harrington who stood watching as their luggage was removed from their carriage.

"Certainly," she replied, stepping away from the bustle of the busy street.

"I will not journey further with you. I have received news that calls me back to Rome, and so my visit to England must be delayed," he began, once they were alone.

"I am sorry to hear that. It is not bad news, I hope."

"No, just a matter that must be handled. Still, that is not why I stopped you."

"No, of course not," she replied hastily. "Forgive me; the matter was no concern of mine. What did you wish to say?"

"It is about your husband."

Catherine turned a hard eye on the man. "Lord Wrexham, I have long guessed at the opinion you have of my husband. I do not believe it would serve either of us for you to voice that opinion now," she warned.

"Even if it is more favourable than you might suppose?" he countered.

"I … pardon?"

"It seems I may have been too quick in judging your husband. Although I still maintain he is not yet deserving of you, he is perhaps not quite as unworthy as I once believed."

"And what, may I ask, caused such a reversal in opinion?" enquired Catherine, surprised by the change in his attitude.

"I had the full account of his dealings in the matter of Miss Harrington and Mr Matthews from my man, Barnes, and that account was decidedly to the favour of the man. I only hope he continues to improve, so that one day he might be the sort of husband who does justice to a wife such as you."

Catherine smiled. "Sir, you are too kind. I fear as harsh as you have been in your judgement on the worth of the captain as a husband, you have been just as lenient in your judgement on my worth as a wife. My sincerest hope is that we both improve, so that, one day, we may do justice to the commitment we undertook and the marriage vows we made. Still, I thank you for your candour and for all the help you have provided us. It is my dearest wish that when we meet again, we shall greet one another as friends."

"I could ask for no greater gift," he replied, raising her hand to his lips before taking his leave.

Garbrae, standing next to the carriage as the last of their luggage was unloaded, watched the little exchange between the pair. He was close enough to see what was happening, but too far away to overhear what was being said. What he saw unsettled him: Catherine's change in colour, the smile about her face, Wrexham daring to take her hand and kiss it!

The man would not survive the trip back to England if he continued in that fashion.

"Lord Wrexham returns to Rome," Catherine said as she breezed by him. "He sends his regards and his regrets, as he travels no further with us."

Some good luck at last, Garbrae thought, the image of the kiss quickly fading into nothing. *Then it is just us three.*

Anna was in a quandary. The captain was not proving to be the easy conquest she had hoped. She had not expected him to bring his wife along on her rescue, and her ladyship was stubbornly of the opinion that the man belonged to her. But Anna had known him longer, she knew him better, and he had loved her first.

What to do?

How to be saved?

How to know where the captain's heart lay, for he was far too honourable to profess love to her while married to another. Lord, how had she managed to be rescued by the one man whose honour and loyalty were not to be swayed by any of the flirtations she could usually employ? Still, his honour may yet serve a purpose if she could figure out a way to test it. She was in a quandary. But she was not yet defeated.

Catherine sat across the deck from Anna, watching in astonishment as the woman flirted brazenly with a young man still heady from the excitement of his first grand tour. She coloured on realising her husband also bore witness to the

EVITA O'MALLEY

display and worried to think how painful such a sight must be – understanding now his shared history with the woman.

Garbrae drew his eyes back from Anna. Lord, what a display. Casting his gaze to Catherine, he paled on seeing her high colour. What an embarrassment for her. She had introduced Miss Harrington as a friend and companion, and there she stood, hardly more subtle in her flirtations than a street whore. How could he ask Catherine to bear it?

"If you will excuse me a moment," he muttered between gritted teeth. Garbrae took his leave from the table and strode across to Anna.

Such anger, Catherine thought. *What encourages it? Hate? Jealousy? Love?* There was no comfort to be had in any of the answers.

⁓

"You have such an adventure of it, John. May I call you John, for we seem like such dear friends now?"

"Certainly, Miss Harrington."

"Anna. Please, you must call me Anna," she replied, gazing at him through thick lashes, allowing her smile to fall into a delicate suggestive pout.

John was lost, all the blood rushing from his head, so he could only stutter her name in reply.

"If you address her so informally again, young man, it will be last thing you do," said Garbrae, having reached the pair just as Anna's name was spoken.

"Oh, captain," Anna responded, "do not be so harsh. John and I are dear old friends."

"Sir, if it is your wish to end this trip without incident and with all your bones intact, I suggest you walk away now, and you stay away. If I see you even glancing in Miss

282

Harrington's direction, I will not be held accountable for the damage that will be done."

The man was gone the minute Garbrae paused.

"What way is that to talk to a friend of mine?" Anna admonished, decidedly thrilled at Garbrae's covetousness. "What brutality, and to display it in front of a lady."

"I see no lady here!" Garbrae snapped. "The only lady I see is the one sitting across the deck currently suffering due to her association with you. You are an embarrassment. As if shaming yourself in this manner were not enough, you shame my wife as well. Cease this now, or I shall confine you to your room for the rest of the journey."

Anna paled; her flirtation had not gone as planned. She had not managed to incite jealousy finding, in its place, contempt instead. Damn him, but he must actually love his wife or, at the least, think himself in love. This was not what she had hoped. *Still,* she thought, having cast a quick look in the direction of Catherine, *there may yet be something to be gained.*

"I am so sorry; I did not think. I have obviously been affected by events of late more than I realised, and I am not myself. Of course, how foolish of me not to see how it must look. You will forgive me? Her ladyship will forgive me?" she implored, her hand reaching for his, her face suddenly the picture of innocence.

Garbrae, confused by this change, was momentarily at a loss and allowed their hands to linger too long together. Back in control, he straightened, withdrew his hand from hers, stepped back, and offered her his arm.

"We shall speak no more of this. Do not give me cause to have to reprimand you again," he managed, walking her back across the deck to the waiting figure of his wife.

∽

Catherine, as Anna had hoped, had not been oblivious to the little scene that had played out. That Garbrae had stormed across to the other woman was pain enough, but then they had shared some secret. She had taken his hand in so intimate a manner, and he had allowed her to do so and for their touch to linger. Well, that was pain beyond measure. And though she swore she would not show it, Catherine's heart ached. She could make sense of nothing, all surety denied her. She could not guess at his feelings, or rather, she would not, for fear she would not like what those feelings were. His reaction to Miss Harrington was too complicated for her to grasp without a better understanding of them, of their history together, and she had only the lady's account of it. She could not read him well enough to know what forces were at play within him. The night of Lord Wrexham's ball she thought they had reached some kind of understanding, but he continued to keep her ignorant of so much, not least his own feelings. There seemed to be nothing but confusion between them, half understood conversations, interrupted moments, and the ever-intrusive presence of that woman!

They were never alone. So what was she to think as they approached her? What hope could she offer to heal the ache in her heart? She could think of nothing. There was no hope to be found.

"Your husband does not seem happy, your ladyship," Anna dared to venture when the pair were alone; Garbrae having left to secure them a table for dinner.

"The situation we find ourselves in is hardly likely to inspire ease," Catherine replied, allowing her tone to bite, refusing to afford the woman more than the barest civility.

The women, though speaking to one another, refused to

look at one another, both staring out across the deck to the vast blue waters beyond.

"You think it is this situation, *my* situation, that upsets him?" Anna asked.

"You think otherwise?"

Anna smiled and leaned back in her seat. She paused a beat before saying, "I think the captain could have arranged for my return to England without ever leaving the comfort of his home. I think he could have arranged for me to travel back accompanied by another, and I think, had he really wished it, he could have seen to it that Mr Matthews married me."

"You and I have avoided this subject long enough, Miss Harrington," Catherine said, finally turning about so as to properly regard the woman. "We both know what it is you skirt so playfully around. You believe my husband to be in love with you. Please, correct me if I am wrong."

Anna continued to gaze out at the sea. "Still. I would make that correction. I believe your husband to be in love with me still, your ladyship. I am so pleased we have finally been able to come to this, to give voice to this understanding. How refreshing to be on equal footing with one another, to have all secrets aired with no room for misunderstanding or confusion."

"Indeed," replied Catherine, "and what do you believe that gains you? He is, as you so casually mention, my husband. What do you hope to accomplish by pursuing him?"

"Quite simply, I hope ... I intend to take your husband from you," Anna replied, with such bluntness that Catherine was staggered.

"You intend on what? We are married. It is too late to set yourself up as some sort of rival. Have you sunk so low that you pursue the position of a kept woman?"

Only now did Anna turn to face Catherine, her usually soft gaze as hard as flint.

"I have the man's heart; it has been mine since we were children. I have no intention of being a mere mistress. I shall be his wife. I shall provide him with the life and the happiness he was forced to forfeit when he married you."

"I am undone!" exclaimed Catherine. "I had not imagined you would be so bereft of reason. We are married. Have you lost your senses?"

"You are married now, this is true, but he is wealthy enough to secure a divorce. It can be done. You have no children, so what is there to tie him to you?"

Catherine coloured. She knew Miss Harrington was unaware of the fact she and the captain had not yet shared a bed, but she was embarrassed, nonetheless.

"I do not think my husband will be quite the easy conquest you suppose, but even discounting any objections he may have to your schemes, do you suppose for one minute that I shall stand idly by and watch as you simply take my husband from me?"

"I think you are a sensible woman. I think you may have grown to care for the captain, certainly, but I challenge any claim you make for love. If you truly loved him, his happiness would surely rank above your own. I think you have wealth and connections enough to ensure your acceptance in society as a divorced woman—"

"And you have neither," cut in Catherine, "nothing that would ensure your acceptance in society as a fallen woman." She spat every word at her companion, with no mask on her disdain.

Anna's lips curled into a cruel sort of a smile. "But I have him. I have never questioned his devotion to me. If anything, his running to my rescue rather proves that point. And I am not quite the innocent he left behind. I am altogether aware of the power of my beauty; it was sufficient to inspire one man to run away with me."

"Although not sufficient to inspire him to marry you!"

Anna's smile tightened, now seemingly cut into her face. "Well, you have spirit, I grant you. I had not expected such an ardent battle on your part. Still, I should warn you, I have learned much about pleasing a man, and I will employ every little trick I know. If you think I will be dissuaded from pursuing him, when he offers the greatest hope of my salvation, then you greatly underestimate me."

Catherine stood. "Miss Harrington, I have not underestimated you since the moment we first met. You, however, have not been so astute. If you had, you would not have exposed your designs on my husband quite so completely, nor would you have hinted at the full extent of your disgrace. Still, I cannot thank you enough, for the information is most welcome. I warn you that your arrogance will be your undoing."

CHAPTER 40

*T*he mutual understanding between the ladies had given rise to a curious civility, so that the remainder of the boat journey was completed in a display of extraordinary politeness, neither failing to appear anything but pleased in the company of the other, neither allowing a hint of their true feelings for the other to slip beyond their mask of perfect contentment.

Anna's flirtations ceased immediately. Instead, she paid her attentions to Garbrae, while always keeping an appropriate distance. She was courteous and attentive but, above all else, proper. She completely controlled her impulse to charm with coy glances and girlish giggles and was surprised to find genuine interest worked better at maintaining his notice. It also seemed, she noted, with no small measure of pride, that she was surprisingly adept at feigning genuine interest. He talked with her, seemed pleased with her, smiled warmly, and was never cross – all of which she observed with decided satisfaction.

"Do not think I do not see what you are about," Catherine said cheerily at their final breakfast together. She kept her tone light and breezy, as though nothing were amiss.

"I cannot imagine what you mean," replied Anna, her tone as pleasant, and her face brightening into a smile.

"I see how you play up to the captain and how you have curbed the worst excesses of your true nature. It has been a most interesting show," Catherine finished, with a smile just as winning as her companion's.

"I had not thought to fool you with my little game, for I fear we see each other too plainly for that," Anna responded, allowing a light laugh to fall from her lips, drawing Garbrae's attention from across the room.

"No, I suppose you did not hope to fool me," Catherine said, nodding politely before waving at her husband, "though I suspect you hoped the effect of your amiability would have been rather different."

"I thought the captain quite charmed."

"Yes, but I failed to turn into the harpy that I rather suppose you hoped I would in response to seeing how favoured you were with my husband's time and attention."

Anna smiled wider still. "Yes, that was disappointing. Having you bitter, jealous, and nagging would have been such a pleasing contrast to my own sweetness. Still, it was naive of me to think you would play your part in my little drama exactly how I would have wanted it."

Conversation paused as fresh tea was served. Both women acknowledged their thanks with an appreciative nod.

"So, what do you propose to do next?" Catherine enquired. "What other games and schemes, intrigues and masquerades will you employ in your effort to take my husband from me?"

"You do not think I shall be foolish enough to unmask myself to you again?"

"Well, there was always the hope," said Catherine.

Anna poured them both a fresh cup of tea and added sugar to hers before saying, "I underestimated you once; I shall not do so again. I think that had I not warned you, I might have succeeded in inciting the jealousy I wanted. I have learned from that particular mistake."

"It is heartening to see you are capable of learning from your mistakes," replied Catherine, lifting her teacup and taking a sip. "Oh, captain, all is in order, I take it?" she continued, sweetening her tone as her husband approached.

"It is. We dock in two hours and shall not wait for the luggage. I will take you home at once. No doubt, a little home comfort will be a welcome relief to us all, so I shall not delay it."

"And what becomes of me when we are back in London?" entreated Anna.

"You will stay with us." Garbrae replied.

"And our current houseguests?" Catherine enquired, unhappy at the thought of Rose being exposed to Anna.

"I have sent word ahead; Fitzgerald will stay with friends, and Lady Rose and Miss Dunne should already be on their way to stay with Miss Dunne's family. We will be quite undisturbed."

"I cannot hope to thank you enough for all you have done, for all you continue to do for me. My lady," Anna gushed, overjoyed to learn of their plans, "I could not have hoped for a better friend than you have been to me. Your friendship throughout the blackest period of my life is worth more than you can imagine," and then, adding with undeniable flourish; "I feel as though I have found in you the sister I so always longed for."

Surprisingly, Catherine found a glimmer of admiration for the woman; she really was quite something! Allowing the admiration to shine through, she regarded Anna. "My only regret is that you should have ever found yourself in this position at all. If the little I could do has been of some comfort, then I am glad. Now, captain, shall we make for the deck, so we may enjoy the first sighting of England?" Catherine stood so she could secure her husband's arm.

"What a wonderful idea," he replied.

"Indeed," added Anna, presumptuously taking the captain's other arm. "I shall join you, if you have no objection."

"None at all," replied Catherine, "for who knows how much time we shall have together once our journey is done."

CHAPTER 41

Grosvenor Square, London. December 1813

"She will be left in the care of her family?" Catherine asked once more. "You promise me she will be left in the care of her family."

"Do not concern yourself. I shall see that she is not left without protection; she will certainly need it once it is generally known that she has returned."

That was not quite Catherine's meaning, and his response did not quite allay her fears.

"I did not simply mean to see to her protection, although of course I wish to see her safe, but she will be left to her family; she will not return here?"

"No, she will not return here. Your patience, to this point, has been exemplary; I would not care to see that tried. While the second half of our return journey was certainly more pleasant than the first, I was not completely unaware of the strain put upon you. You bore with exceeding grace a burden I had no right to place upon you; I will not soon forget that. I am aware of the impropriety of keeping her here more than

292

the week already spent. I know Miss Dunne assured us that Lady Rose could stay with her as long as was needed, but I do not think your sister was happy at having to leave this house, especially as we could give little good reason for it. Miss Harrington will be returned to the care of her father this afternoon, I will return to you, and Lady Rose will be returned to us both – I give you my word."

~

"I cannot look at you," bellowed Mr Harrington, his voice bouncing off the walls in the front drawing room, unsettling the other occupants and resulting in further sobbing from Anna.

"Mr Harrington, I realise this is distressing, but she is still your daughter, your only child," Garbrae said, appealing to the man.

"God, I wish she were dead!" Harrington cried in reply. "I wish she had not survived to this day, was not ruined, had not brought such shame to us. I am grateful her mother did not live to see this, for it would have broken her heart."

"Father," Anna pleaded, "how can you be so cruel? How can you say such things? You cannot mean it; you do not mean it."

"It is my fault," Harrington continued, as though his daughter had not spoken. "I was too lax with her. I afforded her too much freedom. I could not refuse her when she begged anything of me, feeling I had to make amends for her being without a mother, as though bowing to her every whim could somehow accomplish this. It is my fault. I have brought her to this."

"I am right here, Father," Anna argued, stepping into his line of sight, stepping closer to him than she had dared before. "Why do you talk of me as though I were not here?"

Harrington drew his eyes up from the floor just long enough to hold her gaze. "She is nothing to me now."

Anna all but screamed and threw herself at her father's feet. The man turned on his heel, not willing now to even look upon the woman kneeling before him.

"You cannot mean it; you cannot mean to abandon me," she implored, her voice high and panicked. "I am your daughter. You cannot cast me out!"

Garbrae, completely undone by the scene before him, prayed only to be gone. He had no business here. He barely recognised the two people in front of him as those persons he had grown up with. The thought that a childhood of happy memories should be eclipsed by this unpleasantness was more than he could stand. He moved toward Anna and picked her up from the floor. He was surprised by her lack of resistance, all her strength drained by her final plea to the mercy of her father.

"I shall leave," he said quietly, having seated Anna. "You cannot want me here."

"Take her with you. I will not have her here," Harrington said, his back still to them both, his voice hard and flat.

"Take her where, Mr Harrington?"

"Anywhere, but do not force me to have her removed. Do not force me to have her dragged out." A slight pleading broke into the voice that had been so resolute but moments before.

Garbrae took hold of the other man's arm and spun him about so they faced one another.

"You speak as though she were my responsibility, sir, when you know this is not so. I offered myself as a suitor once, and you refused me. You cannot now thrust her upon me as though I were under an obligation."

"Just remove her from my house; that is all I ask of you, Garbrae. Let the man who ruined her see to her beyond that."

"That man is in Italy, and although he has promised to support your daughter, the arrangements are not in place. It will be a discomfort for you, but you could see her protected until all other plans are made."

Harrington wrenched his arm from Garbrae's tightening grasp. "If you are so concerned, why can you not keep her? You brought her back from Rome; she is your charge now."

"I never said where she was found … You knew? You knew where she was, and you did not send for her?"

"Of course I knew. Do you think it was difficult to track a man such as Matthews? His fondness for high-living makes him an object of remark, even on the Continent. I may not have your resources, but those I do have were employed in the pursuit of her. I hoped to reach her before too much damage was wrought, but she was already lost to me when my agents uncovered her whereabouts. My daughter was lost to me."

"The damage to her reputation is severe, but she swore to me she has not been … that is to say, she has not been completely compromised. A marriage is still possible."

"Not compromised? You cannot believe that. She is with child, man! She admitted as much to Matthews and that man talks when he drinks. He laughed about it to my agents. Laughed about it! He has ruined her and cast her aside as the nothing she is. Get her out of my house!"

Garbrae sank into the chair opposite Anna. He tried to formulate a response, though had he even managed a reply, Harrington would not have been in the room to hear it. For on his final declaration that his daughter be removed, he had left, the door closing lightly behind him. All anger gone from the man and from the room in that final moment, leaving nothing but an emptiness in its stead.

"Is it true?" Garbrae finally managed. "Will you bear this man's child?"

Anna could only nod.

Garbrae rose from his seat and rang the bell. He asked the young maid who answered to have his carriage brought around. He did not look at Anna and paused only long enough at the door so that she understood she was to follow.

～

"I will see to it that a suitable home is found so you may see out your confinement in comfort," Garbrae said, once they were seated in the carriage, away from the attentions of the servants, though he suspected there was not a maid or stableboy who had not heard Mr Harrington yelling.

Anna looked out of the window, staring blankly at the street outside.

"Matthews knew,' said Garbrae, 'and yet he remained so unaffected when we spoke. He must have assumed I was aware of the full measure of your peril, but he made no mention. How pleased he must have been that the matter could be so easily done away with. Had I known the full circumstances, things might have ended differently."

"You would have seen me married to him, despite knowing how he would have hated me for it?" Anna asked, her voice barely carrying over the sound of the carriage.

"No. Not even the knowledge of your being with child would have led me to force you into a marriage with the man."

"Then how would the situation have been any different?"

"The difference is I would not have left him sitting quite so comfortably."

Anna fell to her knees on hearing this, her hands resting on Garbrae's thighs. "Then you do still love me!" she exclaimed, the sudden hope that all was not lost compelling her, that something might yet be rescued from the day.

"Miss Harrington! Right yourself this instant," Garbrae cried out, pushing her away from him and back toward her own seat, grateful they were in the chaise and not exposed to the world in a phaeton. He doubted that even the threat of being seen would have been sufficient to prevent her from making such an embarrassing display.

"But I do not understand," she mumbled, clearly at a loss to explain his displeasure with her. "You must still love me if you speak that way about the man who has wronged me. You must still love me, and so it is not too late for us."

"Love you? Woman, I can barely look at you," he replied, stunned by her delusion. "What did you think would happen? For the final time, I am married."

"But you do not love her. You cannot – not after all you have done to rescue me and not after all you have risked so that I would be safe. You think I am insensible to the passion you have for me?" she continued, her manner and tone switching between pleading and playful, uncertain as to whether the part of victim or seductress would better please the captain.

"How was I ever so stupid as to believe myself in love with you? Cease your games; your seductions will not work on me. No amount of sweet talk, coy glances, or appeals to my boyhood affection for you could ever make me forget what you have done. Did you honestly think I would declare myself to you? Abandon my wife and run away? To what? Raise Matthews' child? Are you really that deluded, or just so desperate? Was I simply the best ... no, the easiest option for you?"

Anna sat back in her seat, both surprised and wounded by the viciousness of his attack.

For a moment, Garbrae thought he could see a flash of the girl he had loved before lies and schemes had corrupted her, and he could almost feel pity.

"I never imagined it would end like this," Anna said at last. "I thought he would marry me. I felt certain he would marry once we ran away together. I loved him madly, unreservedly, and quite foolishly. I placed a trust in him, in his honour, that was wholly undeserved, and he has ruined me."

"Did he ever say he would marry you?"

"He never promised marriage, never made such vows, and yet, he did make such promises, if not in words then by his actions. He made me his own, caused me to bear his child. Is that not promise enough?"

"You know it is not."

"Then what am I to do? I have nothing. Mr Matthews, Father, and even you have turned against me. If you demand I leave your home, as my father demanded I leave his, then what hope is there for me? I do not have the money, power, or connections to fend for myself."

"Is that why you pursued me? Is that why you called on my help? Did you think I would be persuaded into loving you again? Perhaps even leave my wife for you? Did you think your hold over me so complete?"

"Perhaps I hoped for it. You always seemed so sincere in your affection for me. I think a part of me hoped to find that unchanged."

"Why did you not say that you had bedded Matthews?"

Anna paused before answering. When she did, she could not look Garbrae in the eye.

"I was afraid you would not help me if you knew how far I had fallen," she said, hoping the lie was more convincing than it sounded, fearing no matter what her reply, Garbrae would see the truth.

For a time, there was silence between the two as Garbrae wondered at the lie, for he had seen it instantly. Why would she continue to lie to him, even now? As he considered the question, one possible reason for the deception dawned on him, but the possible truth of it was painful to think on, underlining, as it did, how completely Anna had fallen.

"Good God! Please tell me you did not think to bed me so that you might pass the child off as mine? Not that, please!" he begged, daring her to contradict him, to rail violently against the mere suggestion.

She did neither.

"How could I have been so blind? Did you hope to seduce me? You knew, had I believed you were carrying my child, I would have found a way to marry you. Has this been a game to you? Was my marriage and my happiness a game to you?"

"No, of course not!" Anna cried in reply, finally finding a voice. "I never wanted to hurt you. Please, you must believe me. I was just so frightened, and I convinced myself it was best for you, that I could make you a good wife and that you could be happy with me. Please do not turn me out now, I have nowhere else to go." Her face fell into her hands, her crying uncontrolled, and her entire being given over to fear and the certainty now of all being lost.

CHAPTER 42

Catherine stood at the library window, grateful for the perfect view of the street, the comfortable seats, and the possible distraction of a good book, though, she had no heart to read and no desire for distraction from her sentry duty.

The captain would return after leaving Anna with her family, and she would bear witness to it. As he left, that morning, he had assured her the disruption Anna's presence had wrought would be at an end. Catherine knew her future comfort lay in the removal of the woman's insidious influence from their lives.

She stared anxiously out of the window, starting at every sound, all peace of mind and feeling of comfort driven out by the unease that knotted in her stomach, fearing the captain would not return alone.

He promised me, she thought, *and this will be the measure of his feeling for me. If he can rid us of this woman, as he has sworn to do, I shall know he has made his choice.*

Anna had family in England. The situation was quite different to Rome where she was alone and unprotected.

Here, she had her father, and he would be made to see to her. The captain had even arranged for Rose to rejoin them by the end of the week. He would not risk Rose's reputation. Yes, if there was nothing left but the ghost of boyhood feelings, he would see to it Anna's father took her in.

And if he does not? A small voice at the back of her mind challenged. *If he returns with Miss Harrington still on his arm, what then? What do I make of it? What do I hope for, plan for? How do I think to win back a heart on which I never truly had a claim?*

Catherine sat, her unease growing as she distractedly flicked through the pages of the heavy volume she had pulled from the shelf, foolishly hoping to occupy herself.

"Do I even try to win him?" she asked aloud, her eyes filling with tears as the room filled with the question. "Do I scheme and plot as she has done? Do I demand and rail against whatever decision his heart makes? If he does not love me, can I hope to be happy in the knowledge he stays with me out of duty?"

She moved back to the window, sinking her body against the rich velvet drapes, allowing the soft material to brush her cheek and soak up the tears that had begun to fall as she realised she would not trap the captain in a marriage of duty.

Better to be alone, she reasoned, for though the thought of leaving him cut her to the bone, better a quick resolution, better they end it at once, better that than living with the knowledge he loved another. What torture would be found in forcing him to stay with her? Nothing but a slow death to the love she bore him could result, her hope fading away to nothing. For watching her dream of a life and a passion shared evaporate would surely kill her. She thought of Captain Fitzgerald; she thought of her father.

"It would end me," she whispered. "Being with him

without having his whole heart would rend my soul in two. I will not suffer such obliteration."

He may yet return alone, a quiet hope offered, springing up from the despair that gripped her.

"But if he does not, I know what must be done," she spoke aloud once more, steeling her resolve but silently praying she would not have to see it through.

Garbrae, certain that Anna was settled, and that he would have some time alone with Catherine to explain to her all that had occurred in the few hours since they had breakfasted, went in search of his wife. He found her in the library with a tome on economics in her hand, her attention fixed on the book. Indeed, such was her focus, he was not certain she had heard him enter, and he took a moment just to look at her.

He had, he admonished, treated his wife poorly. He had been distracted, and she had borne the brunt of his distraction, but he was determined such failures would be atoned for. His attention would, at last, be given completely over to the woman sitting not ten feet away.

Before he could announce his being there, Catherine surprised him by saying, "You are returned then?"

"I am," he replied, noticing she had yet to draw her eyes from her book.

"Should you not have said 'we'? Should you not have mentioned Miss Harrington returned with you despite your assurances this morning that she would not?"

"Ah, you are aware of her being here. Please, allow me to explain," he said, moving closer to where she sat, anticipating a brief, though thoroughly awkward, conversation.

"You need not trouble yourself with an explanation," Catherine continued, cutting the man off.

"But I …" Garbrae began, determined to explain, nevertheless.

"I will give you what you want," Catherine cut across him again, her resignation plain, her resolution not to hear him evident.

He paused, uncertain he had heard her correctly. "I am sorry, but what will you give me? What is it you think I want?"

"Why Miss Harrington, of course."

"Miss Harrington?" he replied, his voice a mix of surprise and confusion.

"Happiness then, if you think my referencing the lady herself too bold. I will help you to be happy."

Garbrae tugged off the hat he had not stopped in the hallway to remove and tossed it onto the nearest seat. "And how do you propose to secure my happiness?"

"We shall get a divorce."

Catherine slammed her book shut on the declaration and a loud thud boomed into the silence between them. Garbrae was staggered. He had wondered how this conversation with Catherine might go, but never in his wildest imaginings had he foreseen this. He had walked into the room fully determined to declare himself once and for all in love with her, and there she sat talking of divorce.

"Did you say divorce?" he asked, when at last capable of speaking.

"I did."

She was completely unmoved, speaking with a casualness that astounded him. Loathe as he was to admit it, she had evidently been thinking on this for some time, for he was certain no decision newly made could have been delivered with such ease.

"You cannot mean to consider divorce?" he challenged. "What of the scandal? What of your family or the effect on your sister? Have you even considered what it would do to her prospects?"

"Of course I have."

Catherine's head whipped back, and she glared at him, but Garbrae noticed a slight tremor in her lip and wondered whether her resolve was as steeled as he supposed. He stepped toward her.

"What is it you want, Catherine?"

On his approach, Catherine stood, dragging the back of the chair to her side, holding on to it as though it were a shield.

"What I want, James, is for one of us to be happy," she replied, "and you deserve the chance of it – with her. A divorce can be obtained. It will not be easy, but we have money enough to see it done, and there are no children to consider. You will be free."

Garbrae stood but two feet away, staring at her.

"But you love me," he said. "I know you love me."

"And you, you lied to me. I told you once I could bear any pain, so long I was not kept ignorant of the truth, and still, you lied to me."

"Though I did not tell you all of the history between Miss Harrington and me—" he began.

"All!" Catherine cut him off, her voice loud with amazement at the nerve of the man. "You did not tell me any of the history between you – the lady was not so delicate."

Garbrae's stare hardened. "What exactly did she tell you?"

"It hardly seems to matter now. Divorce me, marry her. Have the life you thought denied to you."

She shifted awkwardly under his gaze, and when she could bear it no longer, fearing her resolve would shatter, she offered him a final sure sign of her intentions – she locked her arms across her chest, turned her face from his and stared vacantly into a distant corner. He was dismissed.

Garbrae took a step or two back from her. She heard him move away, heard the sound of his boots as they kicked out against the couch.

He was leaving.

She stood resolute.

"What did you call me?"

Catherine turned her head in his direction and was surprised to find him sitting on the couch he had seconds ago kicked out at. He was the very picture of a man at ease, with a wide smile across his face.

Catherine looked directly at him, confused. "I did not say a word."

"Not now. Earlier. What did you call me earlier?"

She paused, trying to remember. "James. I called you James. It is your name."

"Yes, but you never call me James. From the moment of our first introduction, you have called me 'captain'. Why choose now to call me James?"

She sighed and rubbed at the pain forming behind her temples. "Does it really matter?" she asked. "What is it you expect me to say? What is it you want?"

"What do I want?" he asked quietly, leaning forward.

They stared at one another.

"What do I want?" he asked, slightly louder than before.

"Yes!" Catherine demanded. "What is it you want?"

"You started this conversation so certain of what I wanted, and you only think to actually ask me now?"

"James, you are being tiresome, and I have a headache."

Catherine leaned on the back of the chair behind her, suddenly exhausted. Garbrae rose from the couch and crossed the room to her in slow, easy strides, until she was trapped between the chair at her back and her husband.

He traced the fingertips of his right hand down the bare skin of her arm and watched as goosebumps formed under his touch. When he reached her hand, he entwined their fingers together and smiled at the heat he could feel between their palms. With his free hand he tilted her chin, so she was looking at him, the agitation and anxiety of his day melting away under the uncertain, blinking gaze of her dark brown eyes.

"I want you, Catherine," he whispered, brushing his lips across hers on saying her name. "I have wanted you for so long now I can barely recall a time when I did not."

A tiny gasp escaped her lips as he made a trail of light butterfly kisses across her cheek. She could feel the warmth of his breath against her ear as he continued. "And I want you to want me – not out of duty, but because you choose to."

He sucked gently at her earlobe, and Catherine's knees buckled. On feeling her body shift against him, Garbrae released his hold on her hand and wrapped his arm around the small of her back, taking her weight, and drawing her closer toward him.

"I want you to tell me your feelings are so different now from when you once professed to hate me that you cannot account for hating me at all. Damn it all, Catherine," he said, softly, "but I want you to love me."

Catherine stood, still being held up by him, and said nothing in reply.

"Have you nothing to say?" he asked.

She remained silent.

Garbrae, suddenly embarrassed by the emotion he had poured out, and increasingly uncomfortable with her continued silence, leaned back so he could see her face. The thought that she might not love him struck a cold fear into his heart. Lord! What if she had offered the divorce not only to allow him his freedom but to secure her own?

He released his hold on her and stepped back, allowing some space between them. If she did not love him, could not love him, he would be gone, gone from the room, from the house – Lord! To escape from the county would scarcely provide distance enough if she did not love him.

"Catherine?" he said.

She looked at him, her face flushed, tears streaming down her cheeks.

He reached out and swept away the tears with the brush of his thumbs.

"What is it you want? Tell me, and I will give it to you."

"I want to go home. Leave Miss Harrington here until other arrangements can be made."

"Back to Manchester? We can be gone before week's end; I will send word to your sister."

"No," Catherine said. "It is time for Rose to go back to Westbury. You and I will return to Manchester – just us two."

Her breath stuttered, and a small smile raised up into her tear-stained cheeks.

"I want you, James. Not out of duty, but because I choose to," she said as she took hold of the lapel of his jacket and pulled him to her. She cupped his face with her hands, and her fingers slipped up into his hair as she drew his lips so close to hers that they almost touched.

"I love you," she said. "With every beat of my heart and to the very depth of my being, I love you."

"You love me," he said.

She smiled once more. "So much so that I cannot account for ever having hated you at all."

Please read on for the opening two chapters of the second book in
this trilogy:

An Unkindness of Ravens

Due to be published in Autumn 2021.

CHAPTER 1

Grosvenor Square, London. April 1814

"Must you go?" Lady Catherine Garbrae asked once more of her husband, the fourth time she had done so since he mentioned business called him back to Manchester.

Captain James Garbrae grunted in response, his body bent over his desk as he rifled through the lower drawer for the last of his papers. "You know I must," he replied on retrieving the pages and standing to his full height, "but it will not be for long, a few weeks no more, and before you even ask, no you cannot come with me. If you come, your sister will come, and we cannot pull her from the season now, not while she is enjoying herself. Could you even ask her to leave? And what of Miss Dunne, would you send her back to her mother's? You know how good she has been for Lady Rose … and Fitzgerald."

Catherine aggressively fluffed the small cushion she held in her lap. "You know I would not ask it of either of them; at the mere suggestion, they would both be packed. You know how Rose is about seeing everyone happy and how Miss Dunne is about not being a burden."

"So, you will trade a few weeks at a cotton mill for parties and the theatre. Your sacrifice is great," he teased, knocking the cushion from her hands before he drew her out of her seat and up against him. He kissed gently at the base of her throat, enjoying the goosebumps rising up under the swirl of his tongue.

"Cease your distractions," she said, pulling his face to hers. "You know it is not time in the mill I sacrifice; you know how I will miss you."

"Of course I do, and it is as hard for me to leave you. This business cannot wait, but I will not disrupt the lives of everyone in the house. Fitzgerald needs to become accustomed to the full force of society again, and Lady Rose deserves this season. Ill health keeps your mother in Westbury, and what was it she begged of you?"

"Oh, you are a hard man, James!" Catherine exclaimed, pushing him away.

"Is that guilt I see at play about those beautiful eyes?" he asked, pulling her back into his embrace.

"No," she said, guilt washing over her as she recalled the latest letter from home, in which her mother had laid claim to every bond of maternal and sisterly affection to ensure Catherine watched over Rose whose beauty, good nature, title, and newly returned wealth left her ever in danger from unscrupulous men.

"I will not be gone for long, I promise," he said, releasing her before going back to his desk.

"Will Captain Fitzgerald be staying with us?" Catherine asked, staring at her hands, always hesitant to raise the topic of the ill health of her husband's dearest friend.

"Do you still worry about him?"

"He seems much improved, and you are right when you

say Miss Dunne is good for him, but there is something ...
Sometimes I worry his healing is only skin deep, that if we
were to scratch at the surface, all the terror and anger from
the war might still break through. I know you love and trust
him, and I love him more every day, but I do not always feel
..." Catherine struggled for the right word.

"What?" Garbrae asked.

"I do not always feel safe," she admitted, hating having to
make such a confession, "and I will not put anyone in harm's
way. I still recall the sight of you holding him down, the man
thrashing about, wild and terrifying, in your arms. I will not
risk exposing my sister or Miss Dunne to such a scene when
you are not here."

"And I would not put any of you at risk. I know sometimes it feels as though Fitzgerald is a wire that is pulled too
taut, ever in danger of snapping."

"Exactly!" Catherine exclaimed. "Then you feel it too."

"I do, for all his great strides, my friend is not yet whole;
he is not yet himself. I had few such concerns in Manchester
for he was secluded away with us, and I could watch over
him. When he watched over Lady Rose and Miss Dunne
while we went to Italy, London was quieter, and the ladies
were careful about not asking too much of him. But now,
with all the claims on his attention and the endless clamour,
he seems strained."

"But you will still leave us?"

"I will, but I have made arrangements," he said.
"Fitzgerald will remove himself to the house of a friend of
mine – Henry Sinclair. I should say, Lord Sinclair, for he is
the Viscount of Lindley. Sinclair has promised Fitzgerald
will be watched in case his night terrors return. And so he is
not forced to attend every event Lady Rose has planned,
Sinclair and our mutual friend, Mr Winter, have promised to
go with you. I am sure, between them, they will see you safe

and protected, though Heaven knows, you ladies hardly seem to need it."

He smiled, recalling the few occasions in recent weeks he had stridden purposefully across a ballroom to rid the ladies of the unwanted attentions of some man, only to find the man already turning tail after a verbal thrashing from his wife.

Catherine was surprised by this revelation. "And why are you smiling? When did you make these plans? Did it not occur to you to discuss this with me?" she queried, fixing him with a glare she reserved for when he had most displeased her.

"Stop dissecting me with your eyes!" He laughed. "I am smiling, my dear, as I was recalling the rather splendid manner in which you dispatched that unpleasant little man last Saturday. What was his name? Cheshire? Chessington?"

"Chesterfield," replied Catherine. "He was, I own, beauti-fully dealt with. He should think himself lucky I only announced his ruin to my sister and Miss Dunne, and not to the room. Imagine him thinking to seduce Rose so her status and wealth might save his own crumbling reputation and grand house."

"You were spectacular, you know," Garbrae added, coming around his desk once more and sweeping her into his arms, pulling back the curls that had fallen forward so he could trace a line of kisses along her face, "like the first night I saw you, with your shoulders pulled back and your head held high, preparing for battle. The man did not stand a chance."

"I have long been able to handle the dangers of a London ballroom, but," she said, drawing his gaze to hers, "none of this distracts me from my original questions. When did you make these plans, and why did it not occur to you to discuss them with me?"

Garbrae pulled her tighter against him. "I have scarcely begun to distract you this afternoon, wife," he teased, "but let me assure you, before I do, I only came upon the idea last night and had a hurried word with Sinclair at the club. The details will be fixed this evening."

"But I do not know this man, or Mr Winter. How well do you know them?" Catherine asked, forcing her attention to the matter at hand, rather than the delightful thrill she felt at being crushed against her husband.

"You will meet them at Lord Cosgrove's tonight, and I will be surprised if they are not favourites within minutes. I have known them both for several years. Sinclair is a good, decent, and fair man, a widower with two sons—"

"Enough," interrupted Catherine, already losing interest in talk of any man who was not her husband.

Sinclair and Winter were no threat; an ageing widower and his old friend were the perfect sort of companions.

"I trust you. Thank you for taking such care." She paused a beat. "We will meet them at Lord Cosgrove's?"

He smiled. "Lady Rose was sure you would claim a headache to get out of this evening's obligation, so I made certain you could not."

"But Miss Cosgrove," Catherine implored, almost whining at him. "A whole evening with the Honourable Henrietta Cosgrove," she added, feeling the headache she had planned to fake taking full form behind her eyes. "I do have a headache—"

"Oh no, now is not the time for that," he jested, lifting her off her feet and twirling her about before he laid her down gently on the couch.

"But Miss Cosgrove," she whispered once more, before her complaint and the rest of the afternoon were lost to the wonderful distraction of her husband's ardent attentions.

CHAPTER 2

"*H*ow is your head now?" Susan asked sweetly.

"Quite well," mumbled Catherine, still unhappy at being in the carriage on the way to the Cosgrove's when she would much rather be ... well, almost anywhere else. "I know you all planned this," she said, her eyes narrowing and her glare darting between Susan, her sister, and her husband.

Rose did not even have the decency to contain her delight. "I could not allow you the opportunity of wriggling out of tonight's engagement; you know Lady Cosgrove throws the most spectacular parties."

"And what is your excuse?" Catherine asked Susan. "You are no more in favour of the Cosgrove's party than I."

"That is true, but I promised Lady Rose I would attend, and I have no intention of suffering alone. Besides, I find you are at your most entertaining when you are most put out."

"It is so cruel. I thought better of you Miss Dunne, for you know how I loathe Miss Cosgrove," Catherine replied. "She is so—"

"Petty?" offered Rose.

"Mean-spirited?" offered Susan.

"Prone to jealousy?" offered Garbrae.

"Well endowed?" sighed Fitzgerald. "Did I say that out loud?" he added, noticing the silence and the heads all turned to him.

"Fitzgerald, my friend, you have rendered these ladies speechless – that is quite a feat!" Garbrae exclaimed, his eyes wide at his friend's admission.

For a second, everyone else in the carriage was still until, without warning, Susan burst into laughter, followed closely by the others.

"I have never been so stunned by a slip of the tongue," Catherine managed, once sufficiently in control of herself again. "I am quite certain I will be hard pressed to glance at Miss Cosgrove without recalling it. You know I might enjoy this evening after all."

The party was, as Lord and Lady Cosgrove always promised, nothing short of spectacular. Their large ballroom had been converted into a travelling circus; small tents set up at one end housed fortune tellers and other little sideshows, a contraption hanging from the ceiling foretold a display of acrobatics at some point, and dotted about the room, their costumes glittering in the light of hundreds of candles, were jugglers and dancers, jesters and magicians.

Not content for the entertainment to be the only spectacle of the evening, tables had been laid out in the side rooms, full and heavy with food, platters piled high, glasses overflowing. In the centre of it all – the plateau, the Cosgrove's gastronomic crowning glory, a towering creation in sugar, a representation of their own garden, complete with revellers.

It was gaudy and gloriously decadent, and Rose squealed in delight. Taking hold of Captain Fitzgerald's arm, she pulled him toward the nearest performers.

Even Catherine could not help but be carried away with it all. "Well, if we are going to be here, we might as well enjoy it," she said, beaming as she grabbed her husband and followed Rose, the room swallowing them up as they made their way into the throng.

Susan did not immediately follow but chose, instead, to shrink back against the wall, finding herself a seat, almost hidden, in a quiet corner from which she could enjoy the various scenes at play from a distance. She needed a few moments of quiet where she could be still and observe, as had been her custom before her friendship with Lady Catherine and Lady Rose had thrust her into London society.

Perhaps that was why the nightmare has returned, she thought as she sat, her fingers tracing the scar that ran the length of her face. She checked the curls remained in place, masking as much of it as possible. Being looked at again, noticed after so long being ignored, was unsettling. Her heart raced at the recollection of the night before, of her waking, gasping and shaking as she had done in the months after her injury. Always the same dream, the same man, the same voice. His voice – she knew but refused to admit even to herself. His voice calling to her, professing love as she fell away into pain and darkness. Susan shuddered. Now was not the time to dredge up those feelings. After all, it would not be long before Rose noticed she had not followed behind her, and Susan's friend was never happy when she tried to hide.

Susan looked about her, certain Rose would already be hunting for her and was surprised to see it was Captain Fitzgerald who had been sent in search of her.

"You will not join us, Miss Dunne?" he asked as he approached her seat.

"Crowds," she grimaced, trying and failing to chase away the disquiet she felt. "They sometimes unsettle me. I needed a moment."

"You worry about being looked at," he ventured, allowing his gaze to settle for a moment on her scar.

"I am accustomed to being looked at, or rather, I am accustomed to my scar being looked at," she replied. "It is being questioned or scrutinised that unnerves me. If people would be content to peek, I could ignore it, but when you are stared at, when people fix you with their eyes, their jaws practically hanging open. Or when they ask how it happened, as though dragging up such memories were nothing. Oh, but you need not stand here; you need not miss the fun," she said, aware of their being left most conspicuously alone.

"I would rather stay with you, if it is not too much of an imposition," Fitzgerald replied, offering her his arm. "I have little patience for these sorts of crowds myself and was quite happy to be sent in search of you."

By taking his arm, Susan granted her consent to his continued company, happy to spend time walking the edges of the little circus that had formed in the centre of the ballroom, comfortable with a man who did not stare, who would not question unless invited, and who, she was certain, would never pity.

The Cosgrove's ballroom was a good size, perfect for entertaining, having large, glassed doors that opened out onto a pretty walk. As always, torches were in full blaze, lighting a trail those in need of a little fresh air could follow, and the party split its time between enjoying the entertainments of the ballroom and the peace of the gardens, coming back together to share stories and gossip.

"Where are the gentlemen who are to take up the burden of keeping guard now you are abandoning us?" teased Rose, having learned of her brother-in-law's intention to leave for Manchester in a few days.

"I see my wife has been telling tales," Garbrae replied, grabbing Catherine about the waist and pulling her to him.

"It is hardly telling tales." She giggled, despite trying to sound severe. "Not when it is exactly what you are going to be doing. Now, let me go before someone sees you."

Garbrae relented and released his wife, turning instead to Rose and assuring her she would meet Lord Sinclair and Mr Winter soon enough, for they were to attend that evening.

Susan stiffened.

"Are you alright?" asked Fitzgerald, noticing the change in her manner.

"Of course," she said, smiling. "I knew a man called Winter once. Silly, there must be ..."

The rest of Susan's sentence caught in her throat, for at that moment, the door opposite them was darkened by the figures of two men, and she could only stare.

"Miss Dunne?"

"I need air, captain," she gasped, almost panicked. "Why is the room so hot?"

Fitzgerald, shocked by her high flush, placed his hand to the small of her back and led her away. As he did, his eyes darted in the direction she had last been looking, where they fell upon the figures of two men entering the room. He walked her out to one of the seats in the garden and refused to leave her side despite her protestations.

"Do not think for one moment I will leave you – not unless it is to order the carriage brought around. I have never seen anyone take such a turn; you are shaking for Heaven's sake."

"I am not," she insisted, her claim undercut by the obvious waiver in her voice.

"And I am not leaving."

Susan swore silently, knowing she would not be able to escape without some explanation of her maddeningly silly behaviour. "As you wish, but can we sit for a minute or two first? Perhaps my nerves are a little rattled. I had thought I should never see him ..." she began before her voice trailed off.

Fitzgerald sat next to her in silence. He was unhappy Miss Dunne should be so upset by the mere sight of a man from across a room. A man, he noted, who had joined Garbrae and Lady Catherine, a man who was young, and handsome, and smiling at Lady Rose.

Fitzgerald was most decidedly unhappy.

"Shall we walk?" Susan asked at last, rising from their seat.

"Will you talk if we do?"

"I will."

"Then we shall," he said, rising to join her and offering his arm.

The walk started with the same silence Fitzgerald had endured as they sat, until believing herself sufficiently removed from the house and the many ears there, Susan began, "The man, Mr Winter, I knew him once," she managed, before pausing, struggling to say more.

"That much even I had guessed," Fitzgerald replied, his tone assuring her this was not explanation enough.

"It was six years ago, my first season in London, before all of this," she said, motioning to her scar. "I was believed to be quite pretty once, you know."

"I do not doubt your beauty must have made you quite the favourite."

"I will not claim beauty or favouritism, but there were offers made, men whose interest was keen. To my parents' delight, among my suitors were some of influence and money."

"And was Mr Winter among those suitors?"

"He was. Indeed, for me, Mr. Winter was first among them."

"But not for your parents I assume, for I have never heard of him or his family."

"Lord, no, they never even knew about him. A second son from a good but unremarkable family who secured attendance at the parties we were at because of his friendship with a well-positioned family. Mr Winter was so far from the match my parents hoped to make that it was laughable to contemplate."

"But you welcomed his attentions?"

"I did."

"You fell in love with him?"

"I did," she replied, unwilling, unable to admit more.

"And?"

"And nothing. Nothing came of it. We realised the folly of our feelings; we knew the objections my family would have to the match. I did not marry him. If I am not mistaken, he married someone else, a woman of decent money and property in Spain. Shortly afterward, I was injured, and that is all," Susan continued, rushing to finish the story, her mood lightening as though she were no longer affected by the man or their shared history. "Such a silly reaction to seeing him after all this time – I can hardly account for it. I am quite sure, after six years, he will not even remember me."

"Yet, you remembered him," Fitzgerald persisted, certain there was more to the tale.

"Well," she replied, flustered by his inquisitiveness, "until I was fortunate enough to meet you, the Garbraes, and Lady Rose, I had little to distract me from recollecting my one successful season in London. Is it any wonder I should remember him?"

"And that is all there is to tell?"

"Of course, what else could there be?" Susan said.

She pushed back a half-remembered dream forcing itself forward – a hand tracing the curves of her face, the feeling of falling forever, a softly whispered, *I love you.*

"There is nothing else."

"Well, speak of the devil, there are the very gentlemen in question," Garbrae said, raising his hand to call over the two men who had entered the room.

Catherine and Rose glanced across at the main door and spied two gentlemen waving in acknowledgement.

"Ruin a girl with a glance," whispered Rose, having turned pale then flushed and, all at once, into a fidget.

Catherine shot a look to her sister before turning to her husband. "This … this is who you suggest spends the next few weeks with us?" she asked, her disbelief plain.

"Yes," he replied, his smile faltering on seeing her expression. "What is wrong?"

"This … these men? A widower, you promised me, and his friend of twenty years. Did they meet in the nursery?"

"Sinclair *is* a widower – his wife died two years ago giving birth to their second son, and—"

"And you knew perfectly well the image I had of Lord Sinclair and Mr Winter, a widower with two sons and his dear old friend. I almost thought to ask you how old Lord Sinclair's sons were."

"Four and two, so I think your sister is perfectly safe from danger there," he teased.

"Do not provoke me, captain!"

"Oh, I must be in trouble if you are calling me 'captain'," he said, unable to resist continuing the playfulness, regardless of how much he might regret it later.

"Have you seen my sister's face? She is half in love already."

Garbrae cast a sideways glance at his sister-in-law and was surprised to see how affected she was – he had not anticipated this.

"I did not imagine," he mumbled, "but it is too late now, arrangements are made, perhaps it won't be as bad as … Sinclair," he said aloud, the two men having reached them at last, "how wonderful of you to join us. Come, let me introduce you. Lord Sinclair, Mr Winter – my wife, Lady Catherine Garbrae, her sister, Lady Rose Montgomery, and, oh," he noted with surprise, "there were two others in our party, but they seem to have disappeared."

Rose and Catherine looked about them equally surprised by the absence of Susan and Fitzgerald.

"I am certain they have simply stepped out for some air. In the meantime, gentlemen, welcome. What a pleasure to meet such good friends of my dear brother-in-law," Rose gushed, her colour having almost returned to normal, her gaze never dropping from the two men opposite.

"The pleasure must surely be ours, Lady Rose," Mr Winter replied, making a low bow and fixing Rose's attention with a charismatic smile.

Catherine looked at her husband and shook her head.

What have you done? she seemed to ask of him. *Whatever have you done?*

~

"There you are, we thought we had lost you," Rose called out on seeing Fitzgerald and Susan returning from the garden. "Come, you must meet our new friends. Lord Sinclair, Mr Winter, meet Captain Michael Fitzgerald and Miss Susan—"

"Dunne!" exclaimed Winter on turning around to greet the new arrivals.

"Oh, you know one another. How splendid," said Rose, clapping her hands together.

"Mr Winter and I met a long time ago," Susan offered. "It must be six years ago now, if I am not mistaken," she continued, her tone light, her manner perfectly composed. "Where have you been all this time?"

"I have been abroad. Spain," Winter managed to choke out before Susan's attention turned to Sinclair and the conversation moved there.

Winter stood.

It was as if the world around him had fallen completely and irrevocably apart, and no one else seemed to notice. He could barely hear them, could barely see them. He thought he could make out the sound of a woman's laughter and was vaguely aware of eyes being turned in his direction. Had someone asked him a question? He smiled and that seemed to satisfy as the eyes turned away again, muffled voices droning on.

She was here.

He could reach out now and take her in his arms, feel her body melt against him as it had always done, reclaim the mouth that had returned his kisses with such heart-stopping fervour, hear the voice that still rang sweet and clear in his dreams, promising love, promising forever.

She was here.

After six years, Susan Dunne was beside him.

Goddamn it, he thought, *how could she be here?*

Susan was grateful to find Lord Sinclair was a charming, interesting man. She managed to give him most of her attention, after the initial awkwardness of meeting Mr Winter was over, for there was little else that would have kept her in their company.

She was falling apart.

Unwanted recollections – Winter's hands caressing her, the swirl of his thumbs across her skin, the run of his tongue across her lips – bombarded her, and she could not douse the fire burning deep in her belly. God, did she look as undone as she felt, was her breathing as rapid as it seemed, did the room seem to tilt to anyone else?

Casting a glance to her right, she saw Mr Winter; he was unaffected, perfectly calm. He was a little quiet. She did not remember him being quiet, but he smiled when he ought to and seemed to nod along with the conversation. He remembered her but was unmoved. She was nothing to him. Her world had crumbled in an instant, and yet, she was nothing to him.

Susan drew her shoulders down and clawed her attention back from the man who stood but an arm's length away.

They had meant something to one another – once.

It had not ended as she had hoped.

He maintained none of those old feelings.

She would not be unhinged by his reappearance.

She would not fail herself again.

No man would ever devastate her as John Winter had done six years ago.

AFTERWORD

When I started this book it was going to be a Pride & Prejudice continuation novel, but every time I sat at my computer to write about the Darcys or the Bennetts all I could hear was a conversation - or rather an argument - between Catherine and her Captain. I didn't know who these characters were but theirs was a story it seemed I couldn't ignore, and so *A Charm of Magpies* was born.

I hope you enjoyed following Catherine and James on their journey to finding one another as much as I enjoyed writing it.

If you did, please consider leaving a review, and keep an eye out for book 2 in this regency romance trilogy: *An Unkindness of Ravens*, which continues the stories of Lady Catherine, Lady Rose, Susan Dunne and the men who love them.

CPSIA information can be obtained
at www.ICGtesting.com
Printed in the USA
BVHW031105110121
597539BV00008B/169